SKIN
FLICKS
#2

Naked Auditions & Other Gay Erotic Tales

Edited by David Macmillan

companion press

laguna hills, california
http://www.companionpress.com

Neither the publishers nor the editors assume, and hereby specifically disclaim, any liability to any party for any loss or damage caused by errors or omissions in *SKIN FLICKS 2,* whether such errors or omissions result from negligence, accident or any other cause.

Hollywood Porn Party: Fund "Raising" © 2000 by Chad Stevens
The Personal Appearance: Dream Date © 2000 by Barry Alexander
Naked Audition: Body Worship © 2000 by Vic Howell
Under New Management: At The Adonis © 2000 by Simon Sheppard
Cyber Sex Site: "You've Got Fan Male" © 2000 by Sam Archer
Discovered Talent: The Next Big Thing © 2000 by Lance Rush
The Talent Scout: A Tiger By The Tail © 2000 by J.D. Ryan
On Location: The Big Tip © 2000 by Bill Crimmin
Gay for Pay: That's Why They Call It Acting © 2000 by Jordan Baker
Casting Couch Coach: Star Power © 2000 by Michael W. Williams
The Right Connections: Big Brother © 2000 by David MacMillan
Script Tease: A Bare Market © 2000 by Ian DeShils
Screen Test: My Brilliant Career © 2000 by Michael Cavanaugh
On The Set: Boy Pussy © 2000 by Alan W. Mills
The Honest Agent: No Small Parts © 2000 by George Dibbs
Rehearsals: Boys And Their Toys © 2000 by Jay Starre
Tops & Bottoms: Tricks & Treats © 2000 by Bryan Nakai
Director's Assistant: Grunt Work © 2000 by Derek Adams

COMPANION PRESS, PO Box 2575, Laguna Hills, California 92654

Printed in the United States of America
First Printing 2000

ISBN: 1-889138-26-6

Cover photo of porn star Chip Noll, courtesy Per Lui Copyright © 1999

Contents

Introduction

TRUTH OR DARE?

Oops! That's the child's game that once got me into trouble...

Okay... True or false? They're all fictionalized, but are the stories you're about to read imagined or did they really happen?

Some of the writers, like Alan W. Mills, work with porn stars for a living. He is the editor of IN TOUCH magazine and lives in L.A.—the gay porn video capital of the world! He parties with the hottest of the hot boys in West Hollywood—and is a pretty hot boy himself—and hobnobs with the likes of Chi Chi LaRue, so you figure it out.

Not all of the writers are fortunate enough to live in Porn Central, USA. Like the porn stars themselves, the writers who contributed to this collection are located from one coast to the other. Take me, for example, living in Atlanta, the capital of the bible belt. Even here I've met a few porn stars in the flesh—albeit as they passed quickly through town on tour. Let's just say they each made an impression and left me with a few tales to tell. These days—hallelujah, praise the lord—porn stars turn up just about everywhere.

I can't verify that some of these writers haven't stretched the truth a bit, but I can tell you that none of these stories have been published before and each is reportedly based on a true story. All of the stories in this collection are new—each written just for this book. This second volume offers up three more stories than the first volume. And, of course, they're all very hot; that was a requirement for being included. I didn't just want great writing. I wanted great writing that would get you—and me— hot and horny.

So how did I decide which stories were hot enough to be included in this collection? Well, that brings me back to Alan Mills. Since 1995, he's been the editor of IN TOUCH, one of the best gay erotic magazines around. He's put his stamp on gay erotic writing in the U.S. That's saying a hell of a lot for a lad who's just turned thirty—but looks like he just turned twenty.

Alan first accepted one of my erotic short stories for IN TOUCH back in 1997. I've learned a lot from him over the years about writing good, and sometimes even great, erotic fiction. He takes chances—you'll see what I mean when you read his story—and he's willing to stand by his choices. He's also very generous. When I sent out a call for submissions, Alan referred many of his best writers my way.

In fact, I think only five of the contributors to this anthology have not appeared in IN TOUCH, INDULGE, or BLACKMALE. So, thanks in large measure to Alan, and the fine writers he's nurtured over the years, you're about to read some of the best gay erotic stories being written today about porn stars and the porn industry.

And, if you're a porn star who has a story to tell, or a writer who has a porn star story to share, e-mail it to me at dtam01@aol.com If it's accepted, you'll receive payment for your story and we'll be reading it in the next edition.

David MacMillan
Atlanta, Georgia

Fund "Raising"

Chad Stevens

IT WAS A PERFECT DAY FOR THE CHARITY POOL PARTY THAT WILL CLARK was throwing for the Bad Boys of Porn.

I didn't have the $75 admission but didn't even think about it. The thought of seeing my all-time idol, Ric Harden, was way too cool to miss. I put on my best, freshly-washed shorts and tank top, grabbed my disposable camera, and drove my cranky old Toyota into the Hollywood Hills. What the heck, I figured, I'd find a way to sneak in. I was resourceful—especially when I wanted something, or someone.

At twenty I was pretty spunky. I liked to live life on the edge. Being 5'7" and 130 pounds I figured I had to make things happen or they'd fly right past me. And, hey, with all those naked porn stars milling about, who would notice me?

I couldn't stop thinking about Ric. His hard, tan body. His baby blue eyes. His square jaw and short black hair. Those pouty, kissable lips and that classic Greek nose. What a stud he was. I collected all of Ric's videos—okay, I rented them. But if I had the money I would buy them. I would kill for the chance to be fucked by Ric.

If I were real lucky, I could even get discovered while I was there. I was sure there'd be lots of directors looking for new talent. It'd be great to get a deal going on a movie—staring Ric Harden and me, naturally. Just thinking about him made me squirm. I tightened my sphincter muscles, imagining Ric's famous nine-inch rod pushing itself up my hot and ready hole, rubbing my eager prostate.

The hot sun seemed to be smirking down at me mercilessly. I kept my windows rolled down since the air conditioning had long since died. I was sort of between jobs at the moment, living on my many "free" credit cards and the kindness of family and friends.

My spiked, bleached hair had begun to wilt and I was dripping buckets of sweat by the time I reached the hills of Hollywood. I pulled off my tank top, hoping it would dry on the vinyl seat.

Steering around a sharp corner, I massaged the pulsing head of my pre-cum-dripping meat, poking its way out of my tight shorts. I let go of my cock and firmly gripped the steering wheel. My raging hard-on had no intention of going away.

The road kept climbing and I was beginning to think I was lost. Just about the time I started thinking about turning around, I saw a sign announcing valet parking. I turned onto the residential street.

It dawned on me then that, just maybe, I was a little bit out of my league here. There was a line of cars in front and one forming behind me. Nice, fancy cars.

The street was too narrow for me to escape and park on my own so I just waited for the valet. He was awfully cute: short dark hair and not much older than me. A cute dimple punctuated his sexy jaw. And he had a basket that would impress anyone at the party.

"Park your car for you, sir?" The valet smiled down at me.

The car behind me honked. "Leave the car here and I'll park it later," he said, pressing a ticket in my hand and pointed to a waiting van. "The van will take you up to the house. Have a nice time."

"Thanks," I said. And that was it. The guy never even noticed my dick. Pity. I didn't feel quite so bad not having any money to tip him later. I climbed out of the car and pulled my tank top over my chest.

"Did you forget this, sir?" The valet held up my pitiful, bright yellow cardboard camera.

"Yeah, thanks." The valet smiled back at me. Was he laughing at me? Whatever. I wasn't sure about the van trip to the party house. The other party-goers were a bit older than I and I felt them all staring. Normally I'd love the attention but I was beginning to get a wee bit nervous. I certainly didn't want to be made a fool of if they threw me out of the party.

I quickly forgot my fears while gawking at the beautiful hilltop homes we passed. It took a lot of bucks to live up here. Someday, this could all be mine.

The driveway leading up to party central was steep and lined with lots of trees and bushes. That was good. I quietly held back as my van mates entered the line to get up to a table of very good-looking studs taking tickets.

Was that Will Clark? Oh my god, I thought. I was in heaven. He was hot, with that short, reddish hair—and those eyes! He wasn't wearing a shirt and his legs were bare under the table.

The trick was getting past this table without being seen. It was still early and there weren't a lot of people around. I thought there must be another way into whatever was behind the tall bushes and hedges. I could smell burgers cooking somewhere inside. I'd skipped breakfast and lunch, more out of lack of anything to eat than nervousness, and my stomach growled hungrily.

I wanted to see the house, the boys and the burgers, not necessarily in that order. I scoped out the terrain from behind the van and decided my best way to the party lay to the far side of the garage. I hid behind some old-fashioned, dented aluminum trashcans as the van finally backed down the driveway for the next horny bunch of boys and boy seekers. I sort of scurried behind the wall of the garage furthest from the fearsome table of party greeters.

Safely out of sight behind the garage, I looked for a pathway. There wasn't any. Just tall bushes and a very steep hillside. Not good. Sex was my thing, not mountain climbing.

I grabbed the nearest bush and began to edge myself along the steep rise. Branches scratched at my legs as I inched upward.

A sharp branch managed to pierce my tank top and tear it without letting go. Damn. I tried to undo the shirt but it was too tangled. I pulled harder on the cloth but to no avail.

My foot began to slide out from under me and I looked behind me. Half the hill, the narrow two-laned road, and a sheer drop-off on the other side. I grasped the bush for dear life. I waited a moment for my heart to stop beating so wildly.

Perhaps this wasn't such a bright idea. I could see the TV news crews scrambling to get a shot of my broken, bloody body lying among the rocks and scrub brush at the bottom of the hill. Surrounding me would be all these naked porno stars.

"No," Ric Harden would say to the cameras, maybe even with a tear in his eye, "I have no idea who he was, poor thing. But don't forget to check out my latest video."

Yeah, that'd be me—gone and forgotten, before I was even discovered.

I decided to lose the shirt rather than my life so I worked the whole thing off with my left hand without letting go of the bush with my right arm. Proceeding ever so slowly forward, I finally saw the end of the garage and a stone-covered pathway around what looked to be a small two-story outbuilding of some sort. I reached the last bush and pressed myself against it, looking around for bouncers. I heard another rip as I pushed myself to my feet.

Fuck, not my shorts too! I looked down at my freshly torn shorts and examined the new hole. A two-inch tear gave a very nice view from my pubes to the beginning of my ball-sac. Of course I wore no underwear. Damn! Maybe nobody would notice.

I reminded myself that I was here to make a splash and that I'd gotten this far. I held my head up proudly and walked towards the side of the outbuilding. I heard voices and plastered myself against the side of the building and peeked around the corner. What I saw shocked even me. Sure, there was a fantastic view of the entire Los Angeles basin and downtown LA. But—

Directly in front of me was a beautiful, blond, genuine porn star. I recognized his face immediately—Peter something. His tall, lean, bronzed body glowed in the midday sun. He was wearing a very small, bright blue bikini. It barely covered his enormous manhood. Another guy, also very hot and darkly handsome, was pulling Peter's bikini down. His hairy body was thickly muscled. Peter's cock sprang up and I swear it must have been at least ten inches long. A third guy was holding a fairly large camcorder. He was filming this little scene as Peter's companion knelt down and took Peter's enormous dick in his mouth. Beyond this amorous couple were a few curious onlookers. There was an old, heavyset man in baggy khakis and a Hawaiian shirt with a younger Asian guy. Both held cameras. Very touristy. The whole scene was surreal.

My stiff cock meat snaked out the bottom of my shorts. I made no effort to cover up, considering the situation before me. I remembered my little camera in my pocket and snapped a few pictures. These were memories I didn't want to forget.

"Yeah, that's good," the photographer said as Peter's tremendous schlong worked its way down the other guy's throat. I could hear conversations and laughter in the background. This was wild. Even beyond what I'd expected.

"Whoa, that's enough," Peter said gently as he pushed the other guy off his glistening dick. He shoved the monster tool back into his bikini and in an instant the whole group disappeared.

I took this opportunity to join the party and survey the area. Men were everywhere—some hot, some not-so-hot—all wearing bathing suits or shorts and t-shirts. I was disappointed that no one was naked.

The backyard was mostly taken up by an enormous pool. It was almost curved into a semi-roundish L-shape. There was even a carpeted bridge going across the pool, leading to the building I just climbed around. Through open sliding glass doors I could see a hot tub that was seeing more action than I was. There was a crowded bar area at the end of the building. It was all open, like at a hotel resort. One guy was actually painting art on a bikini-clad, hairy stud.

The house was a two-story brown wood-and-stucco creation. It kinda looked Hollywood Hills-modern. To the side of the pool was a huge grill area where two hunks in tight shorts and t-shirts were grilling burgers and dogs. I smiled. My stomach growled. That was for me!

"Hi there," the cute grill person said. "What can I get you?"

"How 'bout a good time," I said without thinking.

"Just stick around buddy," he said. "I'm sure you'll have one. How about a hamburger in the meantime?"

"Sure, thanks." I saw Will Clark, the host of the party, heading in my direction and ducked into the kitchen, my naked hamburger clinging to my plate.

"Wow, what a spread," I said to myself. Every available counter top was loaded with food of some sort. Salads, fruit, beans, meat-balls—even a few cooked wieners.

"Did somebody say spread?"

I recognized the voice.

"Ric!? Is that really you?" I asked, spinning around to gaze into the eyes of my favorite gay porn star.

"None other," he responded, his hands sliding into the waistband of his shorts, the tips of his long, thin fingers resting at the top of his slightly visible pubic bush.

"You're looking very sexy today," he said. "Where have you been keeping yourself?"

"I can't believe it's you," I said. Ric looked a bit confused.

"Haven't we done a scene together?" he asked finally.

"Uh, no—maybe you have me mixed up with someone else?"

"Don't worry about it." Ric put his arm around my shoulder and squeezed. My cock pulsed madly in my shorts.

"Let's dress up your burger and chat awhile."

"Sure Ric. My name's Alan, by the way."

"Glad to meet ya, Alan."

Ric planted a big wet kiss on my lips and guided me to the island counter display. "How 'bout some potato salad?" Ric scooped a big helping on my plate. "And here's a bun for that burger. You could use some baked beans too."

I watched in awe as Ric piled all sorts of food on my plate. I was so nervous and excited that I didn't even have an appetite anymore.

"That should do it," Ric continued. He was so sexy in his torn black T-shirt and tight jeans. One tear revealed a beautiful firm asscheek. He packed quite a basket as well. And he was so nice to me I wanted to die right there. Well, not really—I actually wanted to suck face, and more, with the hunk of my dreams.

I caught a glimpse of Will heading toward the kitchen. What's with this guy, I thought. He was spoiling all my fun. "I gotta go now," I said. "Catch you later." Ric looked surprised as I quickly scampered out of the room and into what appeared to be a living room or den of sorts. There was a grand piano, ivory colored. Expensive looking furniture and a panoramic view of the city below.

"I wonder who owns this place," I said to no one in particular.

"Some rich old director," Ric said. He'd followed me. "Let's sit out by the pool while you eat your lunch."

Ric guided me to the crowded pool area. Men were everywhere.

Hunks for days. One skinny, older guy was parading around in a bikini, kinda like he was on a fashion runway. Peter was chatting with an older gentleman, as if making some kind of deal. He fondled his huge dick through his bikini. He could barely keep his hands off himself and I didn't blame him. I wouldn't mind having a piece of that myself. The older guy also seemed very interested and they disappeared together inside the house. Hmmm.

I managed to eat my food while making small talk with Ric. He was very easy to talk with and soon put me at ease. "You know, you're very attractive," he said as I put my empty plate on the table in front of us.

"Thank you," I smiled. "I've had a crush on you since I saw your first video, *Cream of the Crop*."

"God, what a disaster that one was. I was so nervous I almost couldn't even get it up."

"You looked fine to me," I said, then blushed.

"What videos have you done?" Ric asked.

"Actually, I'm a watcher. I haven't done any videos."

Ric moved his chair around the table, closer to mine, and faced me directly. Our knees touched. I was ready to cum right then and there. "Well you might consider entering the business. The money's not too bad and the work can be fun—if you're with the right guy."

He brushed his black hair out of his eyes. He took both my hands in his and stared intently into my eyes.

Help me, I'm melting, I thought. Was it the hot sun or the heat from Ric's body? "I never thought I'd be good enough to be in a video," I said, as if asking for more words of praise and approval.

"Who are you kidding?" he asked, as if on cue. "You have killer looks. Young and fresh. And your smile is so adorable. I could just eat you up."

"Don't let me stop you," I said.

He leaned into my waiting body, our lips brushed together. In moments our tongues twirled into each other's mouth. The electricity between us was amazing. I couldn't believe I was actually French kissing Ric Harden. Ric was practically sitting in my lap. He kissed my eyelids, sucked my earlobes and suctioned my neck. I returned the favor with equal intensity and pinched his nipples, protruding out of his torn T-shirt.

Applause filled the area and I broke away from Ric. I opened my eyes, expecting to see everyone staring at us but instead saw the action taking place on the diving board. Two beefy studs were also sucking face. When the applause stopped they stepped apart, peeled each other's swim trunks off and began kissing again. Their erections dueled each other as the onlookers once again applauded, cheered and whistled. "Head, head, head, head," they chanted in unison. Both studs smiled at each other. One stepped back and the other carefully knelt down before him, the diving board flexing. He then held the protruding cock in his hand and placed his eager mouth on the pulsating member. I could almost hear the slurping above the chanting crowd. I quickly snapped a picture with my camera.

"Do it, do it, do it," they yelled, followed by "cum shot, cum shot, cum shot." With that the guys broke apart, smiled and bowed to the audience and jumped into the pool without a money shot. Damn. Everyone laughed and went back to their respective conversations as if nothing happened. I couldn't believe it.

Ric smiled at me.

"I guess you're not used to this kind of party."

"No. But I could easily get used to it."

"Well, it can be fun. Not as much fun as having a special someone in your life, though."

"True." I wasn't sure where he was going with this.

"To tell you the truth," he continued. "When I first saw you in the kitchen you reminded me of someone from back home."

"Home?"

"The Midwest. Actually Kansas. Terrible place to find a boyfriend. There was this guy I wanted so bad in high school. Turned out he was straight. We became best friends, but nothing more. You look a lot like him. But you're more fun. Can you feel the chemistry between us?" He placed my hand against his chest.

"I'll say." I could feel his heart beating.

"Let's go take a walk by the garden."

"Sure." I had the sudden urge to confess to Ric that I had no money, didn't pay to get in, and that I still lived at home with my parents.

We reached what seemed to be a secluded garden at the back of the house. It was actually kind of hard to tell which was the back or front of the house since the main entrance opened onto the swimming pool and the back was almost all cliff and view. The garden ended at a rocky wall, boasting a mini waterfall.

"This is really neat," I said.

"Not as neat as you are," he replied. I blushed.

"I'm sure I don't even compare to the hunks you've been with."

"Wanna bet?" Ric embraced me and pressed his lips onto mine. Our bodies swayed as if to the shush of the waterfall. The sounds from the other side of the house were muffled into oblivion. Ric's hands massaged my bare back. I held him tighter. Ric grabbed my ass and squeezed my cheeks through my sweat soaked shorts. The sun beat mercilessly on us.

"Aren't you hot in that shirt?" I asked as we pulled apart.

He smiled. In an instant he ripped the shirt off his back.

"Wow!" I stared at Ric's amazingly developed, smooth chest. His firm pecs glowed in the sunlight. I caught a glimpse of his expanding basket. My own cock was very exposed, hanging out of the bottom of my shorts and dripping pre-cum.

He knelt and took my eager cock into his beautiful mouth. I stared in amazement as the famous Ric Harden sucked deeply on my manhood. At the same time his eyes locked onto mine. He held me in his trance. I was his willing slave.

Ric unbuttoned the top of my shorts and unzipped them. My hard cock fell out of his mouth and I eagerly stepped out of my shorts. There I stood, completely naked beside the pre-fab waterfall.

I wasted no time in reciprocating. With shaking fingers I unsnapped his tight black 501's and pulled the buttons open. With little effort I slid the pants down his golden thighs. His famous nine-inch cock snapped to attention. Ric stepped out of his jeans and gently pulled me to the grass with him.

Lying on top of Ric's scalding body felt wonderful. Our cocks stuck together, hard against our stomachs. Like magnets our lips suctioned close. Engrossed in our electrifying joining, I blocked out the whole world. Until I opened my eyes and noticed a pair of sneakers to the side of our naked bodies.

My eyes bugged wide as I took in the scene. At least a dozen studs were surrounding us. Some were in bathing suits, some were completely naked. A few were actually massaging their own swollen cocks. I broke away from Ric Harden, flushing with embarrassment. But my swollen cock insisted we continue where we left off.

What the heck, I thought, quickly getting over my embarrassment. Someone tossed something to Ric. It was a foil wrapped condom. He smiled and tore it open. "Would you mind?" he asked me.

I smiled. "No. I want you to."

He spread the magnum-sized condom over his rock-hard member.

"Here you go, Ric," a middle aged man with longish graying hair and a beard handed Ric a small bottle of lube. "You three guys stand over there, you two there."

Suddenly I was flanked by five naked porn stars, all lubing up their own cocks. I was so hot though that I couldn't resist stroking my own raging hard-on.

From out of nowhere a video camera appeared. It was that same guy from earlier. He sure seemed to be working the party.

"You don't mind, do you?" the kindly man asked. He was obviously a director. "It doesn't hurt to come prepared to these kind of parties. You never know what will happen."

"Sure," I said and shrugged. "What the heck."

Ric looked at me with such intensity I almost forgot everyone else. I felt so free and horny, I didn't care who saw me. He gently laid me back onto the cool grass. He knelt before me and placed my legs onto his shoulders. He sucked on his two fingers and massaged my eager fuck-hole. He then placed a hefty dollop of lube onto my opening.

With one hand Ric massaged my throbbing cock. Fingers from his other hand entered my waiting anus. I could feel them plunge deep inside me. I writhed in ecstasy.

I moaned as he removed his fingers. I gazed into his eyes as he pressed his hungry cock against my tight spincter and gently pushed. Without stopping, he slowly pushed his man-meat deep inside me.

The pressure of that huge tool was a strong mix of pleasure and pain. Ric gripped my cock and massaged the purple head. The pain disappeared, followed by intense pleasure.

He pulled out, almost completely. Then he thrust himself deep inside me. Again and again, he pounded my hot hole. I could feel my cock filling with intense pressure. I was close. But I didn't stop Ric from grasping my dick while hitting my prostate with his huge tool. He pushed ever harder into my bowels until I could bear it no longer. My cock erupted. Jism escaped my cockhead and landed on my face. I opened my mouth to catch the next load. Swallowing the hot, salty liquid was a trick I'd learned through years of practice.

Ric moaned ever louder as he pulled completely out of me. He tore off the condom and grabbed his engorged cock. His face tight and red, he pumped his creamy white load onto my already damp chest. I watched spellbound as his love juice spurted over and over again.

Another load hit my shoulder. It came from the opposite direction. I looked up over my head and saw my onlookers pumping their own cocks. Almost in unison they began to pump faster and faster until they all began to shoot onto me. I watched in awe as five more huge loads of cock juice burst onto my waiting torso. I was bathed in man juice and I loved it. The impromptu audience applauded and I smiled in embarrassment. Ric planted a big kiss on my mouth.

From out of nowhere Will Clark appeared. He looked down at me in my most vulnerable state. This would be a fine time to get kicked out of the party, especially with everyone watching me. Some career move that would be.

"Hey kid," Will said.

"I'm sorry," I offered.

"Sorry nothing."

"But I snuck in here. I didn't pay."

"Forget about it. You're a hit. We'll take the money out of your first paycheck. It's for charity, you know. So get yourself cleaned up inside and let's have a chat. There's a few directors hanging around who want to sign you up to an exclusive deal."

I looked at Ric and he gave me a thumbs up. "Way to go," he said.

I was ecstatic. I'm on my way. Accidents do happen.

the personal appearance

Dream Date

Barry Alexander

309 ROOSEVELT WAS SANDWICHED BETWEEN TWO RUN-DOWN HOUSES. A rusty station wagon sat on blocks at the end of the dirt driveway behind a slightly less rusty Escort. I sat in my BMW and stared in disbelief. Gordy had sent me here??? I double-checked the address. Fuck! It was the right address. Wait until I get my hands on Gordy. I hadn't wanted this job in the first place.

This was supposed to be my day off.

"It's an easy job, Mark. Fifteen minutes and you're out of there—with two hundred bucks in your pocket. And you don't even have to let him touch you. He was so hot just to see you he was willing to settle for that."

"Just a strip and jerk off?"

"Hell, no! For two hundred bucks he doesn't get no cum shot. Do a quick strip and give him a good look. Shit, I didn't even promise you'd get hard," Gordy had said with a big grin.

It had sounded too good to resist. Gordy had never let me down before. He kept my name in front of the public. Thanks to Gordy, I'd starred in most of the top vids of the past year. Between vids, he kept me busy with special appearances and private performances, carefully screening the clients before he booked me. I'd never questioned his judgment

Looking at the house before me, I wondered what had happened to my agent's business sense. The guy who lived here should have spent his money on a new coat of paint. At least the lawn was neat; all the dandelions were the same height.

Fuck Gordy. I don't do charity. OK, so I was lucky to be born with a boy-next-door face and a killer smile, but I've worked hard for this body. People had to pay and pay well for the privilege of looking at it. I'd been pulling a thousand bucks an hour ever since the release of *Hard for the Money*. I'd slept with doctors and lawyers. I'd weekended on the yachts of government officials. And now I was supposed to strip off for some hard-luck case with a hard-on? I thought not. Even if he had managed to scrape together two hundred dollars—which I doubted.

I put the car in gear and backed down the driveway. I heard a bang.

"Wait!"

Shit! The guy ran out of the house towards me. Just my luck. A car was coming and I couldn't back out. I'd been expecting an older guy, but he was only a couple years younger than my twenty-two. Skinny and awkward, his wire rims were too big for his almost elfin face. He'd obviously tried to dress up a little. His mousy brown hair was freshly cut. His T-shirt—so new the package creases showed—was tucked into no-name jeans.

"It's you, isn't it? Rod Cruise?" He stared at me in awe.

I forced a smile. "Just turning around, buddy."

He looked at me for a moment. Disappointment flooded his face, but he tried to pull himself together and behave with a dignity beyond his years. His look told me he'd expected nothing more: "Sorry, my mistake."

Shoulders hunched, he turned and walked back to the house, his hands shoved into his pockets. He stopped at the door and turned for a last, longing look before stepping inside.

I checked my mirror and watched as the next car rolled past. I could have made that one. The road was clear. Nothing to keep me here. I could spend the afternoon shopping, take a nap, then go out for an evening of drinking and dancing with my friends. The kid would probably sit there and watch vids. Shit, that wasn't my fault. What the hell was I thinking? There was no reason for me to feel like I'd just told a five-year-old there was no Santa Claus.

God, you're an idiot, I told myself as I sat on the futon, watching Marty scurry back and forth between the living room and the kitchen. I tried to tell him I wasn't hungry, but the coffee table in front of me was filling up with an assortment of nibbles—celery and carrot sticks radiating around a bowl of dip, Milano cookies fanned across a plate, a bottle of pretentious, but bad, wine. I looked around at the dorm room furniture and wondered how much of his food budget Marty had spent to entertain me. From the sparsely furnished room and his age, I guessed that he had just moved out on his own for the first time.

"Would you like an hors d'oeuvre?" he asked shyly as he held the tray in front of me. This was obviously the piece de resistance, fresh from the microwave: Velveeta on Ritz crackers garnished with olive medallions.

I forced myself to take one. He watched while I chewed and swallowed. "These are great," I lied. "Did you make them yourself?"

He nodded and set the tray in front of me. He stood awkwardly as if not sure what to do now that he had nothing in his hands.

I sat back and spread my legs, giving him a good view. I wasn't aroused, but even soft, my cock is big enough to make an impressive display. I think his glasses fogged up. He took them off and started polishing them on the edge of his shirt, then blushed, and put them back on. He wasn't particularly attractive, but there was a shy earnestness about him that was appealing. And the boner he'd sprouted the second I came in the house showed no signs of abating. I patted the cushions beside me.

"Why don't you come over here and sit next to me?"

Panic crossed his face. I was afraid he was going to bolt.

"I forgot to bring in the cocktail weenies. It'll just be a min—"

The conversation was going nowhere and the day wasn't getting any longer. I caught his arm before he could seek sanctuary in the kitchen.

"Marty, sit."

He perched nervously on the edge of the sofa. I tried talking to him. I'd been with nervous guys before. And I'd taught my share of virgins, which I certainly figured Marty was. But I figured there was only one way to get this guy to relax. I was only a few years older than Marty, but I couldn't remember ever being that shy and nervous. I tried to remember back to when I had been that innocent. I couldn't. There had been too many men in my life.

I smiled seductively at him. "Don't you think it's about time I started doing what you asked me here to do?"

"Right here?" he asked in a voice that was suddenly an octave higher. I smiled. "This is your fantasy, Marty. Where do you want me to do it?"

"Could we—could you—the bedroom?"

"Of course."

"Uh, can you give me a minute, please?"

He bolted up the steps, two at a time. I pictured him hastily shoving dirty socks and porn mags under the bed. But there was no sign of any mess when I walked into the room. The bedroom was as Spartan and neat as the rest of the house. He'd tried to make it romantic. A radio was tuned in to soft rock, but the dozen or so candles burning around the room couldn't compete with the bright afternoon sunlight slipping between the cracks of the drawn mini blinds.

Fully dressed, Marty perched on the edge of a neatly made bed. I could see the hard outline of his cock pressed against his jeans. But he made no move to touch it. His hands were anchored in the chenille bedspread.

"Aren't you going to take your clothes off?"

He shook his head. "I'm only supposed to look. Mr. Gordon was very clear about that. I don't have enough money for anything else."

For $200 bucks, I figured the kid deserved a good wank at least.

I winked at him. "Take it out. I promise I won't tell Mr. Gordon."

"Are you sure you won't mind?"

"Marty, the first time a guy watches me and doesn't get off, I'm going to have to start looking for a new line of work."

Too many men thought they owned me when they put down their money. Whatever they wanted, they wanted with no consideration of how I might feel about it. Marty didn't even take it for granted that he had a right to his own pleasure.

I'd been entertained on yachts. Hand-fed beluga in a bathtub of champagne. Flown to Paris for breakfast. But those were extravagant gestures by men well able to afford them. I suspected Marty would be eating macaroni for weeks to pay for this afternoon. He was a sweet kid. He deserved an afternoon he wouldn't forget.

I started a slow strip, moving in time to the music on the radio. I didn't do my usual routine—the one that had guys drooling and cheering when I humped and strutted across the tables at The Bar. I did the same dance I'd done for my last boyfriend's birthday, when it was just the two of us and I thought it would last forever.

It was just the two of us, me and Marty. I unwrapped myself like a present. Giving him a glimpse of skin, a flash of nipple as I leisurely unbuttoned my shirt. He never took his eyes off me. I kicked off my shoes and opened my fly. I cupped the white mound of fabric and adjusted myself. I was starting to get hard.

Marty's eyes bugged out. It's hard not to be aroused with that kind of appreciation. He hadn't taken me up on my offer, but there was certainly some activity going on inside his jeans.

When I was down to my briefs, I danced over to the bed and put one foot up beside Marty, giving him a close up view. My crotch was inches from his mouth. His eyes were glued to my basket as I undulated my hips and traced the outline of my cock and stroked myself. His breath quickened and lust filled his eyes. I moved away and peeled off the briefs to reveal the bright red jock I wore underneath. While Marty was still panting over that, I turned around and bent over to take off my socks, giving him a nice long look at my famous bubble butt.

I stepped out of the jock and tossed it over my shoulder like a bride tossing her wedding bouquet. Marty caught it. I turned and showed him the last surprise. A black silk thong cradled my cock and balls. I walked over to the bed, shaking and thrusting my cock into his face. He made no move to touch it, but I could see his knuckles whiten as he locked his fingers into the bedspread. I unsnapped the side of the thong and draped it around his neck. He touched it reverently for a second, as if it were a holy artifact.

Fully erect, my cock stabbed the air. I moved as if I were a sword dancer, dueling with an invisible opponent. Mesmerized, he stared at my thrusting cock. A tiny trickle of drool shone in the corner of his mouth.

"Go ahead," I said. "You can touch it."

Almost reverently, he reached out and wrapped his fingers lightly around my cock. "I can't believe it—I'm actually touching Rod Cruise's dick!"

I let him fondle it for a minute, then went back to my dance. My inner clock told me it was time to finish and be out of here, but I was enjoying this a lot more than I'd expected. I like showing off my body to an appreciative audience and they didn't come much more appreciative than Marty.

I'm not sure when I made the decision.

I stopped dancing and looked at him. "Did you like that, Marty?"

"It was fantastic. You're even better looking in person."

"You really like what I've got, huh?"

"Oh, yes!"

"Then why don't you do something about it."

"Oh, yeah. Sure. Sorry." He got off the bed, but instead of coming towards me, he walked over to the dresser and picked up his wallet.

Where did this kid come from? "How can I touch you if you're way over there?"

"You want to touch me?"

"Of course. You've got a nice body. But, I still haven't seen your dick. Come here, Marty."

He stood up and walked slowly over to me. He stopped a couple feet away. His breathing was heavy and, for a second, it looked like he was going to faint from excitement. Moisture darkened the front of his jeans.

"Closer."

I pulled his tee shirt out of his jeans and peeled it off over his head. His chest was flat and undeveloped, but there was a breadth to it that made me think in a few years he might actually have a chest worth looking at. He quivered when I put my palm on his bare skin for the first time.

I leaned in and flicked my tongue over one tiny nipple. His breath caught and he pushed his chest at me. My mouth closed over his nipple. I sucked it to hardness, rubbing my tongue over the sensitive peak.

Marty didn't seem to know what to do with his hands, so I took them in mine and put them on my butt. "You can touch me, too, you know. Anywhere you want."

He was a little hesitant at first, but he soon got the idea. At first, his touch was so feather soft it was more ticklish than erotic. But as he got bolder, his hands explored my body. He caressed my shoulders and back. He traced one finger up my sides and made me shiver. He cupped my cheeks, squeezing the hard globes.

I gave his nipple a parting nip and switched to its twin, giving it the same loving care. That kept his attention while I went to work on his jeans. I had him out of them almost before he noticed. I licked my way down his sternum and stuck my tongue in his navel. His stomach sucked in, but he put his hands on my head and held me in place while I rimmed the tiny crater.

His cock was a bit on the small side—well it would have been considered small in the porn industry—but it was hard and smooth and the perfect size for sucking. I combed my fingers through the soft hair of his bush. His cock bobbed eagerly. He was dripping a steady stream of pre-cum. I caught a liquid pearl and smoothed it over his glans, making the dusky pink helmet glisten. Marty suddenly had a hard time standing still for some reason.

"Let's move this over to the bed where we can both be comfortable," I told him. "You do have condoms, don't you?"

Marty nodded eagerly and pulled open the drawer of the bedside table. It looked like the display case at a candy store; condoms in assorted sizes crammed the drawer. "I bought them before I found out I could only afford to have you strip. I got lube, too."

He pulled open a second drawer. Dozens of sample-sized tubes of lubes lay jumbled inside. Scented, flavored—a connoisseur's collection of lubricants. I was speechless.

"Did I get the right kind of condoms?" Marty asked hesitantly. "I wasn't sure what kind you'd like."

"These are all fine. Why don't you pick the one you'd like to see on me?"

He rummaged in the drawer for a few minutes, then held up a bright blue condom. I grinned. "You must have liked *Blue Thingies*."

He smiled happily. "It was one of my favorite vids."

It hadn't been one of mine. Pretending to be an alien space captain with a blue dick wasn't so bad; blue condoms worked nicely. Then the director decided I should have blue balls too. I did not like having them shaved so they could be colored. It took weeks for the dye to wear off. Every time I looked down I was reminded of a pair of Easter eggs.

I settled back against the headboard. "Put it on me."

Marty leaned over my crotch, a look of intense concentration on his face, and started to roll out the rubber. It didn't take long to notice that something was wrong. He was rolling it, wrong side out. He flushed when I pointed that out.

"Don't worry about it. Happens all the time," I lied.

As soon as a new condom was in place, he took me into his mouth. He was so eager, that in minutes my shaft was slick with his saliva. I had to caution him about his teeth a couple of times, but he soon got the hang of it. All the while he was sucking me, his hands moved over my body—stroking my stomach, teasing my nipples, cupping an asscheek. It was as if, now that he had permission, he didn't want to miss touching a single inch of my body.

I pushed him back. He was getting me very hot. For a beginner, he was damned good. I could have taken a lot more without danger of shooting, but what I really wanted was to get inside that skinny little butt of his.

"Toss me a tube of that lube."

He fumbled in the drawer and pulled out the first tube his hand closed over. I looked at the label—wild sweet cherry. Perfect choice, I thought.

Marty got up on his hands and knees and looked back over his shoulder at me. He looked scared to death. I love doggy style. It lets me let go and fuck the shit out of someone, but Marty needed more than a good fuck. He needed someone to make love to him. Even if it was just once.

I ran my hand down his back and cupped one small buttock. He did have a cute butt. His legs quivered. He needed it so bad. "Roll over. I want to do this face to face. Now lie back and pull your knees up."

His face flamed and it took a minute for him to get it right, but he lay back exposing the most intimate part of himself for me. I looked at the virgin bud nestled between the curves of his cheeks. I brushed my thumb over his rosy hole and felt him tremble. I knew how badly he wanted me inside him, but I could also see fear.

The heat from his puckered hole was almost too tempting. I wanted to drive my cock through it with no preliminaries. To sink my cock deep inside the beckoning warmth. To break through his cherry, and claim all of him.

I forced myself to slow down. I couldn't rush this. I circled the opening, teasing it with my fingertips, then worked a generous helping of the sweet-scented lube inside.

I was surprised at how easily my finger slipped inside him. He was so hot and silky. I added another finger, slowly stretching him. When he kept pushing his butt at me, trying to claim more fingers, I started pumping him. His cock jumped every time my fingers bumped his prostate.

I knelt over him, leaning forward until my cock brushed against his. Bracing myself on one hand, I stroked both dicks together. I leaned down and rolled my tongue around his nipple, then licked my way up his throat until I claimed his mouth. He kissed me eagerly, sucking at my lips and tongue and finally slipping his tongue inside my mouth.

I knelt up, moving closer until my cock brushed the bottom of his ball-sac. I tilted my cock down until I felt the heat of his pucker. I love that first moment of sliding inside a man—the way a sphincter resists for those first couple of moments, then suddenly opens and welcomes me inside. I leaned into him, pushing gently until I felt the crown slip inside.

Marty gasped at the intrusion, but he didn't try to pull away. I held still, letting him get used to me, while I savored the heat and tightness encasing my dick. When I felt a slight relaxing, I pushed another inch inside. This time, Marty moaned in pleasure. He pushed his butt back at me and I slid in deeper. He sighed with pleasure as he opened for me.

I felt like I was sliding into liquid fire; he was so hot and silky around me. My hands slid up his thighs as I pressed deeper. Marty wiggled his butt to take more of me. I gave a last push and my balls smacked against his buttocks. I held for a moment, looking into his eyes as he smiled up at me in triumph.

"I really did it! I have Rod Cruise's dick inside me. I've dreamed about this for so long."

I couldn't think of an answer that wouldn't make me sound conceited as hell, so I began a series of slow, deep thrusts. I wanted him to be aware of every inch of my dick. I changed the tempo, bumping his prostate with rapid thrusts of my cock. His face looked like he'd found heaven. Knowing I was the first, that I had gone where he'd let no man before, made me even hotter. I'd fucked prettier guys, but something about this guy was special. He felt so good, so hot and tight around me. I wanted to get deeper and deeper inside of him. To make his first time so wonderful that he'd never forget me, no matter how many men came after me.

I put his legs on my shoulders, leaning over him so I could kiss him. His hard dick was trapped between us. My abs were soon sticky from all the pre-cum his cock was leaking. Our mouths locked together, forming one more connection as we rode towards the peak. I slipped a hand between us and found his cock. His balls hugged the rigid shaft. I wrapped my fingers around it. He started drilling my fist.

My hips drummed against him. He thrust upwards, locking his ankles behind my neck. His body arched, his head lolled back, his face in a grimace of tortured ecstasy. Hot semen gushed against my chest and stomach. His guts spasmed around my cock. Powerful ripples surged up and down my shaft.

I couldn't hold back. I slammed against him, trying to drive every inch of my body into the tight little butt beneath me. I froze, my hips locked against him, as my balls sought to shoot every drop of my jizz deep inside him. Ripples of pleasure shuddered through my body, replacing thought with mindless pleasure. I collapsed across him, my heart hammering against this chest, and spasms of delight still wracking my balls.

"Was I OK? Did I do it right?" Marty's voice asked from a great distance.

I forced myself back to the present.

"You were wonderful," I smiled down at him. "Now let's see how your cock looks in blue."

With his eyes glowing and a smile lighting his face, Marty was almost cute.

I spotted Marty as soon as Jeff and I walked into The Bar. Something about him looked different yet oddly familiar at the same time. It was the clothes. He was wearing a sleeveless Henley tucked into button-fly jeans. The periwinkle shirt didn't look as good on him as it did on me, but I got the point. It was the same exact outfit I'd worn in the opening bar scene in *Raw Talent*.

Marty was on the prowl. But it looked like his nerve had failed him. He sat at the end of bar, pretending to be fascinated by his drink. Hmm, maybe I could stir up a little interest for him.

"Wait here, honey," I told my date. "There's someone I have to see."

I heard my name ripple through the crowd as I walked across the room. Everyone kept his distance, though; I did have a reputation for being aloof. I couldn't keep the smile from my lips as I felt every eye in the place on me. Well, all of them but two—Marty still hadn't looked up.

I slid onto the empty seat beside him. He looked up and his eyes lit up in welcome.

"Marty! Great to see you again." I leaned over and gave him a long kiss. I held him for a minute and whispered in his ear. "You can do it. Pick a nice one and let him take you home."

I broke the embrace and gave him my best smile. "Thanks for last night. You were fantastic."

The guys were moving in on him even before I got back to Jeff. "Come on," I said, "Let's pick another place. I think Marty is about to have himself another night to remember."

naked audition

Body Worship

Vic Howell

DRIVING DOWN TO THE UNIVERSITY OF GEORGIA FROM NEW YORK, I started seeing this stupid billboard every ten or so miles, beginning somewhere in South Carolina. Five or six football jocks of various races stood around with the same shit-eating grin on their faces and a single copy of the King James Version held between them. The caption read REAL MEN DON'T READ PORN.

That damned billboard definitely brought home the fact that I was entering the Bible Belt. But UGA had been the only grad program to give me a lecturing position, a scholarship, and housing. I'd had my ass humped on at least a mile of video tape to pay for the degree I'd just earned from Columbia. That, and I'd spent too many weekends doing special appearances, grinding my naked butt across stages at most of the gay strip joints on the east coast. I needed a break from the business and Georgia was giving it to me.

Sure, my income was going to take a nosedive; but I wasn't going to be paying Manhattan apartment rates, either. I figured if it got to where I needed a few quarters in my pocket to rub together, I could still go back and do another fuck film and a couple of special appearances.

I arrived in Athens and found the dorm that the University had thrown in as part of my instructor package. By the time I reached the lobby I realized that I was going to be sleeping in Jocksville, USA, every night for the next semester. I was assigned to the athlete's dorm.

I rushed to get my shit put away—fast. What I knew I didn't need was some friendly bubba finding a couple of my toys or my stash of stroke mags. I remembered the billboards on the drive down.

Being surrounded by boys who carried up to three hundred pounds of muscles on their bones and no brains in their heads was not my idea of a way to live long. Oh, yeah... Any one of them and his buddies wouldn't bother stringing me up once they found out I was queer; they'd just toss me out the window of my tenth-story room.

It was September and the first football game was only a week away. Even though the University hadn't opened for classes yet, the football team was already running two practices a day. The dorm was deserted. I was alone.

I'd put the last box in my closet; the 90-degree heat and 100 percent humidity outside had me covered in sweat. I fell into the chair nearest me and wasn't about to move for a million years or so, or until I'd cooled off enough to hit the showers. I was still pumping sweat when the door opened.

The guy who walked in was a hunk. Blond, blue-eyed, more than my six feet, and perfectly developed—his abs and lats and pecs had abs and lats and pecs. This guy was one heavy duty gym rat!

He smiled bashfully and stuck out his hand. "Billy Bob's my name," he drawled with so much magnolia juice and honeysuckle in his mouth I could barely understand him. "What's your'n?"

"Baruch." He stared at me like I was speaking in unknown tongues and, for him, I probably was. I grinned. "It's a Jewish name—it means Bruce in English."

"Can I call ya that, then?" I nodded. "Where ya from?"

"The City." He looked at me with big, blue, uncomprehending eyes. "New York, that is. How about you?"

"A little hole in the wall near on to Macon called Dry Branch." He plopped down on his bed, keeping his eyes on me like some kid seeing a tiger in the zoo for the first time. "What year ya in?" he asked finally.

"I'm starting a doctorate in Philosophy—I've got a teaching assistantship which carried a room with it." I shrugged. "So they put me in an undergraduate dorm."

Now, he did look like a kid seeing a tiger for the first time—it was like I might nosh on him for a snack. "A teacher?" He turned bashful again, twisting on the hem of his T-shirt. "Maybe, ya could—uh—tutor me some? Later on in the semester, I mean."

"Why?"

"I ain't got too much time for studying and stuff with football and all." I almost groaned aloud. "Hey, Bruce, tell ya what I'm gonna do," he said, sitting straight up on his bed and folding his legs under him.

I arched an eyebrow in his direction. Yes, he did look good enough to eat; but he was going to have to change into a Calvin Klein model in one hell of a hurry if he expected me to get into anything with him. The guy could bash my brains in with any of those fucking muscles I could see through his shirt. "What's that?"

"Well—see—I belong to this group that meets every Wednesday night—"

"What's it called?" I was wondering if I might find a cutie there—one who might like to strut his stuff on video, so I wouldn't have to. Fifteen percent for making a few phone calls sounded a lot better than flying out to the coast and having my butt crammed for fifteen or more hours over a weekend.

"The Campus Crusade."

"What the fuck is that?" I asked sharply, breaking in on his slower thinking process.

"Why, Bruce—we're the real Christian student group here on campus."

I groaned. I would have to draw a Jesus freak for a roomie! That frigging billboard from the drive down rose suddenly in front of my mind's eye and I found myself wondering if I'd hid my stash of mags well enough to survive a semester with this overgrown mental midget. "I don't think so, Billy Bob," I told him and tried to smile. "You see, I'm Jewish and that isn't my kind of group."

He continued to stare at me—only now, his eyes reminded me of a lost puppy. "What's Jewish?" he asked. "Sorta like being Catholic or Jehovah's Witness?"

"Sort of," I answered, trying to staunch his questions. It took more than looks in a man to keep my attention. Besides, I'd learned a long time ago not even to think about straight men.

"But, Bruce! There's only one path—"

I held up a hand. "Billy Bob, I don't discuss either religion or politics. We've got to put up with each other for this semester; let's not do something this early in the game to piss off each other."

Several weeks went by after our first meeting in our room. Classes had begun and our lives took totally divergent paths. I didn't have time to find cuties whom I could convince to have sex in front of a camera or even to have sex with me; teaching freshman philosophy was harder than I'd thought. I slipped into the basically sexless lifestyle of a doctoral candidate, studying and teaching. Billy Bob grunted his way through P.E. classes, football training, and football games. He didn't invite me to any more Jocks For Christ meetings and I didn't allow myself to think about my hunky roommate—even if he did insist on getting out of everything but his underwear the moment he hit the room. I'd even forgotten my stash of porn mags—Wittgenstein had me by the balls. It was turning into a boring semester.

I let myself into the room, my mind somewhere between dialectic materialism and Socratic natural aristocracy. My eyes registered that Billy Bob was on his bed in just his BVDs like he usually was, but I didn't think anything about it. It was Friday and I was tired and, maybe, my mind wasn't working as fast as it usually did. What I wanted was a number of cold ones and, afterwards, a warm body snuggled next to mine. I promised myself the cold ones at least. Damn Friday anyway!

He turned as the door shut behind me, his face a bright crimson. "What're you doing?" I asked, chuckling. "Playing with yourself?" His face went white then and I became curious suddenly. "What've you got there, Billy Bob?" I demanded good-naturedly as I crossed the room.

Stopping at the foot of his bed, I realized two things with total, complete clarity all at once. This boy had a boner in his briefs that would leave a prize Angus embarrassed and he had my latest copy of EUROGUY open on the bed in front of him.

Glancing at the desk, I saw the drawer where I'd stashed the mag last week and groaned inwardly. I calculated the distance to the door and the length of time I'd have to open it before this jock for Christ could start to come after me. The problem with that was that he was a wide receiver on the football team and, although I wasn't a fan, I figured that meant the boy ran and he did it well. I started calculating my chances of coming out of this alive.

Suddenly, from nowhere, anger welled up inside me. Why should I accept being torn limb from limb by some hate-filled bigot? Why should I be the one calculating his escape? So what if I was gay? I hadn't done anything to Billy Bob. And the son of a bitch had gone through my personal property to find my magazine.

"Didn't your mother ever tell you it was impolite to go through other people's personal shit?" I growled, allowing my anger to grow. Billy Bob turned whiter, which was hard to do for a lily-white Southern boy.

"I—uh—I was looking for some aspirin, Bruce," he offered slowly. "And, then, I found this—"

"Yeah?" I growled. "So—?" My anger kept me going now; I was on pure adrenaline.

"They sure don't have this kind of stuff back home in Dry Branch."

"That still doesn't mean you've got the right to go through my things—or anybody else's." I stuck out my hand, demanding the return of my magazine. He glanced down at a particularly cute model's picture and, sighing, took a swipe at the two-by-four in his briefs and closed the magazine. He slowly handed it to me.

"I'm sorry, Bruce. I didn't know what to think when I saw it." He glanced down at his hands. "Then, I just plain got curious."

"Well, your mama and the boys at your Wednesday night prayer group wouldn't like you looking at this."

"You're right there." He chuckled. "But, then, it sure ain't none of their business neither!"

I was beginning to wonder just how accurate my assessment of him had been.

"Did you see anything you liked?" I asked cautiously, allowing my curiosity to take me over.

He smiled slightly. "Well—" he drawled even more slowly than usual and lay back to face me. "The story got me to thinking." He glanced down at his crotch and my gaze followed the direction his had taken. Billy Bob still had his boner and I was pretty sure it'd grown some since my last glance at it—it was closer to the size of the Empire State Building now.

I pulled my eyes away and my gaze went to his face, my celibacy definitely getting in the way of sound judgement. "Yeah, well, Billy Bob, your buddies at the Campus Crusade sure aren't going to be happy with you trying out queer sex."

"What they don't know ain't gonna to hurt them," he answered back, watching my face now and consciously playing with himself.

"I'm not willing to be just a warm piece of meat for a straight boy, Billy Bob. So, I suspect we'd better forget it, okay?"

I walked to my desk. I didn't look back at him. I put the magazine away and, plopping down in the chair, turned my computer on to the couple of pages I'd written on the meaning of Kantian metaphysics. Of course, my mind wasn't that willing to change gears; but Billy Bob didn't know that. I was praying he'd say something, do something, so I could end my self-imposed celibacy. I might like reciprocity, but it had been at least three weeks since I had cock. Shit, I was one hungry dude.

After the longest seconds I'd ever experienced, I heard him clear his throat. I still didn't look up from my papers. "Ya—uh—don't mean that ya—uh—want me to—?" I looked up then and saw the biggest, roundest eyes I'd ever seen.

"Billy Bob, that's exactly what I expect."

He fell silent then and I almost had my mind set to get into Immanuel Kant again by the time he spoke again.

"I don't rightly think I'm ready to go that far." I glanced over at him in time to see him break into a real shit-eating grin. "But I sure am interested in finding out more about that shit in that magazine of your'n, Bruce!" His grin became even more shit-eating. "And I sure can keep my mouth shut when it comes to my friends."

My cock made my decision for me. My celibacy was at an end. I found myself grinning in spite of myself. "I guess that's good enough—for starters anyway. Only, I thought you people didn't think real men read porn."

"Shitfire! They just don't know what porn is all about, then." He laughed and stood up. I rose, too, and began to move toward him. It'd been so many weeks I'd almost forgotten how a man actually felt.

Billy Bob grinned as I approached him. "Come on, Bruce. Come to Big Daddy." He held his arms out for me and I slipped inside them like I'd always belonged there.

His paws circled my waist and pulled me against him. I was being pressed against his hairy pecs and was surprised to find the nipples were hard, as my face pushed against them. Tentatively, I stuck my tongue out and pulled one in between my teeth. I smiled as Billy Bob grunted in surprise. I was also willing to swear that two-by-four caught between his belly and mine had grown to the size of Pike's Peak.

I was ready to swoon; it'd been too long since I'd been this close to a man. Shit! Forget reciprocity. I could only think of that monster cock in his briefs and what it could do for me.

"Sweet Jesus," my own personal jock groaned and pulled away from my teeth and what they were doing to his equilibrium. He stared down into my eyes. "That sure feels good, Bruce, buddy."

"Not as good as the rest of it is going to feel," I growled in near frustration at not having him out of his briefs already and me hanging ten on his pole.

"Show me, Bruce," he demanded, giving in to his lust and taking me by the arms and stepping backward toward his bed. "Show me everything. Please?"

I was no longer just another gay boy desperate for a sex-fix. I was this big, panting wide receiver's trainer. I grinned as I helped him direct us onto his bed.

He pulled me down on top of him as he crashed against the mattress. Then he was holding on to me, wrapping his legs around me and gripping me in the warmest, gentlest bear hug I could imagine this side of Moscow.

"Is this gonna make me queer, dude?" he asked.

"Having sex with somebody doesn't make you gay or a breeder," I grumbled. "If you like what we do, it'll just make you realize

that you're bi—and all of us are that to some degree or another."
When I'd managed to raise my head enough to look down at him,
he was gazing at me. My fingers slipped inside the waistband of his
briefs.

He guffawed then. "You ain't no queer until folks know it, boy.
As long as it's just the two of us, all's we're doing is helping each
other out. Ya sure ain't telling. And I ain't neither." He pulled me
back against him and the movement had the effect of forcing my
hands—already inside his briefs—down onto his thighs, pulling his
briefs with them.

He giggled and grabbed for my asscheeks. "Get out of them
clothes, Yankee boy," he grunted and wiggled his bared ass against
his blanket.

I stood up and slipped out of my oxford button-down and jeans.
He stared at my cock and I started to get nervous. "Yer a whole lot
bigger than I'd thought. And yer skinned as well." I looked at his
face and followed his eyes back to my kosher, hard meat.

His briefs were bunched at his ankles and I pulled them over his
size 15 feet. He lay there naked, and he was mine. I looked down at
his dong then, letting myself study it for the first time.

I gasped. All of a sudden I wasn't sure I was all that hungry.

He had the dick of death. The fucker was thick—almost as big
around as my wrist. And long? Jesus! The monster was long enough
to see daylight at the other end when inserted into an ass as deep as
it would go.

I started to pull back, getting as far as putting my feet back on
the floor. His hand caught my arm and stopped my retreat. I was
fucking caught with the biggest cock this side of the Red Army. Oh
God!

Billy Bob was a perfect sample of a corn-fed product of American Phys Ed. I might think he was slightly short of gray matter, but
he had definitely not been slighted in the equipment department. He
grinned up at me and stroked all of it—more than ten inches! "Ya
like it?" he asked, pouring on all the magnolia juice and honeysuckle he could put in his voice. My fingers moved across his hard
belly and wrapped around his cock at its base and stroked upwards,

watching its skin come up and cover that extra-wide helmet of plum-red meat.

I nodded numbly, wondering if I could survive it when it came at me.

"I like the looks of your'n too, Bruce." He studied my cock. He frowned slightly and reached for it. "I guess it'd be all right if I tried receiving first." He stared into my eyes. "That is, before I play quarterback in this game of our'n. You promise to make it feel good?"

I wasn't believing my ears. It sounded like he wanted me to fuck him. I gazed down at him, not yet daring to speak and waited for a sign from that two-by-four that it would give me permission to plunder its backside.

His grin spread across his face. "I want to try it, Bruce. I want to know what your dick up my butt feels like. Ya mind having dessert before you get a helping of meat and potatoes?"

I nodded numbly and started for my desk.

"Where you going, bud?"

"We need rubbers," I told him and found the unopened box I'd brought from New York. Back at his bed, I climbed between his legs and he slid his ass closer to its day of reckoning. Rolling a condom onto my cock, I realized that Billy Bob's was a virgin ass. I glanced around then; only, there wasn't any greasy shit I could see anywhere in the damned room—there never is when that hottest of moments has opened up for a guy. I gulped and spit in my hand and lathered up my cock hoping it'd be enough. "This might hurt a little at first," I mumbled as I encircled my cock with my hand and took aim between his legs. "Push down when I start to knock at your door."

I slid in easier than I had any reason to expect with a virgin ass under me. My eyes were glued to his and I didn't dare look down at my progress. And he was staring right back at me, his face registering nothing as inch after inch of kosher cock made its way into his goyish ass.

I was afraid he'd ball up one of those ham hocks that were his hands and put me out of my misery if I kept going. And I was afraid he'd do it if I stopped. I kept giving him inch after inch of mohelapproved New York prime and he just stared up at me. When my bush was scratching beneath his ball-sac, I couldn't hold my curiosity any longer. "How's that feel, Billy Bob?" I asked hesitantly.

His brows knitted and he wiggled his ass around on my spear imbedded in it. Slowly his face began to break into a grin. "That ain't bad at all, boy," he said. "So far, I mean." He eyed me suspiciously. "Course, ya gotta do a bang-up job on my butt for me, Bruce. Otherwise, I'm gonna be one ever more pissed homeboy. Now, fuck my ass good for me."

I grinned down at him feebly, still imagining a nightmare was going to come up and wallop me when I wasn't looking. But I started to plow that Georgia ass with everything I had. Billy Bob grunted and moaned under me. He grabbed his pud and pulled it with abandon. His ass-muscle grabbed at my cock and made me wonder if I'd ever see myself whole again.

He shot all over the headboard of his bed and laughed as he did it. "Plow that ass, boy!" he growled as his second rope hit him in the eye. I kept on, afraid to stop. And not wanting to, either.

When I'd finally cum up his ass and fallen spent against his chest, he wrapped his arms around me. My cock stayed buried in his butt. A few moments later, he started laughing and didn't stop. Finally, I lifted my head and looked down into his face. His big finger came up and traced its way down my nose onto my lip. "I know why real men don't read porn, Bruce," he chuckled.

"Why?"

"Why read it when you can do it, boy?" He chuckled again. "At least I know how I'm gonna be spending my nights after practice from now on out." He looked down at our connection. "You're still hard—"

"Yeah."

"Do you need another rubber to do it again?"

"Again?"

"I want you fucking me, Bruce. All the time."

I smiled down at him as he ground his ass on my meat. I wondered if he'd fuck in front of a camera. The boys at Jocktime were sure to love Billy Bob.

under new management

At The Adonis

Simon Sheppard

I NEVER THOUGHT I'D BE THE TYPE TO FALL IN LOVE AND STAY IN LOVE, but one brisk fall day a few years ago—

Okay, I'm at this dinner party at my friends Clay and Bri's. There are three couples there, and two unattached guys—me and this other guy who's around my age, 25, and gorgeous. And I suddenly realize that Clay and Bri are playing matchmaker again, the fucks. I hate having other people take charge of my life, always have.

But this other guy, Mike, is—I've got to admit it—a real hunk. Thick brown hair, piercing blue eyes, shoulders that go from here to here. And eligible: he's a young stockbroker, and he tells me he lives in a converted loft in a newly-trendy part of town. I don't want to tell him about my small bedroom in the house I share with three room-mates in an iffy neighborhood near the capitol building. Okay, so the conversation between the two of us seems polite, strained. But when he stands up after dinner, I check him out—he's wearing khakis, with boxers or maybe nothing under them, and it's not hard to tell he has a big cock. Not that I'm a size queen, but—

Anyway, all the married men are cleaning up the table, in their domestic way, while Mike and I drift out to the living room, kind of chatting. I put a tentative hand on his shoulder, he responds by running the back of his hand down my chest, and despite myself I feel my dick swelling. If only he could talk about something besides stock options and the fed funds rate—

We all play some stupid after-dinner game, Pictionary or something. At least if it had been Twister, I could've copped a feel. And then 10:30 rolls around. Time for the marrieds to hit the hay.

"Did you guys have a good time getting to know each other?"

meddling little Bri asks as we're all heading out the door. I could have strangled him. But Mike and I have exchanged numbers and sworn to call each other sometime that week, and I have to admit he certainly is marriage material. Yep, he's a perfect hubby for a gay Republican with a taste for Brooks Brothers clothes and boring, vanilla sex once a week with the light turned off.

Bri and Clay (and their friends Juan and Parrish and Jay and Luke) are all nice guys, but they keep trying to fix me up with straight-arrow, looking-for-monogamy-and-a-Golden-Retriever types. They're probably already planning the reception for my Commitment Ceremony. Thing is, there's a whole side to my life they know nothing about. They're the types who would never dream of setting foot in some sleaze palace like the Adonis Showroom. Whereas I've done more than just dream of it. I've gone there. And often.

When Mike calls a few days later, I'm in a trouble making mood. So I suggest the Adonis as the place for our first date.

"Sure," he says, never missing a beat.

Maybe I've misjudged him.

We meet for dinner at a really nice restaurant that serves really small portions on really large plates. After cremé brulée, we take a taxi to the Adonis. It's in a not-very-nice part of town. 20 bucks apiece at the door is a nice piece of change, but it does give in-and-out privileges till the hand stamp wears off. The thirtyish guy who takes our money isn't bad looking in a kind of shifty, rough trade kind of way—but Jesus, he's sullen. Not a word, not even "thanks." Not an auspicious start to the Big Date.

The main show is about to start, so we go to the theater. About half of the 40 or so seats are filled. Some of the guys there look bored, some look desperate, and a few look better than okay. But none is as handsome as Mike. I start to think of him as "my Mike." I want to show off the prize I'm with, so I guide the two of us to the front row.

"You know, I've always wanted to come to a place like this," my Mike says as we sit down, "just to see what it's like." Uh-oh.

Double uh-oh, because just at that moment, a young guy with a big, curved cock, a cock that I've sucked several times in the video arcade downstairs, strolls over to us.

"Hello," he says, and says my name. He's remembered my name. Whatever possessed me to give him my real name? "Who's your sexy friend?" he says. I can see Mike clenching his chiseled jaw.

Fortunately, at that moment the lights go down and the recorded music comes up. "Gentleman," says the oily P.A. voice, "let's give a big Adonis welcome to the star of such red hot videos as *Hung Hunters* and *Stud Hungry*, superstar Vin Stroker!"

Weak applause. And Stroker comes out in a worn pair of jeans and an old T-shirt. I recognize him, of course—as would any gay man with even a passing acquaintance with porn videos. The smile on his face is frozen, a mask semi-disguising his boredom at having to shoot three loads a day for rooms full of strangers. I hope he at least has Mondays off, like an art museum.

It's not that I find Stroker unattractive, just that his looks are those cookie-cutter good looks that so many porn actors have. In fact, I notice, he looks a lot like Mike.

Stroker's dancing isn't as good as his fucking, at least not the bits of his fucking I'd seen flickering on the screens downstairs. But he gamely swings his hips in time to the music, turns his back to us, rips his T-shirt open, and whirls back around to show us his perfectly-muscled well-shaved chest, his famously big nipples. He smiles even more broadly, then shifts gears to a come-hither-then-get-lost scowl as he starts to unbutton his jeans. He's wearing a white jock strap—no surprise—and he almost-gracefully kicks off his engineer boots so he can peel off his pants.

I look over at Mike. His face is unreadable. His crotch isn't hard. I put my hand on his thigh. No response. I take my hand away.

On stage, Stroker has turned his back to us and is bending over, offering up a remarkably flawless bare butt, glutei maximi perfected by many an hour doing squats at the gym, I suppose. He doesn't bother to spread his cheeks.

A new song, same insipid disco beat, and Stroker starts fiddling with his jockstrap, teasing us rubes with glimpses of his well-trimmed pubic hair. Then the jock comes down all the way, revealing the often-photographed Vin Stroker dick. It is, unsurprisingly, soft, but I have to admit reluctantly that, even soft, that fucker is impressive. In one of those awkward moments that can happen amidst even the best-planned choreography, Stroker bends over so he can slip back into his boots and tie them up. I kind of like the moment, it's real. Then the porn star dances over to the wings, disappears as the stage lights dim. A disco fanfare thuds from the second-rate sound system. When the lights come back up and Stroker reappears, his cock is nicely hard and glistening wet. He has, apparently, been fluffed by an expert. One hand jacking his cock, superstar Stroker dances over to the runway, down the stairs, and straight over to us. Uh-oh.

Vin Stroker heads right for my Mike, and I figure I'd better explain. "You're allowed to touch him, but not his dick. And you're expected to tip him," I hurriedly whisper.

"Uh-huh," Mike says.

Stroker is straddling one of my date's legs, waving his hard-on in my date's face. Mike doesn't move a muscle. Maybe he's a Republican. Well, a muscular thigh is a terrible thing to waste. I reach over and touch Stroker's sweaty leg. My fingers move toward his ass. I open my palm and grab a hunk of butt. Stroker maneuvers himself off Mike's leg and onto mine. His cock is inches from my face. Instinctively, I open wide. Pavlov's cocksucker.

I glance over to Mike. He's pulled a 20 dollar bill from his wallet. "Where the hell should I put it?" he asks me.

"In my sock," Vin Stroker says. Ever the shrewd businessman.

Mike bends over and does the deed. Having been paid, Stroker dances off to his next lapdance target, a well-dressed Japanese businessman three seats down.

"Twenty dollars," I say. "That was generous." And premature, I'm thinking.

"I wanted him to go away," Mike says. I notice he's blushing. This evening was a mistake.

"I gotta go pee," I say. The wine and after-dinner coffee have done their work. I stand up and light out for the men's room.

There's just one other guy in the bathroom. It's the surly ticket-taker, standing at the trough, playing with a very nice, uncut cock. Must be on his coffee break. In other circumstances, I would have joined him, but hell, I'm on a date. A date with a stockbroker. Even I can resist temptation, every now and then. I go into the none-too-clean stall, pull out my dick and drain it. When I leave the men's room, Rough Trade is still there, still stroking.

The music in the theater has changed again in my absence. Now it's the disco version of that song from "Titanic." I walk down the hallway and back into the theater.

Mike's seat is empty.

Could he have deserted me for the pleasures of the Shower Room? Unlikely. Gone downstairs for a blowjob in the booths? Nope, not my Mike. I sit back down and wait for Mike to return. Meanwhile, Stroker has come back on stage, beating his meat.

The Japanese businessman leans over. "Your friend say to tell you he go."

Yeah, Mike probably *is* a Republican. Well, I guess I can hang around for the cum shot. Might as well get my money's worth.

Stroker closes his eyes tight, thinking of something, anything, I suppose, other than the fact that he still has a midnight show to go. My heart will go on... His hand works furiously. He clenches his butt muscles, thrusts forward, scrunches his face up. The tension in the room is palpable. It's as close as I've ever gotten to a bullfight. Will he be able to Do It?

But, damn, the guy is a pro. He shoots ropes of cum high into the air. It gleams in the spotlights and spatters on the stage.

There's a round of genuine applause, coming, I suppose, not just from admiration, but from relief.

Stroker struts offstage. The house lights come up. Some guys in the rear rows are rearranging their clothes. One stands up still grasping a wad of Kleenex. Tidy fellow.

I know what I'm going to do. I'll phone Mike the next day, apologize for coming up with such a bone-headed plan, propose brunch, a movie, a walk in the park. But in the meantime, I'm going to go down to the video booths and get my dick sucked.

I head down the familiar flight of stairs. I buy my tokens from the guy at the turnstile, not the surly one, but a pimple-faced boy who looks like he's just turned 18. If he ever gets those zits under control, he might turn out to be cute. The attendant buzzes me through the turnstile, and I enter the maze of video booths.

Okay, so it may seem excessive to some of you to have to pay 20 bucks to get into the Adonis, then pay more for the video booths. But the booths at the Adonis give good value, as these things go, and the place is pretty clean, without smelling so strongly of PineSol that it makes you want to gag. Best of all, although the laws in this state leave most adult bookstores in a kind of legal limbo, the Adonis falls into the category of "private club" or something (or at least a bribes-in-the-right-places establishment). So what you've got is a video arcade where the police never intrude and pretty much anything goes, as long as you keep shoveling those tokens in the slots.

Since the show upstairs has ended, the arcade is starting to fill up. A certain amount of predatory and/or desperate cruising is normal for the place, but spend too much time cruising without dropping tokens and the attendant is liable to object. So I wander around for just a bit, looking at no one in particular, then walk into one of the Buddy Booths and shut the door. I am, for some reason, feeling kind of in-secure, so I lock the door.

The Adonis is a pretty fancy place and the Buddy Booths are a nice innovation. There's an eye-level little window between two adjoining booths, with a curtain on each side. Assuming both of you are interested, you can see whatever's happening in the other booth, but if one of you loses interest or wants to wank in private, he can pull the curtain shut. It's ideal for voyeurs and exhibitionists, but if both the guys want more, the Adonis has thoughtfully provided a dick-level sliding door between the booths, one that latches on both sides. It's much nicer than the awkward, raggedy, let's-pretend-they're-not-here glory holes chopped into the partitions of many a dirty-bookstore arcade. Neat, discreet, and there's no danger of getting splinters in your dick. See, I told you the Adonis is a class act.

The curtains are open, but there's nobody in the adjoining booth. I drop a token in the slot and choose a scene from the menu of video clips. Nothing there really inspires me, so for old times' sake, I choose *Jockboys*, the scene where Trent or Troy or whatever the fuck his name is gets fucked from both ends on a locker room bench. There's something about it that seems a little more real than most of the videos, like the guys aren't just going through the motions thinking of nothing but the paycheck. And the guy doing the face-fucking has body hair, something of a rarity these days, and something that turns me on big-time. As the image of the three-way flickers on the screen, I unzip my pants, pull out my dick, and get to work.

I try thinking of Mike, of his dauntingly handsome face, the tempting bulge in his khakis, his tips on tech stocks. I can hear Clay saying, "It's really time for you to start thinking of settling down, isn't it? I mean, Bri and I are so happy together." I start to lose my hard-on.

I notice a movement out of the corner of my eye. The window. I turn my head. A face fills the window. It's Rough Trade, the sullen guy from the ticket counter upstairs. He's in the next booth, looking down at the progress of my wank. He's dark, maybe Greek or Sicilian, and he looks like trouble. I smile.

I hear the latch on his side of the little dick-door slide back. He tries to open it; it's still locked. I kneel, slip the latch open, and slide back the door. His cock hovers before my eyes, starts moving through the opening in the plywood. Meaty, and, even hard, obviously uncut. I stick out my tongue and lick the already-moist and shiny dickhead.

"Suck it," I hear him say from somewhere above my head. "Suck it, faggot." I open wide and do. His crotch smells funky, musky, high. I love it. He shoves his cock all the way down my throat and keeps it there, till I almost gag. I could draw back to take a breath, but I don't. Face it, I'm not marriage material. I'm a cocksucker and, with that dick in my mouth, I'm happy.

"Let me in there with you," the dark man says. I suddenly hope he'll fuck my face so hard that his whole body will just thrust through that hole in the wall. But, nope, guess I'm going to have to let go of that dickflesh long enough to unlock the cubicle door. I get up, wiping my eyes, and unlatch the door lock. He's already standing outside, his hard dick sticking out of his jeans. Way out.

He pushes me aside, walks into the booth with me, and closes and locks the door. He really does look like a nasty bit of work, as likely to pull out his switchblade as his dick. Just my type. I drop to my knees. Up and to my right, where Trent or Troy or whoever had been sucking locker room dick, the screen has gone dark.

"Put in another token," the dark man says.

I take my mouth from his crotch. I don't want to get off my knees. "But you're an employee...you have to worry about that?"

"I ain't an employee of this shit heap, faggot. I was just filling in up there. I work for Stroker."

"Stroker?" No wonder I've never seen him at the Adonis before.

"Yeah, I'm his personal manager."

"A porn actor gets a personal manager?"

"Yeah. I make sure he gets where he needs to be, groomed, sober, and ready to roll."

I think back to the show upstairs. "And you fluff him?"

"Yeah."

"You do a good job, huh?"

"Don't get any ideas, cocksucker. I ain't gonna suck you, not for free. But you're gonna suck me, and you're gonna do the best fucking job of cocksucking you ever did in your worthless life."

He pulls his T-shirt up and runs his hands over his lean, hairy belly, over his heavily-tattooed pecs, and starts playing with his big, dark nipples. I'm totally squirming with delight. I gulp his cock down till my nose is buried in his wiry, smelly bush. He slams the palm of his hand against the back of my head and holds it there.

"I said, make it GOOD, cocksucker."

My throat muscles do a tango on his cock.

"You ready to eat my load, fag?"

I try to grunt "uh-huh" so it's comprehensible, but it comes out as one long gargle of desire. He takes his hand from my head. I back off a bit, gulp in air, and slide my lips back to the base of his boner. He starts thrusting against the back of my throat.

"You fucking take it," he growls, and brings the palm of his hand down hard on my cheek. "No teeth," he hisses, and brings his hand down again. It stings. I hope he'll do it again. He doesn't. Instead, he squirts a big, hot load down my throat. I hardly have time to taste the saltiness of his cum before it heads for my belly.

Rough Trade pushes my head away, stuffs his cock back in his jeans, turns, and unlocks the door. "Good job," he sneers over his shoulder, but before I have time to say "thank you," he's gone. He's left the door ajar.

I'm still on the sticky floor, and my dick is still hard. I spit on my hand, spread my legs, and stroke my hard-on till pre-cum is flowing from the slit, till I can bear it no longer, till I can't be bothered to reach for a Kleenex from the box on the wall, till I shoot all over the floor, against the half-open door.

"You're gonna have to put another token in, mister." It's the cute boy with zits. He takes a long look at me kneeling there on the spunk-flooded floor, smiles, shakes his head, and walks away.

I really got to stop doing this, I think. What the hell is wrong with me? Clay and Bri and Juan and Jay are right. I'm getting old enough to settle down. I lick my spooge from my hand, zip my fly, and rise unsteadily to my feet. I should settle down with a man like Mike. With Mike. A handsome man. A good man. I'm making my way out of the arcade, up the stairs, into the lobby. A boring man.

I breathe a sigh of relief. He's there. The shifty-eyed man whose cum I've just eaten, the one with a big cock and a switchblade somewhere, is standing in the lobby, looking my way and grinning.

"How ya doing?" he says, not cracking a smile. "Having a good time?"

"Yeah," I say, trying not to grin. "You're fucking hot."

And that's how I met Angelo.

It's been three years now, and Angelo and I are still lovers. He quit his job with Vin Stroker, moved in with me in a cheap new apartment I found, and eventually got a job managing the Adonis. Sometimes, after we've gone to dinner at Clay and Bri's and we're feeling senti-mental, we go back and cruise the arcade. And sometimes we wait till the blond boy's shift is over and take him, now blemish-free, back to our place and take turns working him over.

Oh, and Mike? Well, Jay left Luke for Parrish, and Mike moved in with Juan for a while, but that didn't work out, and Mike got sick of his loft, sold it at a big profit, and moved in with Clay and Bri, where he gives Brian hand jobs when Clay is out of town on business.

I have my Rough Trade, and Christ, we make each other happy. We'll never get married, though. We like living in sin too much.

cyber sex site

"You've Got Fan Male"

Sam Archer

I'M AN ARTIST, NOT A WHORE.

There is a certain art to fucking on film, to projecting yourself into someone else's fantasies. It's not an easy thing to do with even a modicum of integrity.

Generating the right level of heat, drawing people into the intimacy of sex while performing nearly-Olympian acts of athleticism isn't easy.

Take it another step. Remove the image and leave just the cold, hard glow of pixels on a monitor and it's even more difficult. How many people do you know who can give you a hard-on simply by typing words on a screen?

Surely that's worth a $15-a-month subscription?

So, you tell me: when someone logs onto my web site, arranges for cybersex and begins typing, is he paying for sex or art? And does it matter that, in his mind, he's paying for the sex? The question weighs heavy on my own mind these days.

Normally I don't think much during my chat sessions. I just type with one hand and jerk off with the other. I'm a hopeless sex junkie. I honestly find myself getting turned on during the sex sessions.

Oh, not every session, of course. Most of the guys who sign up to chat with me are pretty inarticulate. They've seen a few of my porn films and like to imagine themselves with me. But it's largely a matter of them stroking off while I do all the work. Not that I'm complaining. They pay quite well for the privilege.

With guys like that, I indulge my own fantasies, closing my eyes and typing as I imagine their hands and mouths wandering over my body.

For example: "I twirl my tongue around your nipples, twining it through the wiry hair of your chest and tugging lightly on it. You stiffen under my mouth and I trap your nipple between my lips, fluttering the tip of my tongue over it."

I get that paragraph by pressing F1 on the keyboard. Pressing F12 brings forth: "Cupping your balls in the palm of my hand, I kiss my way along the underside of your cock. I love to play my tongue over the sensitive area just beneath the head before working my way down into the musky scent of your pubic hair and balls. As I bury my face in your crotch, my hand slides over the firm curves of your butt until it finds your asshole. My spit-moistened finger teases you, slowly moving back and forth over the opening, but never quite moving inside."

So, yes, a lot of the chat is pre-scripted routine and typing on autopilot. Even that has a tendency to get me hard. I love the idea that there are guys out there getting off on the idea of having sex with me. It's a rush to know my fame comes not from wealth or a game that demands equipment and teamwork. My fame comes from the fact that I'm sexy. Drop Bill Gates or Dennis Rodman stark naked in the desert and they aren't that interesting. I, on the other hand, maintain my allure under all situations—even in the sterile wasteland of cyberspace.

It's an added bonus when the person I'm chatting with actually has imagination and writing skills. I might get one or two of those a week.

When it happens, though, it's well worth the wait. At that point the hot keys go out the window and the chat session becomes a duel. I feel myself getting hard and pull out all the stops to make sure my partner gets his money's worth. It's a race to see if I can make him cum before I do.

There's this one guy—he calls himself White Dragon—who beats me every time. I don't know that much about him. His screen name is taken from a mah-jongg tile and according to his credit card information he lives in Seattle.

He writes beautifully, though. Or, at least he does when typing sex fantasies in chat rooms. He shows up about twice a month. In the meantime, I find myself thinking up new fantasies to try out on him while I work with other subscribers.

Here's the scenario I plan to use next: A limo picks me up and I'm ushered into the back seat. As soon as the car begins to move, I'm blindfolded and stripped naked and my hands are tied behind my back. Someone kneels over me, straddling my legs. I barely feel rough denim brushing the outer edges of my thighs. A hand twines itself through my hair and my head is tilted back against the seat so that the stranger can kiss me.

There are no preliminaries. It's a long, hard kiss. My lips are crushed against my teeth as the stranger pulls my face hard against his own. His tongue presses past my lips and into my mouth, slithering over my own tongue as they caress each other.

I'm getting hard as he kisses along the line of my jaw to reach my ear. His warm breath against my ear almost makes me faint as he whispers: "Who owns you?"

"You," I whisper. "I'm yours tonight."

"Just for tonight?" he whispers, the palms of his hand lightly pressing against my bare chest. His teeth seize my earlobe and tug on it gently as he awaits my answer.

"Always," I gasp. "I'm always yours."

By this time, I'm getting hard and my cock is standing straight up between the stranger's legs. I feel rough, dry denim rasping along the head. The stranger stretches slightly, drawing his thighs together just enough to give the tip of my cock a quick squeeze.

"Shouldn't you get undressed?" I ask.

A sharp pain follows the question as he tweaks my left nipple.

"You belong to me, remember?"

The rest of the ride is unbearable. The stranger licks his way over my entire body. I feel first his breath and then his lips on every inch of my being. It lulls me with a sense of rhythm. First the warmth of his breath on my flesh as he exhales. Then his slightly parted lips making contact with my skin. A moment later, his tongue probing the area before he moves on and begins the process somewhere else.

He crosses my neck and shoulders, then my chest—spending an eternity on my nipples—before drifting down to my navel. When the stranger begins kissing my hips and thighs, I expect to feel his lips on my cock at any moment. Instead, he continues to kiss his way down my legs. You never realize how sensitive the human knee is until someone plays his tongue along the depressions on its surface. The stranger even kisses my feet, slipping his tongue between the toes and sucking on each one in turn before beginning the return trip up my shins.

This time, when he reaches my cock, the stranger gives it his full attention. He kisses along the length of it for a few moments, lingering just long enough to make me buck my hips against his face before skipping to a new spot. He tickles the head of my dick a moment, just scraping the skin with his teeth before pulling away.

When I can't stand the tension anymore, he swoops forward again, swallowing my entire cock in one swift motion. I almost pass out from the pleasure as his tongue trashes the underside.

"Oh, my God," I call out, as he strains a bit further, pressing his face into my pubic hair. The back of his throat rubs the head of my cock.

As swiftly as he swallows me, he retreats.

"Now that you have an idea of how it's supposed to be done," he says, "you can give it a try."

In the darkness, I hear his zipper being undone. He straddles my legs and I can feel the cold metal of a belt buckle falling against my thigh. A cock brushing my lips soon erases the sensation.

Opening my mouth, I strain toward it with my tongue, but the stranger moves away. Again, his cock brushes the side of my face and I turn toward it only to have him retreat. The game goes on for several minutes.

I see myself as the stranger must see me, blindfolded, hands tied, fruitlessly chasing his cock while my own hard-on rages between my legs. I should be humiliated, but it only turns me on more.

I finally catch the pattern of what he's doing, the way he alternates angles before slapping my face with his cock. I let him run through the pattern once more to make sure, then anticipate his next swing.

This time, I catch his cock in my mouth, trapping it between my tongue and cheek. The stranger's startled gasp rewards my effort. Immediately, I go to work. Unable to move my hands, I resort to bobbing my head furiously while sucking hard on his cock. At the end of each pull, I strain just a bit more as if trying to pull his cock loose from his body.

His hands tangle in my hair and the stranger is humping his hips against my lips. The face-fuck is brutal. He seems to have completely lost control. Meanwhile, he's clamped his thighs together over my hard-on and the violence of his movements is jerking me off.

We cum together—his hot seed filling my mouth as his cock spasms against my tongue and my own load bathes his inner thighs. The stranger collapses on top of me and I kiss his chest through the thin fabric of his cotton shirt.

Moments later, he gets up. I hear his zipper closing and the door of the car closes. I never even see his face.

See what I mean?

Admit it, you've got a hard-on just from listening to the idea. Can you imagine what White Dragon will feel like when I take him through the whole scenario online, weaving more detail and working his own ideas and comments into the story?

It's what I do best.

It's an art.

So why do I feel just a little bit like a whore now that I've decided to take things to the next level?

I mean, I've decided to run a "Win a Date With a Porn Star" contest on my web site. All the names of my subscribers will go into an electronic hat, I'll pull out a name and—voila—some lucky guy will get to meet me in real life.

It's legal. My lawyers say it isn't prostitution. No one is promised sex for cash. It's not even gambling. No one has to buy a ticket. I just enter the names of people who paid for a real subscription. It's actually more legal than the average church raffle as far as gambling laws are concerned.

All the guy gets is the pleasure of my company for an evening. I'm not saying I won't have sex with the winner. If he's cute, clean and carrying a condom, it's a possibility. But I won't be doing it for the money.

I'll be having dinner and going clubbing with him for the money. If I have sex with him, it's because the guy's able to charm me into it.

Granted, that's not the most difficult thing in the world to do. I'm usually pretty horny. Besides, I've been spending a lot of time chatting with White Dragon and I'd love to see what he's like in a real life bed instead of a virtual reality one.

Oh, did I forget to mention the contest is rigged?

How else am I suppose to meet the guy?

I'll do a legitimate drawing next month. This month I've already made up my mind, "drawn" the name, and e-mailed White Dragon for a phone number to set things up.

Now all I have to do is make the call. His E-mail says to ask for Ben.

"Mad Dog's Harley-Davidson," the voice on the phone growls. Definitely not a good sign.

"May I speak to Ben?" I ask.

"I'm Ben," the voice barks. "What can I do for you?"

"I'm—ah—Ryan Dylan," I begin. "I e-mailed you this morning—"

"Hold on."

A button clicks and I'm on hold. I fight the urge to hang up. This was obviously a bad idea. Mad Dog certainly didn't sound like the charming, ingenious youth I'd been chatting with online.

"Are you still there?" a soft, well-modulated voice asks. "I had to switch to the phone in my office."

"What happened to Ben?" I ask.

A low, seductive chuckle answers my question.

"Ben is a good persona for dealing with the Harley riders," the voice continues. "You might say I'm in the closet—or just that I play a part when dealing with customers. I guess a guy like you wouldn't understand that. I mean, you put yourself right out there every day."

It's my turn to laugh. "You'd be surprised how different I am away from the office."

"Don't tell me you don't like guys?" Ben asks in mock horror.

"It would be my luck to win a date with my favorite porn star just to learn he's only gay for pay."

"Oh, I'm really gay," I explain. "I just don't hang from chandeliers away from the set. In real life, I'm a little on the conservative side."

"There's nothing conservative about raffling off a date on the Internet," Ben points out.

"I planned on it being my on-screen persona on the date. Most people would be bored to tears with the real me. I'm not into the club scene."

"How are you on Egyptian antiquities?"

"Huh?"

"Do you like mummies and scarabs and stuff?"

"I never gave it much thought," I answer.

"Before I inherited the family Harley dealership, I studied archaeology," Ben explains. "I still get off on museums. There's a showing of artifacts this weekend at the Rosicrucian Park museum in San Jose. I thought we might take a look at the exhibit and then catch a movie. One of the local theaters is showing an all night mummy retrospective in honor of the exhibit."

"That's a lot more original than dinner and dancing," I point out.

"Well, if you'd rather hit the clubs—"

"No," I interrupt. "Your plan's perfect."

So, here we are, snuggled together in the balcony of a thinly-peopled movie theater in San Jose. There are maybe 30 people downstairs, but we have the balcony to ourselves. The movies themselves are dreadful. After an afternoon's education in artifacts, I'm amusing myself by building a list of errors in the scripts.

Ben seems to be taking a different kind of inventory. Glancing up, I realize he's stopped watching the movie and is studying my face.

"Like what you see?" I ask.

"Uh-huh," he says, only slightly embarrassed. "I love that little glimmer of disgust you get when you spot a mistake in the archaeology."

"I never realized how painful these things must be to a professional," I murmur.

"I'm not a professional," Ben sighs. "I sell motorcycles."

His arm is around my shoulders as I sink deeper into the red velvet seat. It's a dark, comfortable feeling and it makes me careless. I forget he's just another client.

"So why not lease out the shop and go back to archaeology?"

I feel, rather than see, his face cloud over. It's in his voice when he answers. "Do you really want to spend your life making fuck films?"

Silence looms large between us, but our bodies don't change. The comfort of holding each other isn't worth disturbing over a dumb question.

"If I were to make a sex vid about ancient Egypt," I finally say, "I wouldn't confuse Ra and Osiris. And I'd lose the eunuchs altogether."

A rich, warm laugh bubbles out of the darkness and Ben turns my face to meet his. This kiss is long, but gentle. We play with each other's lips for a few moments while finding the most natural place for it to deepen. Warmth spreads through my loins, as I become aroused.

"Is this work or play?" he asks when he breaks the kiss.

"Play," I answer. "I'm not a whore."

Again silence settles over us and Ben's arm tightens around me.

"The guy on video and in the chat rooms is just a character," he sighs, his voice tinged with sadness.

"Would you rather be with him?" I ask.

Ben snorts.

"He wouldn't fit in very well at the shop."

"But he'd be a lot more fun in a darkened movie theater?" I suggest.

"I didn't mean it that way."

"I did," I say, sliding my hand along his thigh until it reaches his crotch. Rhythmically, I begin squeezing him until the bulge begins to grow. "In real life, I'd never do something like this with a guy I just met."

"This isn't real?" he asks, choking slightly on the words.

"No," I say. "This is a fantasy. This is what makes real life worth putting up with."

He accepts the answer—or just decides not to argue—as my hand discovers his zipper. His fingers are gentle as they play through my hair. Instead of pressing my face toward his cock, he simply pets me as I find my own way there.

His skin is salty with nervous sweat. "Better than popcorn," I think inanely while licking his shaft.

Above me, I hear Ben's jacket rustle and the faint sound of tearing paper. A moment later, a condom is pressed into my hand. I continue kissing his cock and thighs until it stiffens enough to take the condom. There's a faint chemical scent to it as I roll the rubber down his shaft. On a hunch, I give it a lick—grape. At least that's the flavor they intended. It's fairly obvious no one at the plant bothered to taste them on the way out.

Still, it isn't bad, and I soon lose myself in the act of bobbing my head up and down on this enormous pseudo-grape lollipop and luxuriating in the feel of Ben's fingers massaging my scalp. He cums all too soon, filling the condom's tip with his load. I peel it off slowly and deposit the skin in an empty popcorn container.

"Have I executed my duties as a drawing prize properly?" I ask.

"Oh, yeah," Ben sighs. "You make a great drawing prize, a great chat partner, and a great sex object for jerking off to."

"Well, that's my goal in life," I sigh.

"Why not add buddy and houseguest to your resume?" he asks.

"Kept man?" I say, arching my eyebrows. "Can you afford that on a motorcycle salesman's salary?"

"I thought I might find a good man to manage the shop while I go back to school," he says. "I really can't afford you on a student's stipend."

"I might stay with a student for free."

"Charity?"

"Play," I explain. "If you're just a poor student, it would be 100 percent play."

Again, he turns my face into a tender, wistful kiss that seems to last for ages. Our mouths open naturally as our tongues meet in a sort of playful wrestling match and I feel his hands slipping over the buttons of my shirt.

"Are you insane?" I gasp.

"No one can see us," he laughs, pressing the advantage, and soon we're naked, coiled in each other's arms in the red velvet darkness of the balcony.

His lips and hands are everywhere, bringing my body to life with a kind of passion I haven't felt in years. There's a difference between having sex on film and making love in the dark. You can't really understand it until you've done both.

In my videos, I normally top. It's just a preference I have. Allowing someone to enter me makes me feel a bit too vulnerable, so I don't do it. Tonight, it feels like the most natural thing on earth to bend over a row of seats and beg Ben to take me.

His hands part my cheeks and I feel his thumb working lube over my asshole.

"You brought lube into the theater?" I ask in mock disgust.

"It's one of those little packets of butter for the popcorn," he says sheepishly. "I didn't expect to be doing this."

I laugh as he enters me, the grape-flavored lube of the condom mixing with the cheap margarine as his cock slips into me. I gasp at the size of him. He feels bigger now than when I was blowing him.

Soon, however, the discomfort fades into the familiar rhythm of lovemaking and I lose all track of where I am as I live within the sensation of his cock sliding in and out of my ass and his strong, cool hands grasping my hips and pulling me closer.

A few moments into the act, Ben slips his other hand around my waist and pumps my cock in time with his thrusts. I wonder for a moment why his hand is so slick and then begin laughing when I realize it's more butter.

That's what makes up my mind. It's been a long time since I laughed during sex—or made love to someone who hadn't come prepared to fuck me.

I'd forgotten how good that felt.

It's definitely worth blurring the line between work and play.

discovered talent

The Next Big Thing

Lance Rush

"STARS ARE MADE, NOT BORN. SOMETIMES, IT ALL COMES DOWN TO sucking the right dick, jamming your cock up the right ass, and fucking the right way. No shit. Hell! It happened to me."

Those are my words to the new kid on the set after I'd fucked him sore. I like him. Young, cute blond with eyes so blue, and a face so pretty you want to drown it in a Titanic surge of cum. Which I would've. But it isn't in the script. He calls himself Chad. He should have picked something more original—something like Donatello or Dante. Chads are as common as tan lines and swimmer's builds in this biz. He walks away, a little more bowlegged than when he'd stepped on set.

Strange. He reminds me of myself, a few years back.

Only I wasn't quite so innocent then.

As I sit in the director's chair bearing my now-famous stage name, recuperating for my next scene, I stroke my dick and think back to my own beginnings.

It had started out being just another Manhattan night prowling the Chelsea Pier. It was the cool, drizzling, annoying sort of night that made me wonder: What the fuck am I doing here? I'm better than this. Must be a better way to meet a john.

And I wasn't the only one. The night was thick with boys like me, posing in wet denim and leather, our shadows shifting against the slow cruise of oncoming headlights.

"Yo! Yo, Joey. Over here!" I called out. Joey and I had been buddies from day one. He'd sort of showed me the ropes. He'd been hustling since he was barely 18, a long time ago. Just how long, he'd never tell. Joey had a street-tough Italian edge. More man than boy, he wasn't "pretty" like me. But he was hot, and big in the pants— and that night he seemed even bigger.

"Hey, dude. How's it hangin'?" he asked as he came up to me.

"Damn! It ain't hanging like yours," I teased. "You packing socks tonight?" His cock was a long, slumbering pipe forced against his thigh. It was a money-maker's bulge, and it paid to advertise.

"It's the jeans. Got 'em in a thrift shop in the Village. Must be from the '70s, right?"

"The '70s? How the hell would I know? That's your generation, right? Ya old-ass stallion!"

I got off teasing Joey about his mysterious age. Plus, I knew it pissed him off.

"Yeah, right. Funny motherfucker. You should be in the movies. Remind me to kick your ass later. But check it. I'm like John fuckin' Holmes in these babies. See how they hug my johnson?"

"Oh, so, it's your johnson tonight, huh?" I said, surveying his fat Italian rod.

"Yep. In these pants, it's a fucking johnson. Now shut the hell up, and let me bum a smoke."

Most nights I did a little better than him. Johns liked 'em young, or at least young-looking. I had that going for me. The best tricks drove nice suburban rides. Joey tagged all of them a "Mr. Brady." They were family men with kinky little secrets. These dudes were nervous, and real quick to shoot the wad. That night, we stood in the drizzle, praying for a Brady. They were Joey's bread and butter.

"By the time I jump in the ride," he said, "a Brady's so busy mentally doin' it, he's already hard and juicin.' Saves time. Get 'em off, and move 'em out. Just give me nine or ten Bradies, and I'm set. But you? You walk the streets with all these goofy dreams, like a fuckin' gay Cinderella. You expect some prince to cruise by, wag his dick, and sweep you off to his shiny kingdom. You need to grow the fuck up. There ain't no Mr. Right. Only Mr. Get-This-Thing-Off-For-Me-Right-Now."

Joey had a cynical streak. Every man was a potential john, and every john a piece of meat.

Dark, beefy, hopelessly butch, he'd tell anyone who'd listen that he was straight and just a hungry actor. But we all got down, at least for a few minutes, on our knees. I stood 5'11," and weighed all of 150 pounds soaking wet, and most of that was dick. I'd just turned twenty-two the week before. If you were blond, thin and waif-ish enough, you were as young as they wanted you to be under neon. That night, I felt like being honest. Sometimes, honesty can be a great gimmick.

Maybe the shine of my new leather jacket first attracted the man in the silver sedan. The window lowered, and a pair of dark, smoldering eyes molested every inch of me. "What are you into tonight?" he asked.

"Fun," I said. "Wanna party?"

"Get in!" he said, his voice a hard, no-nonsense baritone.

I checked his face. He was leering back at me. Not scary, but real intense. His eyes were like two blazing stars, shining under steel-and-midnight hair. Aged machismo. Thick 'stache.

Mmmm! Talk to me, I thought. A big gruff Daddy! The night became electric.

All I heard was that hot sound: Smack, smack, SMACK! With an air of forceful dominance, he motioned my eyes downward. I looked, and there it was. Naked. Exposed. Smack, smack, SMACK! It shone like a bar of bronzed gold as he slapped it hard to his burly thigh. The Thickest One I've Ever Seen that wasn't multiplied 25 times its unnatural size up on some porno screen.

"Are you going to hurt me with that thing?" I joked, beyond being impressed with his meat's measure.

"Get in!" he repeated.

"You ain't a cop or anything, are you?" I asked.

He could've been. Sure looked kick-ass tough enough. But I'd been hustling for three years. I knew a cop when I sniffed one. They smelled like the street—gritty, dangerous, tricky—with an edge of something righteous they tried like hell to hide. Still, I had to be sure. He shook his head. I glanced back at Joey as he stood by a lamppost, holding his long denim-clad dick.

"Ask if he wants to double the fun?" Joey called.

"No. Just you," the stranger said. I shrugged at Joey and got in as he cracked: "Just don't fall in love, ya fuckin romantic."

We zoomed down the avenue. I looked over for another glance of his big, thick, economy-size meat. He'd put it away. But a bulge the shape of Florida (my favorite state) lay across his beefy thigh. He was silent. Too silent. But my time was money, so I ran down the menu.

"I get 30 for a blow-job. 60 for straight sex. Anything else, we can barter. And I don't kiss." I hated the sound of that. So harsh, and emotionally empty. But it wasn't me. It was what I did.

"How much for the night?" he asked, his shining eyes never leaving the road.

"The night?" I had to compute. Not many asked for the night. "Ummm ... five bills, up front."

He looked at me then as if I was kidding.

So, my eager side, the cocky salesman, kicked in: "Hey! I've had rich men offer to leave their fuckin families for me. I'm worth it, Daddy."

We stopped at a light. That knot in his jeans looked like a fistful of quarters. He grabbed my chin and looked at me, the way food inspectors looked at meat. Had I passed his Pretty Boy Whore Test? I thought next he'd ask to see my fucking teeth.

"How many men you been with tonight, huh? And don't lie to me," he said sternly.

"Two. Just two. Honest," I said, and that was the truth.

He released my chin, reached into his wallet, and slammed 3 balled-up Benjamins in my fist.

The light changed and we headed into the night.

Instead of parking on a dark street for some quick head or checking into some cheap motel, he chose a theater. One that wasn't just any gay porn house. This place only showed those classic loops.

The 8 mm ones, made way back in the supposedly good ole days I'd only heard of, before the onset of AIDS and condoms. I dug those flicks and the nasty men in them. They had flaws, and those flaws were hot and appealing. They weren't all pink and shaved and pretty. Naw. These were no beauty queens. These dudes looked like fucking truck drivers, and Hell's Angels. Big, sweaty, mustach-ioed—and hairy as all hell.

Against the flickering glow of men fucking mano a mano, he pawed my thigh. Mmm. A large, hairy hand. Hello! I watched his large skull, his virile profile catching the shifting light. Hot. Sudden-ly, I was very glad the big galoot had chosen me.

Reaching over, I slowly massaged him. Instantly, I felt his mem-ber growing harder and thicker by the stroke.

"Unzip me, and take out my dick," he demanded, loud enough for most every man sitting there to hear. The funny thing was that he'd said at the exact same time and in the same way the hot, dark stud on the screen said it. My mind whispered: Okay. I get it, now. He's seen this flick before. And he's a freaking exhibitionist.

I took that big meaty column in my grasp, sliding my hand slowly up and down, working the dewy foreskin back and forth. He gripped my neck and brought my lips to it. Holding the wedge by its burly root, he fed me his big bloated dickhead, throbbing shaft and all. He began to roll his hips, pumping slow, pumping deep. Then he found his groove inside my mouth, and took my tongue on a long and vig-orous ride. He humped and I sucked until my jaw hurt from his width.

"Damn, Daddy, you're a whole lotta man," I groaned.

"Just suck it!" he growled.

I skated down, slithering all around his warm dick skin.

It had a thick, zig-zagging vein at its husky base, like that dude on the screen. Straining my neck, I forced my nose deep into his wild bush and promptly gagged as the swollen tube slid down my throat. I could feel every throbbing inch of his meat. I gazed up. He was smiling as I slurped. Men were looking at us.

Looky Lous and horny boys were jerking their hard cocks and cranking their necks to see what it was this Daddy possessed. His dick goo mixed with my slobber as I thought: They should all taste like this man in my mouth.

"Suck it, boy. Oh shit! That feels fuck—fuck—fucking FANTAS-TIC," he purred.

He threw his head back, and let me swirl. He yanked his pants way down those bushy, thick thighs, and I licked them too. I ran my wild tongue up and down his fat shaft, then hummed on his balls as they surged in their long warm sac. A boy-whore knows when a man is close. He pulled me up by my slobbery chin and I sat beside him. Men were cumming, shooting, spewing loads all around us. They were gawking, groaning at the hulking silhouette of Daddy's hefty dickmeat.

"No. Don't touch it," he said, sitting back and letting it waver. Must've been the thickest cock in that whole cock-filled theater, and I had a feeling he loved the attention that fucker brought. "Come on, kid. Follow me," he said, tucking his fame away.

He led me through the dark to that shaded area behind the flickering screen. We stood, face to face. I panicked. It looked like he wanted to kiss me. Standing, rubbing cocks in slow, heated frottage, he whipped it out.

Mmm... Daddy's hard, thick raw meat lunged between my thighs. He tugged at my jeans, and unleashed my cock. It snaked sideways up my taut, brown belly. I closed my eyes. AH! Oh! The heat! No fucking. No need. Just two lust-swollen masts, thrusting.

I kept track of what was happening on the screen. I listened as I gave myself to what Daddy was doing to me. For me. Soon I was imagining everyone's eyes on the other side of the screen, those hungry, voyeuristic eyes, all watching us. Men were staring as if this Daddy and his dick were stars.

I opened my eyes and saw shadowed faces creeping near us. That dark space was a land of peeking eyes—shining, watching our sliding, half-naked dance of lust. A strange hand gripped my ass. It didn't belong to Daddy. He pushed it away, and kept pushing, lunging between my trembling thighs. The sound of hard, slick, jacking cocks filled our ears. The horny tribe of voyeurs was adoring him. Just as I thought he was getting his rocks off, he said: "Let's leave."

It was his cash, his trip; so, we stuffed our stubbornly rigid dicks away, and left.

His place. Over cold beers, we sat in facing chairs. He didn't want to fuck right away. No. He wanted conversation. "Why sell yourself for chump change? Hell. If you're gonna do it, a pretty kid like you should demand top dollar," he scolded. "Where do you see yourself in five, even ten, years?" he asked, his brown eyes writing me off as some punk with no future.

"I'll be a writer then. A successful author, with a hot bestseller, and Hollywood-types licking my ass for the motion-picture rights. Man! You want stories? I've got stories. Hot ones. Funny ones. Stories that'll make you fucking cry," I snorted. "But mostly, I just like to fuck, and get paid."

"So you're ambitious. Good. That's a good thing," he said, eyes suddenly gleaming.

"Yeah. That's me. I'm just an ambitious hustler, with all these goofy dreams," I said.

"Know why I picked you over the others? You remind me of someone. My boy. Chris. We met in that theater. He had your sweet face. Same optimistic eyes. I like that. The streets haven't tainted you. Yet." He pushed himself out of his chair. "Let's grab a shower. I don't know where you've been, but I want you clean."

I thought he'd just insulted me. But I didn't care. Under the shower, with his gray-black hair slicked back, and those eyes leering beneath dense, satanic brows, I was falling into his face, drowning in its ridiculous masculinity. By its earned lines and creases, I figured him for forty, forty-five, maybe older. But physically, he was in his prime. Yes. I've seen my share of naked men. But his wide and flopping nakedness aroused me like no other man before or since. He turned, and I washed the high wet slopes of his back. He washed mine. Pulled me slowly against his strong, turgid meat, heat and suds ran down my ass, and I tingled.

Turning me around to face him, his bare body welcomed my gaze. His chest was a swirling land of mixed-gray fur—so smooth, wet, expansive. His nipples were large, rosy, brown coins, the size of lucky quarters. His foreskin was a brown shroud I could've fit a pocketful of change inside. And that dick. So fucking erect. The damned thing was practically cinematic.

"You like this dick, boy?" he asked. "Did you like seeing all those horny guys beating to the sight of it—on the screen?" He grinned at the memory.

"Yeah. That was hot. They all wanted you. Wait. You mean, BEHIND the screen, don't you?"

"No, kid. I meant ON the screen. That was me up there, kid. That Patrolman, who stopped the blond speeding in his pickup. Remember? The cop with the 'stache, who said—"

"Unzip me, and take out my DICK!" we both repeated at the same time.

I looked at him again. Really looked at him. Shit! It WAS HIM! Older yes—but just as hard and studly as that man—that brute—on the screen. Oh, shit! Oh, fuckin' A! How lucky could one hustler from the mean streets of New York City possibly get?

I wanted to play that scene. I wanted to have him stop me on a lonely road, in that tight, painted-on trooper's uniform, that mountie's hat cocked at a dangerous tip. Yes. Did he know I was a sucker for men like him?

Did he know how I nearly creamed in that theater chair, when that cop on the screen barked to that man in the truck: "Get your ass up"? Shit! How his machismo shone through behind those mirrored shades. All I wanted was to hear those hot, magic words: "Unzip me, and take out my dick!" But I didn't have to. It was already there, and poking out from a dank mess of pubic fur, all big and hard and wet before me. Yes! Shit, yes.

The thick rod's skin dribbled under the jetting water. I had a whole new respect for him. I admired his broad width in both my hands. I dipped down slowly, opened wide, and worshiped his lengthy shaft with my hot, curling tongue. Oh! In a warm, moist swoosh, he owned my throat—owned my lust and every heaving, jutting part of me. My slurping echoed against the shower walls, as he gasped, enthralled by the slickness of my suck.

He moved just a little, slowly dancing his hips to my liquid motion. God! I loved this man's body. My hands sailed over the tower of him, through ocean of fur and suds, and latched on to his pointy nipples. He shuddered and pitched that once-famous, and still-mighty dick down my hungry, cock-starved gullet.

Then, he pulled it free and slowly went down on me. Oh!

He sucked my dick with all the passion and serious intensity of a lover. My fucking knees wobbled.

Standing up and peering deep in my eyes, he said: "I don't give a damn about your rules, kid. I AM gonna kiss you." His full lips moved slowly towards mine. I had no will to refuse him. We kissed, tongues darting, swimming. Mmmm! It was a long and levitating experience. It was all at once needy, greedy, desperate, and hot.

Without leaving my mouth, he shut off the water and lust floated us—like men with two rigid compasses pointing north. Kissing and walking, he guided me to the room where he took his whores, his boys, and his lovers.

If I had any doubts about his identity, they vanished the moment I was in his bedroom. The walls were covered in framed posters depicting his porn career. Daddy in jeans, and shirtless. Daddy in leather. Daddy in that trooper gear. Shiny porn gods draped their burly arms around him, as he gave that sneer. One of those, I'm-gonna-fuck-the-shit-out-of-your-faggot-ass looks. Oh!

Take me, now.

His bed was as I'd expect—king-sized. He lay first, and pulled me down on to the damp heaving land of his body. In a playful wrestle, our hands slow-danced along chest and biceps, nipples and hips. His dick was a rising brown cobra. Its crown, a perfect pearl, glistened for me, as he rolled a rubber down its shaft.

"Now, we fuck," he announced as if I'd now somehow earned the pleasure of his invasion.

MPPH! Fat club's crest, then his extra-thick shaft slowly pierced me. OH! AWW! He wasn't just another big-dicked john! No. This was a fucking Giant of Porn sliding his cock in me.

I grunted. He smiled, liking that look of sudden pain that only a cock the size of his could bring.

My mind's cinema recalled the way this big woolly beast had taken his little blond prey in the back of that pickup. Years ago in video land, he'd slammed the fuck out of him. Now he was slamming me. Punching that cock through my ass again and again and making me squirm and shudder.

That big club of a dick hurt. But I'd been hurt before. He pushed both legs behind my head, and tore deeper, harder, as I sizzled—and winced from it. He moved and he fucked with the rhythms of an aging tough guy with something to prove.

But I clutched on to him as that rigid prick pounded, pounded through the slick groove of my asshole. A versatile fucker, he pushed me to my side, his cock never leaving my anal eye, and rigorously pumped as he jacked my dick. He began to fuck faster, splitting me deeper, harder. Prick punching, body scratching the blissful hell out of me.

He took me on my belly, my dick grinding into the sheets—his large, furry balls slapping my cheeks, the shanks of my thighs. Finally, I was on my back, legs wrapped tight to his torso and he continued his sweet Daddy attack. I gazed at his face, its tortured masculinity. He fucked as if he were mad at someone. His boy, Chris, maybe. His dick was blazing then, aiming deep, pushing towards my stomach.

I grunted, wanting to scream, but I didn't think he wanted me to, and muffled my scream into his pillow. Did Chris scream when this big porn vet of a Daddy fucked him? Did his belly fill with fire like mine did?

He went with the flow—rippling, trembling, every lunge swimming past the pit of me. I could've sprayed like a geyser without ever touching my raging cock.

He stopped then. Just stopped. I knew he hadn't cum. A cock that size, I would've felt the fucker surge and pelt white-gold into the latex in my gut. He wrangled that swollen tube out of me, and said: "Now. Let's see what you got, kid. Put a rubber on that thing, and earn your worth."

"Cool with me, Daddy," I panted, sliding the safe down my elongated bone.

"How big is it? he asked. Then, with all his previous experience, he told me. "8-inches, right?"

"Yeah. Exactly. How do you like it? Smooth and slow? Or fast and rough?" I asked, my latexed cock poised at his furry ditch. He looked up at me like some tough, seasoned ass-kicker, and I knew.

I pulled his cheeks wide open. No easing in for Daddy. I stabbed him with one quick jab through his mounds. His furry muscular body lurched forth. I pulled back, and his asshole latched on to me.

"Fuck it," he growled. "Fuck it good, boy!"

He wiggled against my jimmy, like it wasn't quite enough. What he didn't know was that I fucked like a jackhammer. I held onto his shoulders, set my hips on overload, and vigorously sent my prick to work—jabbing, stabbing quick and hard, as his body jolted beneath me. Ripples of ass-flesh shook like gelatin as my hips flew and my dick drilled his guts. His mounds were shaking—quaking to the speed of the fuck. He must've liked it 'cause that club of a prick stayed hard as it slapped his belly. "Oh yeah, boy. Fuck! Fuck my ass. You fuck even better than Chris," he grunted.

Determined to give him his money's worth, my speed excelerated as short, choppy thrusts overtook my fuck.

I watched the changing grimaces of his mug—the thrill, that hot, painful thrill of a well-fucked man was enough to set me off. He didn't want to be made love to. No. This Daddy wanted a hard and violent bone thrown to his ass. And I blasted into him, balls banging, prick bombarding his reddening butthole. There was no stopping my assault and battery. His body moved and squirmed—writhing, sliding up and down, finding—catching my quick, nasty rhythm. Yes!

Then, IT happened within the emotional THRUST of that charged moment. It happened, when he said those magic words to the cadence of my dick in his ass. Everything changed, and the whole world happened when he gasped and grunted out: "Kid? How would you like to be in my next video?"

I thought I'd imagined it, but then I heard him sigh. "I could make you a big porn star." He gasped as I stomped his prostate. "Fuck me," he growled. "Fuck me. FUCK!"

"Star?" I stopped in mid-bang. "If you can do that—hell—this night is yours, for free."

"You got a future, kid," he answered, smiling up at me. "Bigger than Chris,' if ya want it. Now, give me with that fuckin' dick!"

And so, I did. I gave him my best—the fancy, swerving, hip-rippling, ass-clinching, thigh-bucking best I had in me.

When he heaved and shot, fuck-star jism flew up high in a rockets stream from that big dick of his. He cried: "I love it! Shit, kid, you've got raw talent. I oughta know. You should be fucking ass, sucking cock, getting fucked for the masses."

That really spurred me on. With a few thundering bucks of my hips, and then a massive jolt, I pulled out and exploded. Oh! My cock just erupted, shooting my hot, splattering cream to his belly the way the men of porn were paid to shoot. It thrilled this man, this Daddy, this finder and maker of stars, to wear my jizz on his belly. "The name's Ron. Ron Masters," he said between labored breaths.

Sometimes shit floated out of men in the heat of the thrust. But this dude was legit. By morning, he'd made the calls to the right people—in front of me. He showed me a gallery of hot photos and said I had my pick of boys. He gave me his card, his cellular number, the works. I floated out of his place the next morning with a sore ass, a drained sac, and a pay-to-play deal.

Later, I told Joey about my encounter with Ron Masters. I ran down the whole crazy, lucky story of how that big beautiful actor-turned-hot-director promised me a shot at the porn galaxy. Of course, to him, I was just a gay Cinderella with goofy dreams. He refused to believe me.

"Bullshit!" he laughed. "When the sex gets hot, a john's just a ventriloquist with a hard on. Only they're talking with their dicks. They don't mean it. Man. What? A john? I'll teach you yet."

The fuckin' cynic.

So, years later, as I'm fighting off shiny boys who want to suck me, fuck me, get sucked and fucked by me, I have to laugh.

But I don't forget my friends.

After a few best-selling videos, I sent for Joey, and now he's here in LA with me. Every good video needs "a hungry actor" ready and willing to provide a hard, strong, utility stunt-dick for the closeups.

"Cut!" Ron shouts, pulling me from my memories. "Okay. Bring in Joey. This scene screams for a big money shot."

the talent scout

A Tiger By The Tail

J. D. Ryan

"WHAT'S A FLUFFER?"

The question seemed to echo across the set. I locked gazes with my cameraman for a second. John had spotted the new guy instantly—was probably already designing the perfect camera angle for his lean good looks. John and I shared a taste for the dark, exotic types.

"When you gonna quit bringing in strays, Boss?" he asked.

I held up a hand, still watching my new discovery, until my assistant had him inside the dressing room and introduced him to the others returning from lunch break. I counted the seconds on my fingers: 1...2...3...

On five, an indignant squeal sounded from behind the door. "I don't NEED no stinkin' fluffer!"

John let out a short guffaw. "And another prima donna at that," he said, shaking his head.

"He'll figure it out," I replied, my gaze still on the door.

J.T. Pierce stepped from the dressing room, a slightly stunned expression on his face, to pause at a jumbled stack of backdrops leaning against the wall. His silky black hair tumbled over his dark eyes, and he shoved it back with a quick movement of one hand. I was certain that nearly every crewman in the room was watching him.

John snorted. "I think you picked up a bantam rooster there, Boss."

I raised an eyebrow. "Street rat, you mean."

Then I took a second look. J.T. did resemble an arrogant cockerel. The top of that dark mop barely reached my chin. His muscles were lean and wiry, rather than bulky. He strutted instead of walking— most likely a habit picked up from his time on the streets. I chuckled, seeing the rooster instead of the rat.

Well, his street days were over anyway. Nobody who worked for Bettencourt Studios had to hustle. I smiled as my young find strutted about the set, investigating the props, the cameras, the lighting. If my instincts were right—and Armand Bettencourt's instincts are always right—J.T. would soon have more hot men wanting that tight ass of his than he'd ever had on the streets.

The rest of the crew straggled in from lunch. I left J.T. to his own devices and called a quick planning huddle.

"I want the new kid in a bit part," I told them. "Let's see if he's as good as I think."

"We haven't shot the pep rally scene," John offered. "Maybe he could be one of Bart's school buddies."

"What about a pizza delivery?" somebody quipped. I shot a glare in that general direction without spotting any guilty faces. Pizza boys!

One of the light men laughed. "You could put him in as the school mascot." John elbowed him, and the rest of the men chuckled.

My eyes narrowed. The crew fell silent. I let them stew for a moment while I stroked my goatee. I thought about fake fur... tiger stripes... and bronze skin.

"Perfect!" I finally bellowed. Across the room, J.T. flinched at the volume. Then I was moving, striding across the set, snapping commands to the right and left. I liked watching the crew scatter in front of me.

"Get me that tiger suit from the football video. John, I want a new angle for this—show me something different. And the lights need to be golden, like sunlight. I want you to play up his coloring."

J.T., sensing that his big scene was being plotted, swaggered over, thumbs hooked into the belt loops of his jeans. The prop man returned, dragging the costume. J.T.'s eyes widened.

"No way!" he squealed. "You said you were gonna make me a star—not some dumb mascot!"

I stared down at him, hands on hips. J.T. straightened to his full height. His bangs brushed my bottom lip. Black eyes shot sparks from beneath thick eyebrows drawn into a frown.

"Has Bettencourt Studios ever made a lousy video?" I growled, leaning over him.

His scowl only got deeper. This was one rooster who wasn't going to back down without a good reason. I felt a slow heat building within my groin. I realized that I liked the feeling. Few had ever thwarted Armand Bettencourt.

"You want to dress me up in a fuckin' tiger suit!" J.T. snapped.

"And I want you to be the hottest fucking tiger anybody's ever seen!" I bellowed back. "I want every man who rents *Bart's Big Game* to run out the next day looking for goddamn college mascots! I want the costume shops to have a run on cat costumes! I want you to make that fucking tiger suit look GOOD!"

A rebellious gleam sparkled within the black eyes. "This is another test, isn't it?"

"Goddamn right it is! You pass it, and I'll see about a bigger role in the next video."

J.T. stood there, eyeball to chin, for a long moment. I felt my cock thickening. I hadn't realized how much I'd missed working with somebody who'd give me back as good as he got. Lord, but I was tired of mindless obedience!

J.T. shrugged. "Give me the damn suit," he grumbled.

The lead I'd hired for this video returned as J.T. was still struggling into the costume. I'd had my reluctant mascot strip before climbing inside—the camera crew was watching his lithe, bronzed body appreciatively. The lead raised one perfectly plucked blond eyebrow at the scene before him. I ignored him—after a week, Mr. "I Only Top" wasn't very high on my list. I gathered my players and outlined the game plan.

"Bart's going to sneak into the concession stand for a drink. He spots the mascot—I want you sweating like a pig, J.T.—"

"I'm already sweating!"

"Bart won't be able to resist the temptation. J.T., you'll have a blowjob scene to start with. Next picture we'll give you more screen time—if you do a good job."

J.T. shot me a disgusted glare, and pulled the tiger's head on. The rest of us moved into position. At the cue, J.T., pretending not to notice the lead watching from the doorway, slowly removed the costume head. He shook his dark mop, flinging sweat across the room. He was supposed to turn and notice Bart, but he reached for a bottle of water from the ice bucket instead. The gasp as he threw back his head and emptied it over his face seemed to come from every man in the room. Even the lead was breathing more heavily.

J.T. turned then, slowly. He looked at the lead for a long minute, his eyes moving from the size 14 sneakers to the blond buzz cut. A smile blossomed over his wide lips. His hand moved to the crotch of the tiger suit, rubbed slowly up and down.

"You need some—refreshments?" he asked.

Hey! I didn't give him any lines! Ah well, it was a good come-on. The lead moved forward as though pulled by a wire around his hardening cock.

"I think I do," he muttered, reaching for the young man. They kissed deeply. J.T. then sank slowly to his knees, his fingers busy at the zipper of the lead's jeans. It took a while—those furry gloves made him a bit clumsy. I liked the impression it made though: coltish eagerness. Bart turned slightly, playing to the cameras as J.T. leaned back to admire the nine-and-a-quarter-inch cock standing nearly straight out from the blond pubes. Slowly, J.T. reached out to stroke the organ, his long fingers dancing lightly over the shaft.

The lead fished a familiar foil packet from his jeans, flashing the logo for the camera. I grinned at John—that tie-in concession with the condoms had been one of our best moves. John pointed silently to the monitor. What the hell was J.T. up to now?

My new actor, after fumbling in a hidden pocket of the tiger suit, brandished another Bettencourt Condom package. He grinned, held his find up to the lead's packet, and winked. Winked! Just like a goddamn commercial. When did I tell him to do that?

I loved it.

Bart ripped open one package and slowly rolled the condom over his massive tool. J.T.'s eyes never left the cock inches from his face. He seemed almost mesmerized. Now he looked more like an eager puppy than a strutting rooster. He licked his lips, then a slow grin spread across his face—the grin of a man who's been given a studio full of gorgeous cocks to play with.

As soon as the condom was in place, J.T.'s head dove forward. Too fast—I stood up, ready to yell "cut." But J.T. merely brushed his lips across the glistening head, making the cock jerk upwards. Then he raised his fur-covered hands.

The lead groaned at the touch of the gloves. J.T. wriggled his furry fingers, tickling the balls and underside of the long shaft. He closed one fuzzy fist over the fat balls and tugged gently. His other hand slid beneath the lead's T-shirt to tickle his nips.

Throughout the performance, J.T.'s nose remained a scant inch away from the hard cock. Either he was truly fascinated with the thick organ, or he was an even better actor than I had given him credit for. I watched the lead as J.T. stroked his cock and balls. The big blond made all the right moves and noises—grunts, thrusts and "do me babies." It hit me then. I was goddamn tired of typical fuck flicks!

Maybe that was why I'd picked up another stray from the streets. I wanted something new, something you didn't see in every other video. I was tired of prima donna porn stars, tired of their just-give-me-the-paycheck attitudes. Sure, my stars did what I told them to do, but that wasn't good enough. I wanted surprises—people who could see the potential in a scene and exploit it. If I ever wanted to do anything with the awards I'd gotten, I needed more thoroughbreds in my stable. And J.T. might just turn out to be the dark horse in that barn.

He was enjoying the blond I'd given him to play with. His hands were all over the lead's body, like he wanted to touch everything at once. He'd moved his lips to the glistening cockhead, and was teasing it—flicking his tongue in and out like a snake. John zoomed in for a close-up, shooting over the lead's shoulder.

I loved the look on J.T.'s face. Eyes closed, a smile tugging at the corners of his mouth—he slurped that big dick like a kid with a stick of candy.

He opened his eyes suddenly to look directly into the camera lens. In close-ups his long lashes looked as thick as a woman's. He pulled back for a long, slow smile, then opened his mouth.

I found myself holding my breath as he struggled to take in the big cock. I'd hired the lead solely for the size of his organ. J.T.'s small features made the thing look even bigger. It looked too large to fit into his mouth. And I was getting hot just thinking of it happening.

J.T. worked the fat cockhead past his lips, slurping noisily. He slid his furry hands between the lead's legs. I could almost see the cock swell even larger. I knew it was rock-hard by this time. J.T. took a deep breath and dropped his mouth open. For a moment, I thought he'd unhinged his jaw like a snake.

He worked that cock into his throat until his nose was buried in clipped blond pubes. I swear, his neck looked swollen with all that man-meat stuffed inside.

Then, he started the blowjob.

Everything up to this point had been foreplay—that fact was suddenly obvious. J.T. showed the camera what a professional could do with his mouth. I had no idea how he managed to breathe with nine-and-a-quarter inches of fat, hard cock down his throat. I didn't even know how he'd gotten it all inside in the first place—it looked like the thing ought to reach about halfway down to his asshole.

All I knew was, within thirty seconds, Mr. "I Only Top" had come alive, shoving his cock into the waiting throat like a jackhammer. J.T. dove forward to meet him. He let out a string of muffled grunts that had my cock standing straight up in my jeans.

J.T. shoved both arms between the lead's legs, forcing them apart. His fur-covered hands clamped on the quivering ass-cheeks. The force of the larger man's thrusts tossed him back and forth, but he clung to the blond like a leech.

I slid a hand between my legs, trying to ease my aching cock into a more comfortable position. It'd been ages since a scene had turned me on this much. I thought I was immune. I glanced at the cameras— John was rubbing his own hard rod. Our gazes met, and he gave me a sheepish grin, then shrugged.

The lead pulled out, stripping off his condom for the cum shot. J.T. wilted onto all fours, panting like he'd just run a marathon. Thick manjuice spurted onto his dripping hair as the blond aimed his firehose onto the smaller man. The lead managed to get his exit lines right, which should have surprised me. But I barely noticed—I was watching the next Bettencourt Studios star.

J.T. grabbed onto the edge of the counter, barely missing the paper cups that made the counter a concession stand. He hauled himself upright, still breathing like a horse after a race. Cum dripped from his hair. One thick rope of cream slid down his right cheek. He stood facing the camera, his lean chest heaving—I finally remembered to mutter "Cut!"

"Oh, man," John muttered from across the set.

"Yeah," I agreed.

The two of us met over J.T.'s tiger-striped body. J.T. had wilted back against the counter. I was relieved to see the perky bulge tenting the front of his costume—I'd been a bit worried that he'd gone too far with his scene.

He glanced up as we approached, and a crafty look crossed his face. "So," he asked, "was that hot enough for you?"

I snorted. "Look at the new kid, John! One scene and he's thinking we're going to reward him."

John smirked. "Yeah, you'd think that big, fat cock would be reward enough."

J.T. glared, not quite sure if we were kidding. John and I put on our best scowls—not an easy expression when your cock's trying to poke a hole in your jeans.

"Well," I drawled, tugging at the tail of the tiger costume, "maybe we could think of some reward we could give him."

"Seein' as how it was his first time on screen and all," John added, rubbing absent-mindedly at a cum stain on the fake fur.

J.T.'s eyes narrowed. "I want the same reward I got last night!" he demanded. Giving me a coy smile, he turned, showing the zipper on the back of the tiger suit.

I had a better idea. I'd had the prop department put a piss-flap into the costume, so that the mascot wasn't forever climbing in and out of the thing during a performance. It was just a triangle of fur, wrapping backwards from crotch to tail, but it saved a lot of time. I reached down, tugged the Velcro strips loose, and slid my hand inside.

J.T. squirmed, but I kept a tight hold on that tail. John grinned and moved in close.

My fingers found what I wanted, and I closed my fist over his hard cock, already slimy with pre-cum. He gave up all pretenses.

Spreading his legs, he bent over the counter. I tugged his perky seven-incher out through the flap, still holding onto the tiger's tail.

A finger from my other hand probed the eager hole before me. J.T. moaned, shoving his hips up off the counter. Damned if he *ever* seemed to get tired of getting fucked!

John moved to the other side of the counter. His hand cupped the bulge in his jeans—not quite as large as the lead's, but still a nice basket. "Maybe I ought to reward him a little bit," he suggested. J.T. reached out one furry arm, climbing half onto the counter, and grabbed for John's zipper.

"Damn!" I growled, slapping the fuzzy ass in front of me. "Don't you ever get enough?"

J.T. shook his head. He ground against my hand.

"Well," John said, unzipping his pants, "you can come up for air with mine, kid. I'd feel bad if you passed out in the middle of our reward."

J.T. nodded, his lips already parting. John rolled a Bettencourt condom over his drooling eight-inch rod. J.T. dove on it like he was a cock-addict in withdrawal. I shook my head—he ought to be paying me instead of the other way around!

I grabbed another condom from the drawer and sheathed my eager dick. J.T. spread his legs wider as my swollen rod pressed against his hole. He didn't give up his vacuum suction on John's cock, though. I eased past his pucker, giving him time to adjust to my presence. I still hadn't gotten over the irrational worry that such a little guy would split wide open with my fat cock inside him. Even after spending nearly a week trying to satisfy J.T.'s hungry ass, I found myself checking to be sure he was still intact.

J.T. moaned deep in his throat, wriggling that ass backwards against me. The fake fur tickled my balls. I loved the feeling of his sweaty ass inside the baggy costume. I pulled the suit's tail to one side, so I could watch his hole spread for my cock. The triangle of glistening, bronze skin peeping from beneath orange and black fake fur begged for attention. I slid both hands inside the costume. I closed one fist over the shaved balls and tugged gently. J.T. gave a muffled squeal and pushed against my hands.

Across from me, John grunted loudly. His hands were clenched in J.T.'s sweaty mane. The sight of his red shaft, glistening beneath its latex coat, dripping with ropes of saliva, nearly sent me over the edge. I watched it slide in and out of J.T.'s throat, and tried to time my thrusts to match John's rhythm. As he shoved forward, I pulled back. He met my gaze, and we grinned at one another.

Soon, we had J.T. reduced to a quivering wreck, whimpering helplessly as we pounded him. I held myself in check, refusing to give in to the hot waves pulsing up from my balls. I wanted to watch J.T. while John and I fucked him. I wanted to enjoy feeling his ass muscles spasm over my thrusting cock. I wanted him to keep making those muffled whimpers. I loved seeing him like this: totally out of control with lust.

His hands in their furry mitts roamed over John's body, clenching for a moment on the wide leather belt or around a fold of John's shirt. I loved those hands. I wanted to do an entire video of J.T.'s hands.

Beneath those tiger-striped gloves were long, strong fingers. Wide palms, deep-bronze skin, bony wrists corded with tendons. When J.T. was getting fucked—really, sincerely, deeply fucked—those hands seemed to move of their own volition. They clenched and quivered, slid over every surface within reach. It was as if they were reaching for a lifeline to keep J.T. from drowning in desire.

I couldn't hold back any longer. J.T.'s hands—even covered in fake orange fur—got me way too hot. I leaned into my thrusts, spreading my thick fingers over J.T.'s quivering mounds to hold him steady. His hot little butt spread wide open, red and throbbing. I felt my balls boil up, spewing my hot cream into the condom deep inside my new star. I shoved hard—once, twice—then I leaned over, running my hands over the fluffy tiger stripes covering his back.

J.T. trembled beneath me. His asshole clenched tightly around my wilting cock. I pinned him against the counter, staying inside for as long as I could, enjoying the show across from me.

John was close to losing it. His face was as red as his cock-shaft. I could see his balls hugging the base of his rod. I slid one hand up J.T.'s back, tangling my fingers in his sweaty hair. My hand touched John's. Our fingers twined together.

That did it. John grunted again, thrusting his hips forward. I could see his balls jerk, shooting his load into J.T.'s eager throat. J.T.'s fur-covered hands clamped down on John's cheeks, pulling the camera-man deeper inside him. He fastened his lips against John's sweaty pubes and rode John's cock like a bronco.

When John finally pulled his slimy cock free, J.T. wilted over the counter. I took pity on his quivering body and slid one hand between his legs. I had to step back so that I could see his pretty seven-incher in my fist. Damn, but the man was insatiable!

I liked the sight of his perky cock in my hand. Big enough to make a nice handful, but not big enough to look odd on his small frame. Blessedly, he was uncut—wonderful foresight on the part of European parents, I guessed. The only thing Armand Bettencourt likes better than a pretty cock on a willing bottom is a pretty, uncut cock. And J.T.'s cock was one of the nicest I'd seen in a long time. Seven inches, straight as a ruler, with a head that blossomed from the foreskin like a rare purple flower—all atop a firm, heavy set of balls that practically begged you to cup them in your palm.

J.T. was so close that all I had to do was pump that lovely rod a couple of times before he squirted cream all over my fist. I loved the little groan he gave when he came—a high whimper like a puppy begging for a treat. I loved the helpless quiver his butt gave when I milked the last juice from his cock. John came around to watch the final drops ooze from our next star.

"I almost wish we'd gotten that one on film," he muttered, zipping his jeans. He tossed his slimy rubber into the trash.

An apologetic cough sounded from the intercom box. John and I turned, looking at the sound booth in shock.

"Sorry, Boss," came the tech's sheepish voice. "We were—er—beating off. But as for film... we never heard you yell 'Cut' so the remote camera caught everything."

I looked over at my cameraman.

"Hey," he said with a shrug. "It was your idea to buy that thing."

He grinned, leaning over to help J.T. to his wobbly feet.

"You said they'd leave my hands free, remember, Boss?"

on location

The Big Tip

Bill Crimmin

MOST PEOPLE THINK IOWA IS PRETTY DULL—DOWNRIGHT BORING even—but it isn't true. The scenery and the river boat gambling along the Mississippi attract all kinds of people. There's plenty of opportunity for a resourceful and horny gay boy—if he looks half decent and is prepared to be obliging.

And I'm not bad looking. I'm on the swim team at college, so I stay fit. I've got dark, curly hair, which keeps falling in my face. I'm no oil painting; but I never made anyone puke either. I study hotel management at Iowa State where I'm a senior. During the summer, I work in Dubuque's most expensive hotel, on the bluffs overlooking the river.

I hate my uniform, though. Covered in gold braid and with a little flat hat to match, it hasn't changed during the hundred years the hotel's been open. A lot of guests, however, get a kick out of seeing a guy dressed up like the Phillip Morris bellhop. It often gets me a big tip, so I'm not above milking it.

We had a big party of guys from California come in two days ago, the first of the week. They had already booked the whole top floor, including the Mark Twain Suite. They'd told the manager they were a movie crew and asked for permission to do some filming in their rooms. He'd been quick to oblige, and I suspected they slipped him at least a couple of hundreds. Of course, that wouldn't keep him from inflating their bill.

During the day, they loaded up a couple of cars with equipment and disappeared, probably filming the postcard scenes that made the city famous, like the limestone bluffs and the Diamond Jo Casino.

After dark they locked themselves up in the suite: filming, we assumed, but they were pretty vague about the movie and when it would be released.

Anyway, they rang for room service and, by chance, I was on. They ordered several party platters (the good stuff—smoked ham and jumbo shrimp), mineral water, and a couple of bottles of chilled Chablis. Nice, if you could afford it.

I loaded their order onto a cart, wheeled it into the elevator, and went up to the top floor, swiping a couple of shrimp on the way. Outside the suite, I checked to make sure my shirt was tucked in and my fly was zipped and folded my napkin neatly over my arm.

I put on my best smile and tapped on the door. There was no answer. I tapped again. Silence. If a guest didn't answer the door, we were trained to let ourselves in and discreetly leave the order. After all, they might have been in the bath, or on the john. I opened the door, thinking nothing of it.

I maneuvered the cart into the room and wheeled it to the center of the empty room. Camera equipment and lights were strewn everywhere and a big stack of books and papers sat on a side table. There wasn't a person in sight.

But I sure heard one. The soft, guttural moaning of a man about to cum could be heard through the slightly-open door of the adjacent bedroom. It was a sound I had heard myself make nearly every night of my life since I first learned to jerk off. "You like my big dick in you, don't you?" another voice asked, just as guttural and strained.

I figured I'd walked in on a couple of the film crew making the most of a break in shooting. This wasn't something that was covered in our training manual. I debated my options. Leave the tray and get out quietly? Make enough noise I'd be heard? The second option gave me the possibility of getting a nice tip... They sounded pretty occupied, though. My dick demanded a third option. It was hard and making me definitely uncomfortable.

It'd been a couple of weeks since my dick had anything but my five fingers keeping it company; I could go for seeing some horny action. It wasn't hard to convince myself that they wouldn't notice me if I took a peek.

I padded over quietly and peered through the crack in the door. Okay, it was wrong to go spying... But... well, I was horny. And I was only going to take the one little peek.

Two guys were going at it. A dark-haired guy was plugging his partner and his butt was dimpling nicely as he flexed his hips. His skin glistened with sweat. I slowly realized that it looked awfully bright in the room.

Pulling my gaze away from the fuck on the four-poster bed, I saw huge lights shining down on the guys on the bed. Two cameras were focussed on them and a sound man stood off to the side by a bank of equipment. There were so many people crammed into the room that I was surprised they all had room to breathe.

Porn! They were making a porn movie in the hotel! This wasn't a normal act of love between two men; it was an organized shooting session.

I returned my attention to the action on the bed. Both of them had moved slightly so I could see more of them. A muscular blond I didn't recognize was lying on his back, his heels up around his ears. And a wiry, tall, dark-haired man, whom I'd seen before in the lobby and lusted for, was balanced above him, his weight supported on his hands and his long, thick cock buried to the nuts.

My cock was harder than hard in my uniform pants. Things were pretty cramped in there. Everyone was far too involved to notice me, so I stayed where I was, peering round the door and watching the action unfold on the big bed.

The guy on top was giving his partner a thorough shafting. His substantial cock slid slowly in and out. Its slick, latex-covered surface glistened in the light. He was gorgeous—Brad, I thought he was called. I'd spotted him the first day they were here. He was tall and slender. His body was hard and muscular, yet not overdeveloped. His chest and abs were covered in a mat of dark hair and the ass that was bobbing up and down so tirelessly was tight and rounded.

I wanted some of him. I'd have to try to get friendly with him, next time I delivered an order or brought up their mail.

Who was I kidding? This guy was a porn star; he wouldn't look twice at an ordinary Joe like me.

Brad's bouncing buttocks picked up speed. He slammed his rigid member in and out of the guy's spasming hole. Between their sweaty bodies, the blond had his fist firmly wrapped around his meat. He was pounding it for all he was worth, his hand a blur.

That did it for me. The erection in my pants was in danger of strangling. Taking a quick glance around the bedroom to make sure I hadn't been spotted, I opened my fly. Relief! That felt better. I sighed as circulation returned to my dick.

The action on the bed got hotter. The blond was writhing and moaning under Brad, the hand on his throbbing cock doing overtime.

I was more turned on than I could ever remember. It wasn't every day that I happened across a couple of horny, gorgeous guys getting it on for the cameras. I was harder than I could remember. I just had to touch my dick. Besides, I could always duck out before anyone saw me.

I slid my swollen pole out through the slit in my underwear. My cock practically sighed in relief when it hit the air. I wrapped my hand around it and pulled the skin back off the knob.

"I'm going to cum!" hissed the guy on the bed.

Brad stopped humping for a moment and one of the cameramen came round and set up his tripod close to the bed so that he had a clear view of the guy's dick. The director nodded, and Brad said: "Go for it, Mike."

Mike started jacking himself again. He panted; his eyes fixed on his own groin. Brad was still buried in the guy's ass. He was sitting back on his heels, the blond's lower back resting on his thighs.

"Now," Mike announced, although none of us needed telling he was about to shoot. His face was twisted into a rictus of pleasure, every muscle in his neck stood out as his hand moved frantically on his cock. He exploded then, ropes of white jizz shooting everywhere. Some of them hit Brad; he scooped them up on a finger and fed them to Mike.

My own hand was working overtime now. The sight of the blond eating his own cum was just too much for me. "Yes!" I pumped faster, my balls riding my shaft. "Yeah!" I groaned as I shot my load.

There was complete silence as I came back to earth. I began to realize everybody was looking at me. Me and my still-erupting dick. My presence in the room was no longer secret. My face flushed as red as my dick and the offending member softened in my hand like a deflating balloon.

"Hey," said the guy I figured was the director, "who's that? In the doorway, who is that guy?"

"Uh... Room service, sir,"I said quickly, flashing them my best little boy grin. "I brought up your order."

Everybody laughed. I saw Brad studying me. He smiled slowly. Even in my embarrassment, the beauty of that smile wasn't lost on me.

"It's the bellboy." His smile became a shit-eating grin. "Maybe we ought to see the rest of the menu," he said, pulling his condom off and tossing it on the floor beside the bed. "I've had my eye on him for days, only I wasn't sure he was gay. I guess I know the answer to that now."

Another ripple of laughter ran through the room. I stood there, my limp cock in my hand. I smiled weakly.

"Bellboy, huh?" said the director, scratching his head. "And he's good looking, too. Do you think that dick in your fist would like to see some more action?" he asked me.

"What do you mean?" I asked, nervously. "I don't want to get into trouble."

"It looks like your dick has already got you here. But it's OK. If our little movie got you off, it means we're doing our job right." He pursed his lips. "You're a good looking boy. And you look so cute in that uniform. Why not finish the job you started and let us film it. Of course, we'll pay you for it."

I gulped. This wasn't the first time I'd been offered a bout in the sack by a hotel guest. It was, however, the first time I'd been asked if he could record the occasion for posterity. And the first time I'd been offered money for it. That was prostitution wasn't it? I frowned.

No, prostitution is when you take money for sex. They weren't offering to pay me for that exactly, just the right to film it. Film it and show the results to half the gay world. Every gay boy from Las Vegas to New York would see my naked ass on screen. Did I want that?

Every guy ogling me—my dick. My ass. What could I have been thinking? I'd never have trouble getting a date again.

"OK," I said. "Only—" I couldn't believe I was about to say this, but I knew I wanted it and I probably wouldn't get another chance. "I'll do it, but I want to do it with Brad."

All eyes in the room went to the tall star.

"You bet, boy," Brad whooped. "I'd been wondering how I could get you into bed. And they actually pay me for this! What a crazy business."

"OK," said the director. "We'll film the background later: the bellboy arriving with the cart and spying on Brad and Mike." I glanced at the blond. "He gets spotted and they invite him to join in. That's where you came in. Just get over there and let Brad take charge. He'll make sure you do it right for the camera. All you need to remember is that we want to get the cum shot on film, OK?"

I took a deep breath and walked over to the side of the bed. Mike got up, put on a robe, and sat down on a sofa against the wall. The cameras started rolling. Brad stood up and pulled me close. He was at least 6 inches taller than I; I had to look up to meet his gaze. His naked body was pressed up against me. He felt hard and muscular. He kissed me then and it was good that he was holding me or I might have collapsed right there.

His tongue claimed my mouth, snaking inside; his lips were soft and warm. He pulled away and stripped off my jacket, dropping it on the floor. He undid my bow tie and tossed it on top of the jacket. He unbuttoned my shirt and peeled it away from my body. He smiled at me then and ducked down to tongue first one nipple and then the other.

He undid my belt and flicked the button out of its hole. He moved to biting my nipples as my uniform pants fell to the floor. He pushed his thumbs under the band of my briefs and, kneeling, pulled them down my legs. His lips made little kisses along my thighs and his face moved back up my body.

I stepped out of them. I was naked like him, and I wanted to feel his body against mine. My cock was already at half-mast and his was standing proudly, practically parallel to his belly.

I grabbed him, wrapping my arms around him and holding him to me. We kissed, a long, deep, slow kiss. His cock pressed against my belly, wetting me with pre-cum. He broke the kiss and pushed me gently onto the bed.

I positioned myself in the middle of the four-poster bed and held out my arms to him. He smiled at me then and I practically melted. His even, white teeth practically sparkled and his eyes crinkled with genuine warmth as he got on top of me. His weight felt good, pressing me down into the mattress.

He kissed me again, then trailed his tongue down my neck and over my pecs. His tongue found a nipple, sucked on it, nibbled it. I gasped. He chewed on the rubbery nub until it hardened, then moved across and treated its partner to the same service. I was in heaven.

Then he licked down the center of my chest, over my ribs, onto my belly. He gave my shallow belly-button a good licking and I lay back on the bed, riding waves of pleasure he was giving me. He grasped my cock at its base and rubbed it—a couple of long, slow strokes which made me moan.

"My first uncut cock," he murmured. He pumped my dick again, watching as the foreskin slid over my glans and down again. He cupped my balls, squeezing gently and kneading them. Then he slid my foreskin all the way down, exposing my glans. He swallowed me all the way to the root.

His mouth worked my dick. He bathed my glans with his tongue as his lips nibbled on my shaft. He pushed the tip of his tongue into my piss slit. I already was pretty worked up. Now, I had a gorgeous, horny hunk sucking on my dick. I was in heaven. It wasn't going to take me long.

Brad pulled gently on my balls as his mouth milked my cock. I gazed down at his face. His eyes were closed and he wore a sort of blissful expression as he sucked me. His lips, spread wide by my throbbing shaft, somehow still managed to smile. I stroked his hair, lacing my fingers through the thick, curly strands.

I had moved onto the edge. Sweat filmed my body. My breath came in short, noisy gasps. I was pumping my hips in rhythm with Brad's talented mouth on my dick.

A knot of tension settled in my groin. My thighs tensed. I pressed my heels down into the mattress, slightly raising my ass off the bed. My whole body started to tremble. I was half a dozen strokes away from shooting my load. Got to get it on camera, I told myself. I was making a porn movie and, fun though it was, I was getting paid to deliver the goods.

"I'm going to cum," I groaned.

Brad quickly replaced his mouth with his hand, wrapping his fist around my still wet dick and pumped. My meat throbbed in his hand. As my ball-sac tightened and retracted and my nuts rode my shaft, I moaned. "I—I can't hold it any—"

Volleys of spunk erupted from my cock, shooting all over both us and the bed. Trails of warm jizz decorated my chest and belly. Brad still gripped my spasming prick in his hand. It danced and twitched, struggling against his grip. When I had stopped pumping jizz, Brad dipped his head and sucked my cock clean, then turned his attention to my sperm-splattered belly. I thought I had died and gone to heaven.

By the time the film crew had gone home we'd shot half a dozen segments, as well as the background, non-sexual stuff. I even got a piece of Mike in a three-way fuck.

In the days that followed, Brad and I enjoyed several private performances. In fact, we became quite an item and we've decided that, when I graduate next semester, I'm going to join him in California.

They have hotels in California, too, so I can get a job there as easily as anywhere.

Besides, Brad figures I've got quite a future in skin flicks—that is, if I want to do a little moonlighting from time to time. If I can actually make money from having the guy I love give me his every-thing, I'd be a fool to turn it down, wouldn't I? I kept the bellboy's uniform as a souvenir. Brad loves it.

gay for pay

That's Why They Call It Acting!

Jordan Baker

CHAD'S ASSHOLE TIGHTENED AROUND MY COCK, CHOKING IT DOWN AS I thrust more deeply into him. Slapping his ass, I bent forward across his back and breathed into his ear.

"Relax," I whispered. "This isn't supposed to be a damned rape scene. It's just a job."

Oddly, that seemed to help. I felt some of the tension drain from his shoulders and Chad actually pressed his back to my chest briefly. Closing my eyes, I relaxed as well. No reason to take it out on the kid because I was having a rough day.

My hands found Chad's hips and drew him more tightly against me as I resumed thrusting. It was an even rhythm now, the well-oiled seesawing of two bodies going through motions they'd learned from years of practice. The set vanished—lights, camera and crew fading into the blackness as I rocked. Chad even disappeared and I was alone in my head.

There's a kind of joy that comes with oblivion. The feel of muscles sliding over bone, moving your body in a dance. The pistoning of the hips lull you like the ticking of a clock as hands slick with sweat glide over your partner's smooth cheeks. The heat and pressure on your cock swells like music coming up from an orchestra pit.

You live entirely for the moment, learning to wait for that lovely kick when your cock is buried completely inside someone and his ass is pressing hard against your pelvis. You hold it a moment, savoring the feel, before relaxing and drawing away. No matter how often you shoot porn, no matter how many times you've fucked for cash, nothing ever takes that feeling away.

For a moment, you even forget you're not gay.

You remember, of course, when the pressure builds up in your balls until you can't stand it any more and you signal your partner that it's time for the cum shot.

In my case, I dug my nails so deeply into the flesh of his pelvis that Chad whimpered as I jerked him more solidly against me.

Then the pressure was gone. All that lovely heat replaced by the vacuum of a porn set and the breeze from a box fan washing over us as Chad scrambled to turn around and I pulled off the condom.

He made it to his knees just in time to catch the first spurt on the side of his face. Disconnected from it all now that the hard part was over, I felt a certain sense of accomplishment. It was a good cum shot, thick and visible and easy to film. I splashed him one more time across the bridge of his nose, before Chad managed to get my cock in his mouth and swallow the rest.

My eyes closed involuntarily and I concentrated on the sensation of his tongue sliding along the bottom of my cock, milking it of its last drops. I held position for a couple of extra moments to make sure we'd cleared the scene, then collapsed onto the couch.

"Nice job, kid." I nodded. "You hung in there like a real pro."

It hadn't been, of course. He was young and inexperienced and this had been his first skin flick. He'd taken forever to get hard and had trouble keeping his wood. Working with him had added an extra four hours to my day and I wasn't paid by the hour.

But I remembered what my first time had been like and figured it wouldn't hurt to be nice. In retrospect, complimenting Chad was a mistake. He immediately got that haunted, defensive look, and blurted: "I'm not gay. I just really need the money and—"

"It's OK, kid." I shrugged. "Nobody's gay in real life. We're all just in it for the money and the guys who buy these tapes are just curious. Personally, I think homosexuality is a myth."

Someone snickered behind me and I felt the tip of a towel pop my ass.

"Speak for yourself, bigfoot," the makeup guy popped off with an exaggerated lisp. "I practically have wings."

"Yeah, well, go spread that fairy dust somewhere else, Murray," I snapped, slapping his puff away from my face. "I've got somewhere to be."

"Brute."

And with a flick of his wrist, Murray was gone, ushering Chad off the set while chattering about bone structure and highlights. The kid still had one more scene to shoot and I pitied the poor bastard who had to work with him next. Not quite as much as I pitied the crew.

"Remember, Joe," I smirked, "keep that microphone high. Nobody wants to reshoot a scene because you let that big, black dong drop in from the ceiling."

"Don't even fucking joke about that, Cal," the soundman sighed, rubbing his own shoulders. "I think we're going to set a new record for standing around watching guys jerk off. How come you never have wood problems? An old timer like you shouldn't be able to get it up on demand."

"I pretend I'm doing your wife," I snorted. "Gotta run. I'm meeting with Dean Flynt in a couple of hours to talk about a new pic for Bi-Cameral Video."

"Mention me. My kid's going out for the cheerleading team. It's obscene what the school charges for those uniforms."

And I was clear—off the set and into the shower for a few minutes until I felt fully human again. Thirty minutes later, I was armored in my jeans and boots with an old Louisiana Tech sweatshirt and leather jacket to fight the chill as I rode my Harley toward Dean's beach house.

He was grilling steaks when I got there. It's one of the ways guys like Dean keep you on their side. They figure you never quite stop being a starving actor and the smell of beef cooking on the grill has an amazing effect on a lot of talent. It's particularly effective when you've cum three times in one day and have been surviving on buffet platters.

"Have a seat," Dean gestured. "Dinner will be ready in about an hour. Can you stay?"

I scowled at him, fighting the urge to spit out: No, Dean. I make so much goddamned money I can afford to turn down free meals from producers. Instead, I grinned and said: "Yeah, I'm kind of light on protein today."

"Ah, yes," Dean said, his impeccable British accent making the words sound full of import. "You only top, correct?"

"Correct," I nodded. "I'm not a homosexual. I just play one in vids."

"I don't suppose there's anything I could offer to change your mind... hmmm?" he asked, slowly turning the steaks. A breeze wafted the aroma past my nose. "Your first on-screen anal would be a collector's item. Really, thirty years old and never been buggered. I believe that's a record."

"A dubious honor," I smiled. "But one I intend to keep."

He shrugged, an elegant gesture on the part of the cardigan-clad Brit. I wondered idly if the rumors that he was really from North Dakota were true.

"I'm still working on the script, blocking out the scenes, et cetera. It shouldn't be a problem to keep the character I want you to play pure. As usual, you'll be the strong, silent type."

"Joe Rogers is available if you're looking for somebody to handle the sound equipment. He's a good guy."

Dean nodded thoughtfully, stroked his goatee and said he'd keep that in mind. I'd tried.

It was more a matter of formality than necessity. And that more or less concluded the business portion of the evening. We discussed my pay and what would be expected of me in the film, but it was the same standard agreement I always got when I worked with Dean.

By then, the steaks were done and the conversation turned to more informal matters. The inevitable question arose. I guess after twelve years in gay porn I should have a well-rehearsed answer, but I never seem to know what to say other than "for the money."

"It's what I do, Dean," I said. "I do it because guys like you pay me to do it. You pay me to do it because even at thirty, I still look damn good having sex—and I can get it up when I need to."

"But, as you say, you're not gay," he probed.

"And Dennis Hopper and Gary Oldman aren't psychopathic killers," I laughed. "That's why they call it acting. Otherwise, it would just be people fucking in front of camcorders and where's the art in that?"

"You went to university," he suggested, gesturing to the deathly butch Louisiana Tech bulldog on my t-shirt. "Washed out as an engineer?"

"Graduated with honors," I corrected. "I have a master's degree in speech with an emphasis in theater."

"What on earth do you do with a degree like that?" he asked.

I raised my eyebrows and pumped my fist over a phantom cock.

"Oh, I see."

"I'm not Robert De Niro or Peter O'Toole," I shrugged. "I'm Cal Webb—a very big fish in a very small pond. And I like that. Beats being a minnow in the Pacific."

"But you've never... ummm... I've never seen you have a problem performing."

"I block everything out but the physical sensation. I block out everything but the essential purity of fucking. It's not difficult once you learn how."

Suddenly, Dean's eyes lit up. Snapping his fingers, he came to life. I'd seen it before. Dean's the kind of guy who isn't really there unless he's working on a problem. Writing is his life. Directing and producing are just things he does to support his ink addiction.

"Speaking of blocking, could you help me with a small problem I'm having?"

He was already halfway across the patio before I could gather my drink and follow. I took it the question was rhetorical.

Once inside he snatched a crowbar off his desk and turned to face me.

"Could you take this away from me?"

"If I had to," I replied, carefully examining my escape path in case I was witnessing the unraveling of a person.

"What if you had a bullet in your left arm—right about here?" Dean indicated a spot about halfway between his elbow and shoulder.

"Maybe. Why?"

"I'm trying to plan this scene and need to know if it works. I hate blocking out action scenes—I'm a rather non-physical lad myself—

and am just not up on assaulting people with tire tools."

"That's a crowbar," I corrected.

"See?" His smile was charming. "Anyway, when you workshop stories, the first thing you learn is when in doubt, act it out."

Again, he smiled.

Sighing, I put my left arm behind my back and moved toward Dean. He whipped the crowbar forward—badly. He swung too hard and overextended himself. A twelve-year-old could have slipped inside the swing.

Wrapping my right arm around his neck in a choke hold, I drew Dean tight against me, giving him a pelvic thrust for effect before dropping my mouth to his ear. Making my voice as menacing as I could, I snarled: "Drop it, Dean."

I was rewarded with the sound of iron clattering over terra cotta tile. Dean's body was still tight, straining against mine as if testing for a way to escape.

"You can't, bitch," I whispered, flicking the tip of my tongue against his ear. "I own you now."

"Oh dear," he said.

"You know," I said, continuing to nibble at his ear and jaw, "it occurs to me there might be another problem with this scene. If I've only got one good arm and it's wrapped around your sorry neck, how do I get your pants down?"

On cue, my cock stiffened and I pressed it hard into the crack of Dean's ass. The khakis didn't do much to disguise the fact he wasn't wearing underwear.

"Slut," I whispered menacingly. "You wanted me to take that crowbar away from you. I ought to ram that iron rod up your ass until you taste metal."

Dean was still straining, but now his ass was grinding against my hard-on. Forcing Dean to his desk, I leaned hard on him, bending his body to my will and pinning him in place with my weight.

"This should work," I snarled, biting his earlobe as I released the choke hold. "Unless, of course, you want to lose that ear."

"Oh... my... God..." he gasped as I snaked my "good" hand down to undo his belt. Dean's pants fell free and, for a moment, I was truly impressed. Under those baggy khakis was a body much more toned than I'd expected.

"You have to use a condom," he choked out. "I use condoms in all my films."

"Should I put it on the crowbar?" I snarled, putting my hand on the back of his neck and grinding him into the desk as I fished a condom out of my pocket. I figured my "wounded" arm was good enough to get it out. Pressing it to Dean's lips, I had him tear it open with his teeth.

"See how simple life can be," I chuckled. "Problem, solution."

Lubing up wasn't much harder. I just maneuvered our bodies until my cock was pressed against his lips.

"Why would I suck my rapist's cock?" he asked. "It doesn't make sense."

"Fine," I shrugged. "If you want to take it up the ass dry, it causes me no pain."

He swallowed my head. It wasn't really an award-winning performance. He couldn't deepthroat and only got about a third of my nine inches into his mouth. His tongue felt clumsy as it thrashed around my dick. Somehow, that made it more erotic. I hadn't realized how long it had been since I'd been with a non-pro.

Taking matters into my own hands, I wrapped my fingers through Dean's stylish hair and began rocking his head back and forth along the length of my cock. Gradually, we established a rhythm and I began truly to enjoy myself. The room was fading and I was in the zone—muscle and bone and blood pumping together in the quest for an orgasm.

It was, you have to realize, what I do best.

I don't even remember withdrawing from his mouth and driving my cock into his asshole. I remember being amazed at how tight it was. He cried out as I worked my way inside him.

"You're splitting me apart," he gasped.

I responded by thrusting harder, bullying my way past that last bit of resistance the muscles of his rectum mustered against me—and then there was nothing. The emptiness of the void with all the pressure in the world concentrated in a tight ring around one small segment of my cock as I probed his insides.

Vaguely, I was aware of the legs of the heavy oak desk leaving the floor and returning as I slammed my cock in and out of his butt. From the recesses of consciousness I heard Dean whimpering as I mounted him, holding him hard against my pelvis at the end of each thrust.

Finally, I let go, my orgasm erupting from the pit of my stomach with a sensation like velcro opening or roots being ripped from the ground.

It's a pity no one got it on film. It was, after all, the greatest performance of my life. Too bad it ended with an internal cum shot. I'd have never gotten paid for it on a set. But that's life. Sometimes, you just do what feels good at the moment.

Dean was still bent over his desk, gasping for air when I left to find a bathroom. After dumping the condom and cleaning up, I caught a glimpse of myself in the mirror and wondered what the hell had just happened. I hadn't fucked Dean for money or because the script called for it. I'd fucked him because it felt good. Because at that moment, I wanted to shove my cock up his ass.

Hey! It washes off, I told myself before panic could set in. Shaking off the feeling, I finger-combed my hair and returned to the living room.

Dean was sitting on the edge of the desk, visibly shaken.

"I've never done that before," he said.

"Yeah, well, you were pretty good for a first-timer."

"I'm not gay," he said. "Honestly."

Dropping my hand to his lap, I massaged the bulge his khakis were unable to conceal.

"Welcome to the club," I grinned.

casting   couch   coach

Star Power

Michael   W.   Williams

RIVULETS OF SWEAT RAN DOWN MY PUMPED CHEST, POOLING IN THE valleys of my eight-pak, as I surrendered to the wave of adrenaline my workout had sent rushing through me. I sucked in gulps of air and felt pleasantly drained. Like I did after good sex. My dick was hard, my balls still riding my shaft, and pre-cum oozed from the piss slit.

I pushed to my feet. I was running late and I needed a shower.

Still breathing hard from my afternoon workout, I glanced back at the Nautilus as I opened the shower door. Great machine. I owed my current body to it. When I was in my twenties, I'd work out twice a week to stay fit. At fifty, wanting to look forty, I spent several hours each day on the machine. With discipline and fortitude, it worked.

I had a date coming over in thirty minutes. A business date. A kid who wanted to be in the movie I was casting.

Jett Stanton. The name had a nice ring to it. According to Webster's, one definition of *jet* was "a gushing stream of liquid emitted forcefully through a narrow opening." I wondered if he could shoot his stream of hot, juicy cum with real force.

He wanted to be a porn star like me. So far, I was impressed. It took more that a pretty face and body to be successful, however. It took time, patience, and a lot of hard work.

Jett reminded me of myself when I was young, impressionable, and starting out. Better than just good looking—virile. I had been lucky, though. With the aid of several skin flick stars, I modeled myself after the legendary Casey Donovan and Richard Locke. Under my tutelage, Jett Stanton could start moving in the right direction.

Jett had a very handsome face, beautiful large eyes, a strong nose and chin, supple lips, curly black hair. His smooth body was well-muscled, with broad shoulders, prominent pecs, six-pack abs—everything I looked for in an actor. He had possibilities and I'd already decided to sign him up.

He was twenty-two; a graduate of Stanford where he majored in psychology. He had already proved to be smart the couple of times we'd talked on the phone. He even knew how to get on my best side, telling me how he owned every one of my films on video and that he's watched each one countless times.

I caught myself then. I was dreaming about this kid, creating him out of whole cloth—just on the basis of some bad 8 X 10's and a couple of short phone calls.

My hands soaped my balls and lathered my expanding dick. Closing my eyes, I fantasized my hands were massaging Jett's lithe body as it shifted and bent under my strokes. My fingers wrapped around his manhood, sliding up and down along the shaft, making him feel electrified and wanted. I pretended my moans of mounting ecstasy were his. Soaping my ass and massaging each round, firm cheek, they were his. My forefinger and index slid up and down what I imagined was his smooth butt crevice. Teasing, I poked at the tight sphincter but did not probe too deeply. I'd save that for later. I returned to the cock and caressed the thick shaft, increasing the speed with each downward stroke. The groin muscles tightened. He was going to shoot. The spunk was mounting in his balls.

My hand was unstoppable. I was going to cum. I thrust my pelvis forward. The muscles surrounding the base of my cock contracted. My balls rode my shaft. Aaaaaah! I ejected my load, spraying it onto the glass shower door and onto my legs in large white globs. Mixed with the shower spray, the creamy jizz slowly slid down the glass. I was breathing heavy. I was drained again, but satisfied.

In my bedroom, I picked out a pair of shorts and a loose-fitting tank-top. If Jett had seen all of my films as he claimed, there was no reason to try to overcharm.

There were two steaks in the fridge waiting to be placed onto the barbecue. I hadn't had a good piece of meat in weeks and my mouth watered at the thought of prime beef. As I opened the fridge, my gaze guiltily fell on the tofu and the yogurt that were my regular diet.

Taking a deep breath, I sighed and closed the door. As tempting as the steaks looked, I should never have bought them. It was a stupid impulse; still, they needed to be eaten and I did have a guest coming.

Jett wanted to be a porn star and knew I was casting a new face and body for my upcoming flick. Jett claimed to be that person. I thought he was, too. From what I'd seen, he appeared to be the man. I tended to gravitate toward the smooth, buff physique. No steroids! I looked for real muscles. The types of guys I used repeatedly were those who made love to the lens. A guy's hot, bubbling chemistry needed to draw the audience into the action, making them feel part of what was happening on screen, so that, panting with excitement, they grabbed their cocks and jacked off.

An extremely handsome young man dressed in shorts and a polo shirt gazed back at me as I opened the door. He was a bit shorter than I expected; but the broad shoulders, perfectly proportioned pumped chest, bulging biceps, and trim waist made up for that. His strong, muscular, smooth legs suggested that he was a runner. I liked him very much. "You must be Jett," I said.

He extended a broad smile and his hand. "Gee, you look exactly like you do in your films." Then he added, making with the compliments: "You've been my idol for a long time."

"Come in."

"My favorite is *The Balcony*. I get a hard-on every time I watch it. Seeing you in a sailor suit is hot, extremely sexy. I loved it."

"Thank you, it was fun to do. Glad you liked it," I told him. "It wasn't one my best, but Casey was interesting to work with." I chuckled. "Not sure who had the bigger ego, though."

Jett scanned down my torso and focused on my cock, which began to twitch from adoration. "I don't know about egos, but I know who had the larger cock."

"You a size queen?"

"No." He grinned. "But I know what I like."

I smiled and pointed toward the patio in the backyard. "We can sit outside near the pool. Can I offer you some juice? Water?"

"None, thanks."

"So, you think you have what it takes to be a porn star?" I asked as I led him through the living room.

He nodded his head with confidence. "I've seen a lot of fuck films and I can match any of those guys. I've got a hot body." He passed his hand up and down his chest. Grabbing his crotch, he boasted: "Hung like a bull, 9 inches—thick and uncut."

I almost licked my lips. "I hope you're willing to allow me to check that out before you leave."

"For you, definitely."

"You majored in psychology at Stanford?"

He nodded.

"Why would a Stanford grad be interested in skin flicks?"

"A piece of paper doesn't guarantee a job. I can use the money."

He was honest. I liked that. I decided to get the basics out of the way before I offered him a steak and whatever else we could find to interest us. "Are you married, or do you have a girlfriend?"

I asked because I'd had several boys who were married apply over the years. Like Jett, they needed money. I preferred not to work with straight guys. I didn't want the hassle of girlfriends in the wings.

"I'm gay."

"Then I assume you've had your cock sucked."

He laughed. "What gay man hasn't?"

"I'm probing, that's all," I explained. "You like sucking another man's dick?"

He smirked. "Pass me the salami anytime. I'm not bashful."

I smiled, he had a sense of humor. Last question then. "You've been fucked?"

Six months ago, a sexy, buffed guy offered himself to be in a film. When the time came for action, he was lost. He'd never had his cock sucked—either by a man or a woman—and he certainly wasn't about to suck another man's dick. What the hell did he think I wanted? What a waste! He looked good on film—had a great body, a nice dick, got along well with the guys, but he couldn't perform.

"Yep. I'm quite versatile. I can be whatever you want, top or bottom—from vanilla to raunchy. You name it. What kind of video are you planning?"

"*Russian River Weekend* is the title. Shooting at and around Guerneville and Jenner. Using the redwoods as backdrop. Ever been to Guerneville?"

"Several times. Groovy bars, hot men."

"Why don't you take off your shirt so I can get a better look at your chest?"

Jett pulled off his shirt. Naked from the waist up, he had a fantastic-looking torso, tanned with large, dark brown nipples.

I stepped forward and ran my fingers and hands over his prominent, sculptured pecs. The smooth flesh felt good. I pinched his left nipple and twisted the hard, raised flesh between my thumb and forefinger.

Jett moaned passionately.

"You like that?"

"Uh huh."

I tweaked his nipple again.

He jumped. Good reflexes.

I bit the nipple, first lightly, then with greater pressure.

"Aaaaaah!"

My play and his response weren't part of the interview. I'd made my decision about Jett as soon as I knew he was gay. What I was doing was strictly for my pleasure. I tongued the nib. He cooed.

I moved to his other large, dark brown nipple and bit that one. My right hand stroked his flat, tight stomach. My hand rubbed against the mound of manhood which pushed against the front of his shorts. His hose wanted to be free. "Why don't you remove your shorts?"

He did. The rigid flesh popped out as he dropped his shorts. The massive tool, when freed, cut through the air as though it were a sickle—long, hard, and slightly curved. It was every bit the nine inches he boasted of having. Very, very impressive!

Grabbing hold of the thick pole, I massaged the flesh lightly, pushing back the foreskin from the huge cockhead which was already shiny with pre-cum. I pulled the skin forward so that it slid back over the head. Jett closed his eyes and absorbed the pleasure of the moment. My other hand reached under his large, smooth balls.

"Very nice," I whispered. "You've got the job." I could have sent him home then. Selfishly, I didn't. I wasn't stupid. He'd made me hot and horny. It was my turn to play. "Care to take a swim?" Even before he responded, I ripped off my top and dropped my shorts. I was in the water in a flash.

Within seconds, Jett followed. He dove into the pool, swam two laps, then sank beneath the surface, swam between my legs, and grabbed my semi-hard dick. His mouth wrapped around it and, for a few seconds, he sucked.

Pressing onto his shoulders, I pushed my cock all the way into his mouth. The underwater sensation was incredible. I'd sat on the edge of a hot tub while a guy took me down his throat, but this was totally different. I was standing in the middle of the pool at nearly shoulder-depth while a young, hung stud sucked me off under water. I definitely wanted to use this in a future film.

Releasing me, he bobbed to the surface, coughing water. Wiping his mouth, he said, "That was great. I was on the swim team in college, but I haven't had a good swim in ages." He smiled impishly. "Did you like what I did?"

I grinned back.

Standing in front of me, he grabbed my dick and slowly massaged the shaft.

"You're larger in life than on the screen."

I laughed. "You are a size queen! The water has a way of magnifying objects."

"What's in my hand is no magnification. You're huge."

Since we were comparing size, I seized his stiff tool and stroked. "This is no weenie. I'll bet it's made a number of tight asses sing. In fact, I can feel a song coming on right now. But first—" Not wanting to be outdone, I sank under the water and took Jett into my mouth, his monstrous dick filling me up. With cock and water, I began to gag. Bobbing to the surface, I gasped: "I need practice. I wasn't on a swim team. Lots of hot, horny men on your team though, right?"

Jett grinned. "One or two." As an afterthought, he added: "And one of the coaches from a nearby school. We were sex buddies before he got busted fucking one of the guys in the gym shower. It could have been me."

"You're making me hot. Let's go inside and enjoy ourselves."

"I really like your pool. Two more laps?"

I nodded in agreement. Other than my swims, or when Mickey Gonzales, my superstar at the moment, came to visit, the pool was rarely used. Jett climbed out of the pool and strutted his wet, sleek body with his semi-erect dick flapping between his inner thighs.

I decided he could use the pool whenever he wanted. It would be nice to have a young man lying around the pool. It would get me back to swimming, for sure.

I was definitely interested in learning firsthand how Jett performed in bed. Sometimes I'd asked a third person to join in so I could watch a potential actor be taken through his paces before I signed him. Tonight was different. I wanted Jett. Watching Jett towel off, his indecently huge cock wagging back and forth, up and down, I was glad I'd selfishly kept Jett all to myself. With my arm around his shoulders, I led him to the bedroom.

I sat on the edge of the bed with Jett positioned directly in front of me so I could cup his large, smooth balls with one hand and rub his smooth, pumped chest and flat stomach with the other. I smiled as I appraised my latest acquisition one more time. He was going to make a wonderful addition to my stable of young men. If Jett was exceptional in sexual play and sucked up to the camera, he might very well knock Mickey off his tall pedestal. I liked Mickey—he'd made numerous hot flicks, he'd been very profitable—but he was aging.

Jett pulled at my nipples, tweaking the rigid nips between his thumbs and forefingers. "Yes!" I groaned. "Pull on them. Pull them hard—harder! YES!" I love my tits played with. "Pinch 'em! Pull 'em!" The more wantonly they were pulled, the harder my cock became. I was not masochistic, but I demanded physical, lustful and rapacious attention to my tits, cock and ass.

I grabbed Jett's rigid cock, stroked it several times to make the shaft even harder, then slapped it side to side playfully.

He closed his eyes, threw back his head, and moaned deeply.

"I want you to fuck me," I panted. "I want to feel that hot dick inside me." I reached for the lube and a condom. Tearing open the envelope, I extracted the rolled sheath and placed it beside me. Before smearing his cock with grease, I leaned forward and sucked his monstrous tool. Again he moaned as my tongue slipped into his piss-hole, sucking out whatever pre-cum was there. I licked the underside of his dick, up the shaft along the large vein to the broad, mushroom head. I wanted to feel the helmet pressing against my prostate. Sucking forward the foreskin, my teeth bit down on the loose, excess skin at the tip.

I wanted to feel his impressive ball-sac slapping against my ass-cheeks when he fucked me. I was ready. Pulling myself free of his cock, I lubed it and gave him a condom. Once in place, I smeared the sheath and turned and pointed my ass in his direction.

I didn't have to wait long. He drove his cock into my shit-tube. Given the infrequency with which I'd been fucked, there was pain.

I forced my muscles to relax and accepted him. I wiggled my butt so I could feel every engorged inch as he began to plow me. "Deeper," I panted. "Let me feel it. Pound my ass!"

He did. Pulling out so only his large head remained inside, he rammed his dick back into me. He pulled out and drove forward again. His balls smacked against my ass. He was good.

I cried out as he rammed my prostate. I'd asked for it. He was delivering. "Shove that thick cock up my pussy-ass. Make love to it," I told him. "Shove it in hard. Give it to daddy. Give it up!" I rotated my butt so he could position himself for a direct hit. I growled and yelled as he forced himself deeper and deeper. In and out, he slammed my asshole. I loved it.

When I felt he was about to cum, I pushed him free, lapsing back into director mode, and turned to face him. I wanted to see him shoot. I wanted to see if he could live up to the name I'd decided to give him. Jet Propulsion. I wanted to witness the hot, gushing stream of cum ejecting from the narrow opening of his piss slit. I pulled off the condom and stroked his slicked dick.

His groin muscles tightened. His eyes closed. Growling sounds of ecstasy rolled up from inside his powerful chest. Between my fingers and palm, his cock stiffened. He pulled my hand off his cock shaft and, taking it in his own hand, stroked it with increased rapidity.

He cried out. A huge gusher of hot, molten jizz exploded from his cock, hitting me with force, square in the stomach. The liquid was thick and hot.

"YES!" I breathed. "Wonderful!"

Jett continued to milk his dick, extracting every last bit. When he'd finished, he shook his hand of excess residue.

"It's my turn," I told him. "I want to feel your hot ass around my cock. I want to fuck you, like you fucked me. Can you handle it?"

He smiled. "I can take anything you have to give."

"Bend over." I pushed him onto the bed and began massaging his smooth, bubble-butt. The buns were firm and tight. My fingers rode up and down his ass crevice, stopping several times at his puckered sphincter and gently probing the wrinkled opening. It was tight but surmountable. Applying lube, I massaged the opening, which contracted and expanded invitingly. Teasingly at first, I inserted a finger into the puckered opening, then with increasing firmness and fortitude I added two more.

He whimpered, squirming each time I probed deeper.

He was ready. Donning a condom, I plowed into his hole without any regard for tightness or pain.

He needed to take it like a man. If Mickey fucked him, which I was going to have him do, he would show this boy no mercy. Mickey enjoyed fucking, fucking hard. Mickey was going to relish Jett's ass, as though Jett were fresh meat in a prison of sexually deprived men.

"Give it to me," Jett growled. "I want to feel that big dick of yours. I want to feel like those guys I saw you fuck in your films. Show me no mercy."

I plowed into him. My pelvis bulldozed his ass with brute force. In and out like a precision piston, I plunged into his receptive ass. I felt the hot jism stored within my balls bubbling to be released, but I wasn't ready. I wanted more of his ass. Pulling out, I dragged him to the center of the bed, flipping him on his back. I raised his legs high over his head so that his ass was positioned for my re-entry.

"Grab your legs," I demanded. "Pull 'em back. Pull 'em way back. I'm going to fuck you 'till you scream for mercy. Give daddy that hole." I slapped his ass, then, inserting my dick into the opening of his chute, I forged inward. He was open wide now. I drilled in as

far as I could go. I raised myself over him for maximum penetration.
He howled. "I love it! Give it to me!"

I pumped, driving myself in and pulling out. Driving in again and
pulling out all the way, then jabbing my rigid dick into his hot ass. He
gritted his teeth with each attack. When I couldn't hold back any
longer, I exploded into the condom and his ass. I hollered at the top of
my lungs with pure, carnal rapture. I pulled out and squeezed the rest
of my cum over his stomach.

"That was great," he panted. "You're great too." He smiled
sheepishly. "Do I get the job?"

I blinked. He certainly didn't beat around the bush.

I laughed then. "You had the job as soon as I saw you." I moved
in for the kill, an offer I hoped he couldn't and wouldn't refuse. "You
live in a fleatrap downtown, don't you?"

"An inexpensive hotel off Hollywood Boulevard."

"That's fine for pimps and prostitutes—not you. I have a couple
of spare bedrooms. You enjoy the pool. I like your company, not to
mention your body. If you want, you can stay here for a while—until
you find something else."

"Deal," he said quickly, his eyes misting. "Gee, I never thought—"

I pushed off the bed. "Come on," I called to him as I started towards the door. "We've got steaks to grill."

Who knows, if we got along, maybe he could stay permanently. I
hadn't had a live-in for quite some time. Not that I was looking for
one, but maybe I needed a change.

Maybe Jett could help with production. He was an intelligent guy.
I could guide him and he'd go far—especially if it's all the way down
my body, front and back, and all the way in me. He could go as far as
he wanted—anytime, anyplace. I suspected that he would—again and
again. He knew what he wanted and he knew how to get it.

But then, so did I. We'd use each other; eventually, he'd go on to
bigger and better things. But not for a while.

I was going to make sure he was under exclusive contract to me
for a long time. I learned a lot in this business—the hard way. I
figured that the hard way was the only way to go.

the right connections

Big Brother

David MacMillan

I WAS IN SAN FRANCISCO TO SEE MY BIG BROTHER FOR THE FIRST TIME in three years. Sean was supposed to pick me up. I wondered if he was still as skinny as when he left home. I stood at the empty baggage carousel with everybody else from Boston and smothered a yawn. It might be just midnight in California but my body was still working on Massachusetts time. I was dead-assed tired.

I was also pissed off that I'd not seen Sean yet. The bastard had never been on time in his life.

An arm landed across my shoulders, moved under my chin, and began to pull me backwards.

Some crazy-as-hell fag right out of nowhere was going to hug me in public? My fists balling up, I turned and saw the tall, curly-haired, good-looking—built—guy smiling at me. My brother.

"Wee Willie isn't going to let me hug him?"

"Sean!" I yelped and hugged him to me.

"The one and only, wee Willie."

I didn't punch him for calling me that, not there in front of airport security—even though that had been my standard reaction ever since I was two and understood the thing between my legs was a willie too. But I couldn't just let it pass, either. "I'm not so wee any more," I told him. I couldn't get over how built he was. My big brother had become a serious gym rat. We looked almost like twins now.

A smile twisted his face, and it was like we were kids all over again—something wicked was going through his head. "That might be interesting, little brother—to check out," he answered slowly, shaking his head. "But we've got a lot of catching up to do before we explore that—"

I stared at him. What the fuck was he saying?

He grabbed my arm and squeezed—like brothers do. "I'm glad you decided to take me up on my offer to come out to the coast."

Sean's note said he'd be back late that afternoon and to make myself at home. It also said there was food in the fridge. I'd headed for the icebox straight from taking my morning whiz and made a grilled cheese sandwich and poured a large glass of milk.

I padded through the two-bedroom apartment in just my briefs, getting a feel of the place. I'd been bleary-eyed and numb when we'd gotten in from the airport. I had collapsed on the couch the moment I saw it and was out like a light. Now, I had the place to myself and was awake enough to be curious.

Sean was twenty-two, three years older than I. He was in the west working and going to school part time. He didn't say much about work or school to the folks or me, not in his letters or his phone calls. After a first year of college in Boston, we'd gone west, and it'd been sorta like he'd started living on that Russian space station or something. We knew he was alive because we heard from him and we figured he was making it okay because he never asked for money. But it was like he'd dropped off the face of the earth.

So, yeah... I was curious.

The apartment was a lot nicer than I'd expected. I tried to guess what it'd rent for back home in the Boston 'burbs—and kept coming up with four figures. And he lived alone. I couldn't imagine anybody paying some college kid this kind of cash for part-time work.

I was beginning to wonder if my big brother was selling drugs by the time I started to cross from his bedroom to the one where he'd stored my bags last night.

"Hi," a voice at the end of the hall hailed me. I looked back towards the living room and saw a guy standing there. "I just let myself in. You must be Sean's little brother," he said and started towards me.

"I'm Will," I told him, watching him approach me.

"I'm Alan," he answered, shoving his hand towards me. "Happy to meet you." I shook his hand.

Alan was blond, tanned, slim, and came up to my nose. He

looked to be a few years older than Sean. I realized he was staring at the front of my briefs and, before that could fully register, my dick decided to jerk and start snaking out towards my hip.

"From what I can see, you aren't so little," he chuckled. "Want some help with it?" His hand left mine and moved straight down to brush my equipment package through my underwear.

I jumped back from his touch. "What the fuck?" I growled, gasped, and yelped all at the same time. My dick took that moment to become a full-sized missile, armed for action.

I didn't know what to do. Back home I'd have done plastic surgery on his face. But I was in Sean's apartment and this Alan guy was friends enough with my brother to have a key. And I'd heard about San Francisco.

"Opps—"

Alan was looking directly into my face when I was finally able to get my brain working again. "Does Sean know about you?" I demanded.

"I think so. We're fuck-buddies—"

My brother's what? "Sweet Jesus!" I groaned and felt like I'd just been hit between the eyes. My head hurt.

"Sean's not filled you in at all, has he, Will?"

"You two—" I couldn't say it. I barely could even think it.

"I think you two need to talk." Alan smiled. "I came over to pick up some underwear Sean wanted. I'll just get that and leave, okay? He'll be home later and you two can get better acquainted." He slipped past me into Sean's room and went directly to the dresser. I watched him pull out a red-something that looked vaguely like a jockstrap. Even across the room I could see through the material that was supposed to cover my brother's cock.

"See you around," he said as he re-entered the hall, moved his fingers across my hip, and headed for the front door. "The offer still stands, Will," he called from the living room. "You look good enough to eat, boy." I heard the door slam behind him. And couldn't move. I kept seeing instant replays of Alan's ass as he walked down the hall.

I stared at the blank TV screen and didn't know how or when I'd gotten to the living room. I sat on the sofa, still in my briefs from yesterday, as the afternoon waned. I didn't know what to think.

This Sean—the San Francisco doppleganger of my brother—was a total stranger. He was queer—and a well-off one, too, from the looks of his apartment. This stranger had paid my airfare out here and I was obligated to him for that—almost five hundred dollars worth. And I was three thousand miles away from my nearest friend. What the fuck had I gotten myself into? And how did I get out of it?

I wasn't a homophobe. I didn't beat up queers. I suspected some of the guys I'd known in school were gay. They kept their hands to themselves and I kept mine to myself, and we got along like the buds we were. I'd even done a few circle jerks with my friends when we were young. But I got hard for the ladies.

And Alan.

The memory of that kept me scared and glued to the couch while I tried to understand things and how they were going to work.

I figured if Sean wanted me to pay him back for the plane ticket I would let him blow me—if he really pushed it. I sure wasn't going to tell the folks. It'd be just between us. And it'd only be for as long as it took to pay him back. That kind of shit would stay right here in San Francisco if I had anything to say about it.

But, if Sean could go queer, could I? That scared me as much as me watching Alan's butt as he walked down the hall—every time I shut my eyes. I was scared, but I had finally calmed down—like the guy on death row the night before he met the chair. I didn't know what the fuck was going to be the ending to all this, but I accepted I didn't have any way of bailing out at this late date. Whatever the ending was, I was going to be there, right in the middle of it.

Hands cupped my naked collarbone on either side of my head and tightened their grip. I jumped and started wondering how to dig my finger—and toenails—out of the ceiling. "You've got a bad case of nerves there, wee Willie," Sean said carefully.

I was shaking when I turned to look at him over my shoulder, taking in his hand on me before my gaze moved on back. "You scared the shit out of me!" I growled.

"And you stink. Didn't you even take a shower?" He looked over my shoulder. "Hey, Willie, you're going to get jock burn if you wear the same briefs every day. Don't you have any more?"

"I—"

"You can use some of mine if you need to."

I remembered those see-through things Alan had pulled out of his drawer. "I've got clothes, Sean," I told him. Shit! I might as well go around naked as wear that stuff.

"Alan said he saw you today—"

"That—that guy came on to me, Sean."

"How?"

"He felt my dick through my shorts. He said he'd help me out with it." I turned around to face him. "He said you're fuck-buddies."

"I figured he'd made a move on you. I was surprised you didn't beat him up to prove how big a man you are."

"It's your place and he had a key. I didn't know how good a friend he was."

"Not enough for him to put the make on you, bro."

I relaxed. Sean wasn't the stranger I'd been making him out to be. He was still my big brother. "What did he mean by you being fuck-buddies?" I asked timidly.

Sean sighed, let go of me, came around the sofa, and sat down. He pulled his leg up on the cushion and turned to face me. "I guess we're gonna have to have a talk I'd hoped to put off for a while."

"What talk?"

"Have you noticed the apartment?" I nodded. "Have you tried to figure the rent on a place like this?"

"I guessed maybe a thousand—"

"Those windows there overlook the bay, Will! The whole apartment does. Triple that." I gasped. "Go look. I need a beer. Want one yourself?" I nodded as I pushed myself off the couch and started for the balcony.

"It's beautiful," I told my brother and reached for my beer. We were again facing each other.

"And it's expensive, Will. Anything nice in life is. Don't ever forget that." I nodded, not knowing anything else to do.

"Alan's sugar daddy owns this building. Alan produces gay porn vids. I fuck Alan and let him suck me off. Sometimes I suck him off, too. He's happy and goes home to his sugar daddy."

I'd figured that. I was kinda glad Sean wasn't into spreading his legs for guys, though—at least, not for very many. "How did you start? Back in Boston, you had girls waiting in line."

"I thought with my dick back then, too. I turned and walked away from a guy who offered me a hundred dollars just to suck my dick before I left. That was a hundred I could've used. But I didn't let myself even think it through. I just walked away—"

"But out here?"

"Out here, I was living thirty miles from campus in a three-bedroom house where the rent was eight hundred. There were six of us living there and one bathroom. Two beds to a room and no privacy at all. It was almost an hour into school every day and an hour back."

"That's like it was at home, Sean—before you moved out here."

"Yeah. But I wasn't married and didn't have kids, like Dad. I also have my degree which he doesn't have—"

"You graduated?"

He grinned. "Got the degree back in December, Kid Willie."

"So, you've got a regular full-time job now?"

His grin spread across his face and he was chuckling. "I manage. How does twenty thousand a month last year sound to you?" He held up a hand. "I did have to take two months unpaid vacation though."

I did the math in my head and my eyes bulged. "Two hundred grand?" I yelped. "Last year?" I almost let myself wonder why I'd had to take the red-eye special from Boston. He nodded. "Doing what?" I demanded.

He sighed and sat up straight. There wasn't a bit of humor in his face. "Basically I'm a whore. I do porn shoots and I appear at strip clubs for special appearances—but those only brought in a little more than twenty thousand last year. The rest I made fucking guys who wanted my dick. Or letting them suck me. Sometimes I turned my ass up and they fucked me."

"It sure sounds like it was worth it," I told him and meant every word—even the getting fucked part.

"Would you suck dick or take one up your ass for that kind of money, Will?"

"I—" I almost said sure I would. But then I knew I had to think that one through. "You want an honest answer?" He nodded. "Let me think about it."

"Go take a shower, Will. Think about it while you clean up." He reached over and patted my knee. "I'm taking you out for a steak with the thousand I made today."

By the time I had toweled off, I'd decided Sean had made the right decisions—for himself. Prostitution didn't bother me. If somebody was willing to pay to have sex with a guy, why shouldn't the guy get his nut off and get paid for it? What I wasn't sure of was if I could ever do what my brother was doing.

I was guessing, but I sorta figured you had to be a little gay to get hard for another guy. I was trying hard not to think about how hard I'd gotten just looking at Alan's butt that afternoon. I wasn't gay.

I walked out into my bedroom naked. A fully dressed Sean was lying on the bed watching me. I blushed but kept cool, going directly to my bag and a pair of underwear. "Alan was right, bro." I turned to face him and he grinned. "You're big Willie now." I hurried to my bag.

With briefs covering my equipment, I turned to face my brother. "When did you learn that you were gay?" I asked.

"I'm not gay, Will. I like girls, too. The thing you've got to understand is that I just like sex."

"You do it with guys—"

"Hey! Every guy out there has a prostate gland." Sean sat up and I saw he had a real boner. It had to be almost as big as mine got. "We've got a bunch of nerves right there at the entrance of our shit chute, too. Unless you've bought into all this reactionary shit that the preachers are polluting us with, you'd enjoy getting fucked—just like you'd enjoy fucking. Any guy would because we're all bisexual to some degree. It's just a matter of clearing your head of all the shit that's been pounded into it."

"You're saying that you'd have sex with a guy just as quick as you would a girl?"

He studied me for a moment. "Come over here," he said softly.

I stepped up beside the bed and looked down at him. His fingers moved to the waistband of my briefs. "Sean!" I cried, staring at him, and felt my dick come to attention.

"I'll stop whenever you tell me to, Will." He began to slide the cotton down over my growing dick. I didn't say a word.

"That's really nice," he mumbled as he hooked the elastic under my balls. "How big is this weapon? About eight inches?"

"Seven and three-quarters," I corrected him automatically. I was harder than I ever remembered being. He stroked my shaft a couple of times. It felt good.

I jerked when his tongue touched the mushroom knob. His hands went to my still-covered butt to hold me steady and his lips started down my shaft. I groaned.

He pulled off and pulled my shorts out from under my balls, letting them cover me again. "That's enough for now," he said, sitting back and grinning at me.

"Sean—" I whined, watching him and hoping he'd come back and finish what he'd started.

"Later. After dinner, Willie." He stood up. "Think you'd like to do it in front of a camera?"

"Do what?" I growled. My cock wanted his mouth where it'd been moments before.

"Get a blow job and fuck—it's five bills in your pocket."

I caught on, and my brain took over thinking from my dick. "You can get me into a—a dirty movie?"

"Yeah. Alan mentioned that he thought you'd be perfect for the part he's still got open."

"We aren't talking about my butt here, are we?"

"You're fucking Alan—think you'd like that?"

Remembering the ass on Sean's buddy, I was nodding before I realized it.

"Get dressed, Will. I'm hungry, and Alan's waiting for us to firm up the deal."

Sean lied to me. Alan had two scenes in mind for me. But, at the restaurant, I was enthralled by the thousand dollars I was going to make. I still hadn't started to think when we arrived at the studio.

We started with the second scene because Alan wanted us to do it first. We were in the middle of a bed, sixty-nining with me on top. I was covered in sweat from the lights and had a camera inches from my lips which were sliding up and down Alan's pole.

I couldn't believe it. I was sucking dick. Watching his shaved scrotum come towards me and then move away. Feeling his veiny shaft with my tongue as it slid between my lips. I'd already found a way to open up my throat for his thick knob to get intimate with my tonsils. I was harder than I'd ever been in my life and oozing pre-cum like it was honey.

And Alan was gobbling it down. Deep-throating me. He was under me, his hands on my asscheeks guiding me in and out of his mouth. My helmet plunged into his throat with every downstroke. I was in heaven.

The bed gave as someone crawled onto it. I knew it was Sean. I tried not to think about it. I didn't want to think about what was about to happen. I just wanted to enjoy what Alan and I were doing.

Alan spread my cheeks and, a moment later, I felt cool greasy stuff spread over my pucker as a finger found my hole. Sean didn't waste any time; his finger was buried in my ass before I could even tense up, much less relax. I bucked and Alan swallowed me whole as I grabbed his hips. Another finger worked its way into me and dove for the gold.

Sean's other hand found the back of my head and pushed my face into Alan's pubes. His fingers pulled out of me and I felt empty.

Then something big was in my pucker and pressing against my entrance. I knew it was Sean's dick and that I was about to earn my thousand dollars. I just wasn't sure I wanted to go through with it. His hand kept my face buried in Alan's crotch, though, as he humped his hips forward and his cockhead pushed into me.

Pain seared through me and tears welled up in my eyes. I saw the camera's lens recording them. I tried to scream but it came out a muffled grunt around Alan's dick. My brother's battering ram pushed deeper and deeper into me. I felt Sean's pubes in my spread ass-crack, his balls against mine.

"I'm in, kid," he grunted. "Grind that butt around on my dick and show me you like getting stuffed."

I hoped something would show me that I liked getting stuffed. The initial pain of Sean's penetration had ebbed, but having all of my brother's wide-bodied dick crammed into my tight little hole sure wasn't the funnest thing that had ever happened to me. Alan sucking me from the front was keeping me hard but I was sorta wondering where the sex went. Tentatively, I swiveled my hips and felt his cock move against my insides.

Jesus! The shaft of his dick rubbed against something that felt damned good. My whole body got into the act of finding that one exact spot again and again. Alan started bobbing up and down on my pole, because all I could think to do was to keep everything south of my belly button stationary and grind it—and hold the cock in me just right, so that magic spot got rubbed. I held Alan's meat deep in my throat with my nose buried in his balls.

Sean let me learn about dick all by myself. For minutes he knelt behind me and didn't move, his cock buried in me. I ground my ass all around it and moaned around the knob in my throat. My balls tightened and climbed onto my shaft. I was in heaven.

Sean started to move, fucking me slow and easy. Alan's load crashed against the back of my throat and went right down. He started fucking my face. I'd forgotten about him. I opened my eyes just as the head of his dick expanded again and blew out another load. This time his helmet was on my tongue and I tasted his cum.

It was hard with all the sensations crashing through me, with Sean plowing my ass, but I concentrated on that taste. And the next one. It wasn't bad. I figured it wouldn't be hard to get used to sucking dick.

Sean didn't give me a lot of time to think about the finer points of cocksucking. What he was doing in my butt was awesome. I promptly forgot about Alan's dick still humping my gaping mouth and spurting his jizz.

I was riding the surging waves of pleasure that washed over me. It was like the Fourth of July at Boston Harbor. Sean was still fucking me slow and easy, but I was way ahead of him. My dick erupted. And kept on erupting. There couldn't be anything left in my balls. Alan jerked under me and pushed my hips higher. I remembered he'd been sucking me and hoped he liked the taste of me. I laid my head on his crotch, keeping just the head of his cock in my mouth as Sean continued to fuck me. Alan started to lick my balls.

"Has he cum yet?" my brother asked.

"Has he?" growled Alan. "He nearly drowned me."

Sean picked up his tempo. In moments he was pounding my butt, his groin crashing into my cheeks and his dick taking full possession of me. I started to get hard again. Alan already was.

Sean pulled out of me and, a moment later, I felt his cream splashing across my back. Another wad of Sean's jizz hit my shoulder. "Cut!" Alan called and started to crawl out from under me. I didn't feel Sean behind me, either. I looked over my shoulder and saw him take a roll of paper towels from a cameraman. "We'll shoot the next scene in the other bedroom," Alan told us.

Alan looked at me and grinned. "A fuck from your brother will wear a guy out. Take five and we'll come get you when we're set up for the scene."

Sean came back to the bed, still cleaning his dick. "How was it, Will?"

I blushed but told him anyway. "I can get real used to it—fast." I frowned. "But I didn't like you just pulling out and leaving me empty like that."

"That's what we do on a shoot, bro—" He grinned and his eyes sparkled. "Want to sleep with me tonight? We'll do it the way you want it done."

I looked into his eyes. "I think I'd like that," I told him.

script tease

A Bare Market

Ian DeShils

DAN MOORE'S STOMACH CHURNED, THE ROLL OF ANTACID HE'D CHEWED no help at all in quelling the fire raging in his gut. The *Wall Street Journal* lay open across his knees. Its three-inch-high headline, stark against the white paper, screamed: NIKKI WIPE OUT!

At least they're printing the truth now. Hell! The WIPE OUT was a fact ten days ago. The only news in that headline was that they were finally admitting the undeniable. There was no more bullshit, just the unvarnished truth that Nikki Bank Corp. was as moribund as a rabbit on a freeway, and those heavily invested had taken a bath of monumental proportions.

"Bath, hell!" Dan muttered. Like others in at the top, he had drowned. Last month he'd been a paper millionaire; today he couldn't hustle a buck if his life depended on it.

"What a dumb fucking move!" he muttered again, this time slamming his fist down on his knee.

A guy sitting at the other end of the bench looked over at him strangely. Dan paid no attention. He was lost in the fact that he had brought this on himself. Every last cent he could raise had gone into a deal that was the surest thing he had seen in his eight years at Burrum-Murray.

He'd made 15 million overnight and had just started to gloat over the enormous profits when Nikki's CEO committed hara-kiri and set off the panic. There had been no time to divest, no time to recover a thing. The market opened, the stock dropped like a stone and closed.

By the end of the day Dan was broke.

Not just broke, but out of a job as well. Burrum-Murray fired him when the SEC started poking around. Murray didn't quite have the

guts to accuse him of insider trading, he just called it "irregularities."
"Phony bastards," Dan muttered. Murray and old man Burrum played
the inside all the time. At least Dan's hands were clean. The information about the take-over came from a source outside the companies
involved, not that it helped much in this case. He still needed lawyers,
and lawyers cost money.

As *The Journal* pointed out, this wasn't 1929, no matter how
widespread the losses: no depression loomed. Good news to some,
but hardly comforting to a man who had just lost his last dime.
"Bankrupt," he muttered, the word bitter on his tongue. He had never
known a day without money, but now, even his inheritance was gone.

Thank God my parents aren't alive, he told himself silently. I
couldn't bear to tell them this.

A silver Rolls caught his eye as it whispered past on the far side of
the street. Was that Vitto? It certainly looked like his car. Damn! Vitto
Martelli was the last person he wanted to see.

Hurriedly folding the paper, he stood and walked with the traffic
flow, head down, hoping he wasn't seen. As he neared the middle of
the next block, almost in front of the health club where he first met
Vitto, the limo pulled alongside and the rear door swung open.

"Get in," Vitto said and Dan understood that it wasn't a request.

Dan sighed. Well, I've got to face him someday, he told himself. I
might as well get it over with. He climbed into the Rolls and found
that Vitto wasn't alone. A muscular man dressed in a polo shirt and
Bermuda shorts sat in a jump seat facing Martelli, watching a small-
screen TV mounted on the center console.

As Dan settled down next to Vitto, the man turned from the
screen and smiled. "Nice suit," he said, eyeing Dan up and down. "By
the way, I'm Tony Matson. Vitto probably won't get around to
introducing me, so I'll do it myself."

Vitto snorted. "So far I ain't never had the chance—I ain't quick
enough. Shy devil, ain't he?" Turning to Dan and facing him squarely,
he continued: "So, I heard ya bit the big one. Is that right?" Vitto
looked calm and collected for a man who had just dropped half a
million himself.

Dan nodded. He wondered what Matson was watching on TV. He couldn't see the screen and that was a slight distraction, yet not nearly the distraction he wished for now that he had to talk to Vitto.

"How bad was it?"

"Everything!" Dan groaned. "I've even put up the house to pay the lawyers."

"You're shittin' me!" Vitto stared at him incredulously. "Nothing held back, not even a dime?"

"Five, ten grand—maybe. I'm cleaned Vitto. I stuffed every damned cent into it. It was a sure thing. Who knew that Nikki was a paper tiger or that the billions in assets didn't exist? Hell, Nikki suckered the governments of three countries!"

"You didn't see this coming at all?"

"Well, there were rumors, but nothing concrete. I sure didn't see it coming overnight. That damn take-over was worth millions. All I had to do was sell, only I never got the chance."

"Not too swift, Danny boy." He shook his head in commiseration. "What's on the agenda now? The stock market ain't lookin' so healthy at the moment. Think you can squeeze anything out of it?"

"Fat chance," Dan replied, his voice bitter, "Burrum dumped me. Not that it makes much difference. There's going to be plenty of brokers looking for work after this fiasco."

"You mean you got no prospects at all?" Vitto asked, even more incredulous.

Dan shook his head, slouching deeper into the seat.

"Then how ya gonna pay me back?"

Dan jerked upright. "What do mean, pay you back! That was a business deal, we all got burned!"

Vitto raised his hand. "No, no, Danny. I don't lose money and I don't play the stock market—in fact I ain't got a dime tied up. I only invest in people. Remember that little piece of paper you signed? As I recall, you promised me a twenty-five-percent return on that money. Now, considering how things are, I'm not gonna hold you to that but I sure as hell mean to get my investment back, one way or another."

Dan shuddered. He stared at the other man and thought how like a B-grade gangster movie this was. He'd bought it big time this time.

"Jesus, Vitto—"

"Hear me out. Since you ain't in no position to pay, you're gonna work it off. You're a good looking fellow, Dan, and right now I can use somebody like you. Here's the deal. I put up the capital and, anything you're involved in, you get a share. A damn good share, too, just ask Tony. Course you ain't gonna see any cash for awhile, only credit against what you owe me."

Dan stared at the man with his mouth gaping open and he couldn't find a way to command to his muscles to close it. In the years he had known the man, Vitto never talked about his work beyond saying it was lucrative. They were just racquetball buddies.

Even in the reduced light coming through the darkly tinted windows, Vitto's eyes seemed to glitter. Dan shivered. There was something powerfully commanding about Vitto that he had never noticed before. The man sat absolutely still, his rugged features totally at ease; yet, he radiated an indefinable something that quelled any thought of protest.

At nearly forty, Vitto was a decade older and far more muscular than Dan, a sharp contrast in every respect to Dan's trim build and patrician features. In Dan's memory, Vitto's battered face was always smiling, always genial, only today that smile was gone. Instead, there was an almost predatory look on his face.

A chill ran down his spine. What would—what could—Vitto do if he didn't agree? It occurred to him that Vitto might be in the mob like the rumors around the health club said he was. There was a sudden picture in his mind of the horse's head from *The Godfather* and, as he watched, it turned into his own head. Sweat broke out on Dan's forehead. What could Vitto want from him? Carry drugs? Kill somebody? Shit!

"God, Vitto, I'm not sure exactly what you do."

"I'm a video producer, Danny boy." Vitto grinned. "Tony here is one of my biggest stars. He's going over our latest flick right now. Why don't you show him, Tony?"

The man swiveled the twelve-inch color set to face the rear seat and unplugged the earphone from its jack.

"OH MAN! I'M COMING! OH, GOD! HARDER! I'M COM-

ING! HARDER!"

Tony turned down the volume. On the screen, a slim young man lay on his back, his legs wrapped around the waist of a sweating, muscular fellow. The camera dropped and zoomed to a close up of a cock that looked the size of a fence post as it plunged in and out of a tightly stretched ass.

Dan's eyes popped and at the same instant he popped a boner. Holy Shit, the big man on the screen was Tony! "Jesus Christ!" It was all Dan could say.

Vitto smirked. "Like it?" he asked.

"Ah—ah..." A thousand thoughts raced through Dan's mind, none of which he could articulate. He didn't know how to answer that or even if he should. Tony moved to the rear seat, nudging Dan toward Vitto as he crowded in to watch. The scene changed—now the two men were in a swimming pool. The young man put his arms around Tony's neck and was lifted, carried out, and carefully placed on a blanket. They started kissing, tongues battling for supremacy as a hot sun beat down on hard, damp, naked bodies. Soon, the boy had the upper hand. Pushing Tony back, he laved his nipples, swirling the dark chest hair into little crowns as he worked his way downward.

"Would you believe those two don't even like each other?" Vitto commented.

"What?" Roused from his shock, Dan suddenly felt hot and chilled at the same time. Conflicting emotions gripped him as he realized that Tony's foot, now shoeless, was playing at the cuff of his trousers. Dan couldn't breath, his cock so hard it felt like it was about to burst.

"Yep, they fight like cats and dogs. Kid's got a smart mouth and a lousy attitude. Tony threatened to kill him a couple of times, but they sure can fuck and that's what sells videos. What do ya think, Tony, another winner?"

"Looks like it—only, damn it, I need a change. I won't work with that kid again Vitto. I mean it."

"Well, now, that's where Danny comes in," Vitto said soothingly. "He's got the looks and I know for a fact that he's got the equipment."

Dan jerked. "Wait a minute!" he cried as realization flooded over him. "You don't expect me to do that—that... Stuff."

"Oh, so you don't like it, huh? What's that in your lap then, a summer sausage? Danny, my boy, I know all about you, so cut the crap. I've been watching you since we met. You hang with women but watch men. You're always checking out baskets or ogling a tight ass. You ain't got no secrets from me, kiddo."

Dan's face was flushed redder than a beet. "I don't—"

"Can it, Dan!" Vitto said sharply. "How many times have you checked me out in the showers after a game? You think I'm blind?"

He wanted to deny it; yet, it was all true. He had watched Vitto shower—and just about every other good-looking man at the club. Once, he had even almost had sex with a stranger in the steam room. Only he was too scared, too protective of his reputation and family name, to do anything about it. When the fellow touched him he ran and didn't go back to the club for a month.

"My family—my friends. I can't—"

"Oh yeah, all your good friends. Where the hell are they, Danny Boy? I've asked around—nobody knows you anymore. Something about an SEC investigation, isn't it? What about your girlfriend, Sue Anne—what's she doin' nowadays?"

"I—we broke up." He looked down at his hands, unable to look at Vitto, yet equally unable to move his leg away from Matson's toe massage.

"I'll bet you did. I'll lay odds that you couldn't even get it up for her without a hundred-dollar bill wrapped around it. I know you, Danny boy, I know what makes you tick. It was the deals and money that made you horny, not the broads."

Dan was stunned. For all his denials, everything Vitto said was true. He was totally unmasked, even to himself, and it was like being hit by a truck. He felt dizzy, lightheaded, yet his eyes kept drifting back to the TV screen.

"Vitto!" he pleaded. "I—I can't! I'm not—I've never done that with a man!"

He sat between Vitto and Tony, in utter confusion, watched the tape of Tony and the kid play on, hard bodies pounding away. He was scared, but a part of him was curious, too. A part of him he didn't know, a part that didn't give a goddamn what anybody thought. And that scared him too.

Vitto brushed his fingers along Dan's neck and jaw, gently turning Dan's face. There was a warmth—a heat in Vitto's eyes, a look that he had never seen before. Tony began to stroke his leg—his cock, more accurately, rubbing the length of it back and forth.

Dan's world was a mass of confusion, as surreal and twisted as a painting by Dali. He couldn't protest or even move when Tony began fumbling with his fly and freed his rock-hard cock to the open air.

"God, Vitto, he's got a winner here!" Tony said.

"Told ya," Vitto replied. Then he pulled Dan close and whispered in his ear. "Relax Danny. For once in your life just be yourself. There's nothing out there for you anymore. With me you'll get a whole new life, a whole new outlook. You'll love it, babe—believe me, you'll love it."

He kissed Dan on the mouth, forcing his tongue deep inside and, in that moment, Dan's secret fantasy of Vitto came to life. The powerful man whom he had so often spied on in the shower was forcing him, bending him to his will, and Dan's only response was a moan that signaled his defeat.

Tony dropped his warm mouth around Dan's cock, taking it deeper than any girl he'd dated had ever done. His fear evaporated. A weight seemed to lift from his soul, his muscles went slack and his body melted as a burning, white-hot desire took hold. He had never kissed a man before, never knew what it felt like. No soft-perfumed lips, but firm and commanding, all consuming. Vitto's probing tongue became the center of his universe—so intense, so purely demanding, that he simply had to have more.

Vitto could have asked anything then and Dan would have done it, yet the older man didn't demand. He just whispered encouragement into an ear now ready to listen. "Danny, it's OK. You can be yourself with us. No more hiding, no more pretending."

Clothes disappeared without Dan knowing it was being done. The three sprawled on the leather seat in various stages of nudity—Tony completely bare, Vitto still wearing briefs, and Dan naked from the waist down.

There were more kisses, more encouragement, then Vitto's cock found its way into Dan's mouth, hard, urgent and demanding. The incredible feel of the smooth, silky skin across his tongue—the clean, masculine odor, the unforgettable taste. When Vitto came, it was warm and alive; it danced on his taste buds, imprinting that salty/peppery flavor indelibly in his memory.

Vitto pulled Dan's face to his and kissed him deep. "Better than just thinking about it, huh, Danny? You did real good," he whispered. "Now, it's Tony's turn. Do him, Danny. I wanna see you do him. Take that big cock in your mouth and make him cum."

Dan was hot all over. Sweat rolled down his cheeks. He was about to cum himself, and somehow, Vitto ordering him to do it made him even hotter. His straining cock started to dribble on the edge of the leather seat as he turned. He dove for Tony's groin trying to swallow him whole. It was impossible, of course; yet, he impaled himself again and again. It was what Vitto wanted; and, from the moment Vitto had kissed him, whatever Vitto wanted, that was what Dan was going to do.

He felt warm hands caress his ass and froze as the boiling heat of his freedom began to seep from him. "You gotta relax, baby. Remember, this is mine—just like the rest of you." He relaxed and accepted Vitto's domination as the bandage it had become. He began to bob faster and harder on Tony's meat. Vitto's hand touched his thigh. "Get your knees on the seat, Danny. Bend over Tony."

Dan managed to get first one knee onto the seat and, then, shifting his weight, got the other beside it without losing concentration on Tony's cock. Tony's hands pushed between Dan's closed thighs, spreading them before the man jackknifed under him. Dan gasped as his cock slipped into the other man's mouth.

Dan felt the seat flex even more as Vitto moved to position himself behind him. He felt fingers find his hole and one of them push into him. He flinched before realizing it didn't hurt—if anything—it felt—good!

"This is mine, Danny. I've wanted it a long time and, now, it's all mine. You got that?" Vitto's free hand was open as it slapped across his spread, naked rump.

Even that didn't faze Dan: it wasn't an angry slap or particularly hard, but rather conveyed a possessiveness that Dan found exhilarating. When a second finger began to fuck his butt it almost drove him wild. Lunging forward, he finally took Tony's dick to the root.

"You ready, baby?" Vitto's thumb was slowly exploring the valley between Dan's cheeks.

He couldn't answer, the feeling of Tony's dick sliding deep in his throat was too much—the pulling back to catch a breath, the smooth slipperiness as it slid deep, deep again. Dan was lost in the sensation. He was sex, the very embodiment of it—giving pleasure, taking pleasure—it was all the same and like nothing he'd ever experienced before. He clenched his butt in answer to Vitto's question. The fingers in his hole disappeared and Dan felt a sense of loss rush over him. Behind him, he heard foil tear. He moaned, then moaned again as, a moment later, he felt the blunt, wide head of Vitto's cock find its way to where the fingers were before.

"Press down, baby," Vitto told him, "And relax. It won't hurt if you relax."

He did as he was told, groaning around Tony's thick cock as Vitto's even thicker one began to enter him. Sensations he'd never allowed himself to imagine crashed through his body. He moaned as Vitto pushed in. The man's hands caresses his hips, his sides, slid around and tweaked his nipples. Vitto held him, possessed him while slowly burying himself deep inside.

To his amazement it didn't hurt. Instead, the feeling of Vitto's massive cock took him higher and higher as Vitto began to thrust—deep and slow at first, then faster, putting more power behind each stroke. Vitto's muscular body held him in thrall. Every point where their skin touched tingled like fire; even the gouge of Vitto's nails along his sides sent him into spasms of ecstasy. He wanted more—and more. He wanted Vitto in so deep there was no Dan left to think about. It was in this moment of power, in the moments before his climax that he knew he belonged to Vitto—in every way, Vitto's to command and never be questioned. He had gone beyond any thought of that.

The three climaxed like a cresting wave. Tony moaned loudly as

Dan came in the nearly endless flood of the newly awakened. Tony responded in kind and Dan was amazed at the difference in taste from Vitto—not better or worse, only different—and he realized he needed to suck cock and taste jizz again and again. He loved it—he couldn't get enough. He almost had a second climax just realizing that he could now suck Tony and Vitto at any time, that he could feel those cocks expand and explode, filling his mouth with life force. Vitto's pounding reached a crescendo. He came in hard, deep strokes, the final one collapsing their shaky pile into a heap of sweaty bodies.

They lay unmoving for a few moments, before Vitto extracted himself and sat up. "Good God almighty! Now, was that a fuck, or what?" he said as he fished out a couple of bar towels, handing one to Dan. "Try not to leak on the seat, Danny," he said as he started cleaning himself up. "Well, Tony, are you satisfied?" Vitto seemed all business once again.

"Yeah, I think he'll do," Tony replied, grinning broadly as he reaching over to stroke Dan. His fingers trailed the length of Dan's naked body, causing goose bumps to rise in their wake—tiny shivers of excitement caused the former stockbroker to twitch. He was still breathing hard, yet his breath caught at Tony's touch, then caught again when Vitto tugged him close and began to nibble on his neck. Never—not even when he'd seen his stocks hit the fifteen million mark—had Dan felt as hot as he did at that moment, nothing in his life had ever prepared him for this.

Six months later, Dan sat with Vitto watching Stud Films latest release, *An Officer Not A Gentleman*, an epic featuring himself and Tony in Roman garb, set against fake looking columns.

Vitto nudged Dan with his elbow. "You're right," he said, "those costumes are sexy. Tony looks like he's gonna pop right of that centurion uniform. Good idea, Danny."

The sets were forgettable, the dialogue too, but the scenes steamed. As the camera closed in on Dan nursing on Tony's oversized cock, Dan leaned over and started tonguing Vitto's ear. Vitto glanced his way, winked and leered: "After the film, Babe. Now watch."

The last scene was particularly hot with Tony doing full thrusts down Dan's throat. Vitto swore he could see the head of Tony's cock sliding inside the muscles of Dan's neck. God, that was a turn on!

"Want to try it?" Dan asked seductively.

Vitto didn't answer, instead he stood and shed his robe. His cock jutted hard and straight, a long, thin string of dog water, shinny as a spider's web, drooled from the tip. Dan dropped to his knees in worship, lapping at the head, and in one hard, quick thrust Vitto drove it home. He put his hand on Dan's throat, squeezing to feel his big salami slide in and out. It was a sense of pure power to know this man would take it all, or die trying. He could jam it in, just hold there until Dan passed out—and Dan would love every minute of it, even beg for more. The thought drove Vitto to the edge. He grasped handfuls of hair and began to face-fuck the man with wild abandon. He came in moments and, as if to verify his power, Dan's own explosion spewed warm against his bare legs.

"Damn, but we're good for each other," Vitto said as he pulled Danny up beside him on the sofa. "A quick fuck or an all-nighter, it just seems to get better, don't it?" He kissed Dan, laid him across his knees and began a sweet torture of little tit pinches interspersed with kisses and fondling. Dan purred like a kitten. "You know, Danny," Vitto said seriously, "If you can come up with another script half as good as this last one, I'm ready to go for it."

"Well, there is one I'm working on, just haven't figured out the ending yet—"

"Oh, yeah? What's it about?

"Well, there's this guy, an up-tight stockbroker type who gets in over his head. He borrows money from a handsome—but rather shady—character, loses it all, and ends up working for him making porn films to pay off the debt. I call it *Bare Market*. Do you think it might fly?"

Vitto laughed so hard he couldn't answer. He just nodded.

screen test

My Brilliant Career

M i c h a e l C a v a n a u g h

"TURN DOWN THAT GODDAMN RADIO BEFORE I COME OVER THERE, twist your fucking head off, and cram it up your fucking ass, you goddamn fruitcake."

I spun the volume dial down to a whisper, because I realized that a person who didn't appreciate Barry Manilow was a person who wouldn't listen to reason. I heard some other grunts of approval and an explosive fart.

Before I get down to telling you what really happened the other night, let me introduce myself. My mamma taught me always to say 'please' and 'thank you' and to introduce myself to strangers. "The Hutters've never had anything to be ashamed of, Jimmie Jack," she'd told me. "Except maybe for your Aunt Lula—and that wasn't really her fault. She never would've become a nymphomaniac if it hadn't been for the Bulldogs winning the homecoming game that year. Nobody expected that."

So, now you know. I'm Jimmy Jack Hutter, and my being incarcerated here at the state Honor Farm is just a great big, horrible ugly mistake. Well, unless you've been out of the county for the past two months, you already know I was in that car out in front of the "Big Pit" barbecue restaurant and convenience store. I never disputed that, not for a minute. I was in the car and I was driving, but I didn't have a clue that Lyle and Bobbie had cooked up a plan to rob the place. And just let me assure you that I would never have forced Lula Rose Hicks to strip naked and get into that meat locker. I mean, Lula Rose and I went to school together up until she dropped out her freshman year when she had to get married.

If Juanita Dungy hadn't gone in to get those ham hocks out of her self-storage locker, poor Lula might still be in there. No telling what would've happened. Sorry, Lula Rose.

Anyhow, I was out on my own front porch, waiting for Lyle to come by and pick me up like he said he was going to do when my older sister, Fiona, came flying out of the house like a bad dream. Fiona hates me because I got all the looks in the family, while she got stuck with the mousy hair, the acne and the hips. Tough luck, sister.

"Jimmy Jack! Woohoo!" Tell you the truth, she damn near startled the living shit out of me, but I didn't move a muscle. I just wasn't interested in giving her the satisfaction. "Mamma says for you to come in off the front porch. She says you can't stand out here like that. The neighbors'll talk."

"I'm really not interested in what Mamie and Tootles Jeeter think about me or anything else," I retorted. Mamie and Tootles were sisters, and they kept a close eye on everything that went on down at our end of the street. Mamie'd been wearing the same pink and purple, horizontal-stripe dress every day since I started third grade, so I wasn't about to grill her for fashion tips.

"Jimmy Jack, Momma says you just gotta put something on. What's wrong with you anyway? Momma says that nobody on her side of the family ever acted like that, so you must've gotten it from Daddy. I can see your naked butt. Yuch!"

"Get lost, Fiona. It's hot tonight. Besides, I ain't naked."

"Might as well be, standing out here out in front of God and everybody with your business all pushed out in front like you was advertising it."

"Listen, Miss Prissypants, I'll have you know that these shorts were mail-ordered special from an exclusive catalog with real models in it. They're the 'trimline physique short with action pouch' for your information. You see these in the big city all the time, not that you'd know anything about that."

"Well here's an action for you, Jimmy Jack. Walk around back of the house and stand where nobody can see you. I'm expecting Dave."

Fiona'd been dating Dave Hawley forever and if she thought he was gonna marry her, she was dumber than she looked. He was about the world's biggest loser and the only 'job' he'd ever heard anything about was a Bible character.

"What's with you anyway, Jimmy Jack? Dave says you're one of them queers. Are you?"

"My sex life ain't none of your business, Fiona." I vaulted over the porch rail, down onto the hard-packed dirt. "I'm gonna be famous, Fiona. Rich and famous. I'm fixing to get discovered. Just you wait and see."

"You ain't gonna be shit, Jimmy Jack. That's what Dave says."

"You can tell that dumb fart Dave Hawley to cram it up his fat butt." I had plenty more to say to Fiona about Dave, but she turned and flounced back into the house, slamming the screen door behind her. I might've followed her to say more, but I wasn't about to give her the satisfaction.

I put Fiona out of my mind and turned my thoughts to my upcoming evening. According to the clock in the kitchen, Lyle would be arriving any minute. When Lyle Driscoll pulled into the station for a lube job earlier that afternoon and told me he was a Hollywood agent, I believed him. I mean, I'm just not a suspicious person. Hell, he was driving an imported car and was wearing this big diamond ring and some clothes like the ones in that catalog I keep under the mattress. Well, when he told me he was looking for a guy to star in this new picture he was working on, and mentioned that I was perfect for the part, it sure sounded legit to me. After all, I've been working out real hard for years—and, not to brag or anything, I'd been voted second runner-up for 'best looking guy' my senior year. Anyhow, when he gave me his business card and told me he'd be by at eight o'clock to take me out to meet the people paying for the movie, I just knew he was for real.

Well, Lyle pulled up in front of my place that evening, honking the horn, right on time. I strode across the yard to his car, very tuned into the fact that Lyle was giving me the eye, bigtime. I was wearing that real tight pair of shorts Fiona'd been rattling on about, white socks, my good tennis shoes and a baseball cap, turned around backwards. It was just exactly what Lyle had told me to wear when he told me about the movie. Since it was sort of like an audition, I walked up to the car real slow. When I was about three feet away, he rolled down his window, tossed out his cigarette butt, and flashed me a big, sincere smile. He had real nice teeth.

"Goddamn, dude. You look hot enough to melt paint. Fuck."

"Thanks, Lyle," I replied modestly. "You're looking mighty good yourself." He was, too. He had changed out of his good clothes and was wearing a sleeveless T-shirt that showed off his arms real nice. He had big biceps and dark hair on his shoulders. It looked real hot. I peeked in the car and saw that the fly of his faded jeans was unbuttoned and something that resembled a flesh-colored hose was draped out over the seat between his legs. My heart skipped a beat.

"Get on in the car," Lyle said, jerking his head in the general direction of the passenger seat. I walked around, opened the door and climbed in. Lyle hit the gas and sprayed a rooster-tail of gravel about ten feet in the air. I'd have to remember to rake the yard before I mowed on Saturday. Otherwise I'd risk busting out every window in the damned house.

I forgot all about windows just as we drove past the Tastee Freeze, out near the end of Main street. I was waving real big at Carl and Rudy Macks, hoping they'd see me in Lyle's fancy car, but they were too dumb to look up. "You suck cock, dude?" Lyle asked, right out of the blue. Well, I just snapped my head around and stared, my mouth gaping. "I'm gonna assume that means yes," he said, putting his hand on my neck and pulling my head down into his lap so hard I damn near chipped a tooth on his zipper.

Well, I guess I could've grabbed his balls, punched them up his ass, and ended the whole thing right then and there in front of the Tastee Freeze, but I didn't. I'm not a violent guy, and his balls were so big and furry and heavy in my hand that I just sort of wanted to fondle them instead. While I was doing that, his dick started stirring so I settled down to investigate. I started back at his bush and began working my way out to the end. It was a long enough trip to warrant packing a lunch. I've seen a few dicks in my day, but never anything to hold a candle to Lyle's man-handle. It was as thick as my wrist and had veins twining around it like vines around a tree trunk.

"Get on that damned pole, dude. Show me what you're made of."
I opened wide and got on. "Shit, yeah. Feels fucking hot, man. Suck
that big dick. Lick it. Fuck!"

Lyle bucked his hips and grabbed at the back of my head,
ramming his prick so far down my throat I could practically feel the
fist-sized head pulsing in my belly. I grunted and groaned and
struggled a little, but then Lyle smacked my ass real hard and
jammed a finger right up my hole, which calmed me down consider-
ably. I wondered for a second just how the hell Lyle was managing to
drive that big car while he had both hands busy, but then he started
knuckling my prostate and I forgot all about it.

I have to admit, I've always prided myself on my cocksucking, so
I set out to give Lyle the blowjob of his life. Once I finally got him to
let go of my head so I could maneuver around some, I just got right
down to it. I locked my lips tight around the shaft and came up off
him nice and slow. By the time I got out to where I could knob him,
Lyle was so far away I could barely see him. Hell, if I'd thought
about sucking him before we'd started, I don't think I'd have been
able to manage it.

I was managing now, though. I ran my tongue around the bulging
dome of his glans, swabbed his piss-hole, rasped away at the bundle
of nerves tucked right below it, then started down on him again. I
rode it slow, letting his immense girth stretch my throat muscles to
the max. By the time I was rooting in his pubes, I was beginning to
see stars—and, judging by the sounds he was making, so was Lyle.

I kept on after him, hard and fast. I'd ride the rail from end to end
a few times, then grab his cock with both hands and jack while I
licked all around the end and tried to catch my breath. About ten
minutes into it, Lyle's nuts were trying to climb up on top of his
hard-on, and, judging by the sounds of the engine, we were going
about a hundred miles an hour.

"Unh! Fuck! Jesus!!!" Lyle let fly with his load. His cock slipped
out of my grip and flexed, pointing straight up. A huge gush of white
cream pumped out of him, right up to the roof of the car. It splattered
against the gray fabric and hung there like a big, sticky stalactite.

"Christ!" Lyle let loose with another one. This time, his spooge blasted the windshield, right in his line of vision. He leaned forward to wipe the glass and his big cum-cannon pointed right at me as Lyle squirted out a third shot. It hit me on the neck and sprayed up the side of my face. It was hot and thick and smelled like a man's sweaty balls. I grabbed for my crotch, ready to work myself over, but Lyle grabbed my wrist.

"Save it, pal."

"But I'm horny," I protested. Hell, I was, too. I'd just sucked a cock that was damned near as tall as I was and I wanted some relief.

"Shit!" Lyle slammed on his brakes. I flew off the seat and got wedged under the dash. The floor wasn't any too clean and a whole bunch of dirt and twigs stuck in the gummy mess smeared from my hairline to my shoulder. "We're here. Get out." Lyle opened the driver's door and took his own advice.

"Lyle," I spluttered, crawling out on all fours onto the sharp gravel of the driveway, "I gotta get cleaned up before I meet these—" I looked up and saw a semi-circle of guys, all staring down at me. I scrambled to my feet and crammed my hat back onto my head. My hair was a mess. This screen test wasn't getting off to a great start.

"Hi, guys," I said sheepishly.

"Christ," somebody muttered.

"This is it?" A guy who looked like Lyle, only with bigger muscles, walked around me, staring hard. I felt like some livestock exhibit at the county fair. "Can he fuck?"

"I was fingering him on the drive out," Lyle replied, clearing his throat and hawking a wad of spit. "You could park a tour bus up his hole."

"Pardon me?" I couldn't believe my ears. If I'm anything, I'm tight. Just ask any of the guys down at the truckstop at Four Corners.

"Shut up and get inside," Lyle grunted. All his manners had suddenly gone south on him, causing me to revise my opinion of him. I would've given him a piece of my mind, but I didn't want to act ugly in front of important strangers. I just gave him one of my patented 'don't-mess-with-me' looks and followed him inside.

I'd been expecting an office—what I saw was a big old warehouse with some lights set up around a platform draped in black plastic sheeting. One of the guys had a video camera with him. Another guy walked over and started turning on lights. Several of the others started taking off their clothes. I had no idea what they were going to do, but I had to wash my face.

When I got back—after using a toilet that hadn't been cleaned since maybe sometime during the middle of World War II—there were four guys—all naked, all hard—up on the platform. There was a redhead with great pecs and a scarlet pecker. He winked at me and his dick rose up to point at the sky. Then there was a blond with enough muscles to start his own gym. Right next to him was a Black dude with skin the color of milk chocolate and startling blue eyes. Last but not least, there was a guy who was shaved head to toe, with a cock on him that was bigger than anything I'd ever seen growing between a man's legs—and that includes that truck-driving redhead from Kansas City who I met last month. It was hard as a rock—and let me tell you, it's a wonder the poor guy didn't just up and pass out.

"On stage, buddy," the man with the camera snapped. "Hurry it up."

"Hey, guys," I said, stepping up onto the platform, hand out-stretched. "I'm Jimmy Jack Hutter. I—" My introductions got cut short when the tall Black man gripped my wrist and pulled me up against his hard body.

"Suck me," he growled, his voice deep and sexy. He pushed me to my knees and began smacking my face with his meat. After the first few smacks it was starting to hurt, so I opened wide and he slid in deep, bouncing his balls off my chin.

While I started to suck, somebody grabbed a handful of my de-signer shorts. I reached back, but, by then, my shorts had been torn off and I ended up grabbing my own bare butt. I wasn't the only one with that in mind, as it turned out—within five seconds, the blond and the redhead had followed suit and I had enough hands on my ass to play piano duets. Those hands had fingers and most of them ended up in my crack, pulling my cheeks apart, spreading my ass-lips wide.

"Move the camera in closer, Jack. Get that butt in focus."

"Guys, I—" The Black man's prick popped out of my mouth, only to be replaced by the blond's big schlong. The Black man began prodding at my ear with his spit-slicked hard-on. I was so busy trying not to choke on all that cock while I kept my ass-ring clenched tight that I completely forgot the audition piece I'd been practicing. I was planning to knock 'em dead with this scene from "Little House on the Prairie," but I had a feeling they weren't interested.

"Got those fingers up in him?"

"Yeah."

"Pick him up." Before I could dislodge the huge horn crammed down my throat, the two guys behind me lifted me, suspending me above the platform. I managed to get my feet on the floor and would've stood up and given them a piece of my mind, but the blond guy had a grip on my ears that was constricting my movements. As it was, I snorted and wiggled my butt angrily.

"Okay, men, loosen him up for Harry. Bold Harry, you find that box of 'Like a Horse' condoms?" I looked around. Harry shrugged and wandered off into the shadows. I felt something pressing against my hole, then my ass-pipe was full of cold, slippery lube. I wiggled around, but it didn't seem to slow anybody down. The nozzle disappeared, then I felt furry thighs against the backs of my legs. I looked at the big hand gripping my shoulder. It was bristling with copper-colored fur. A second later, I had the redhead's cock up my ass and I was getting fucked.

"Got a good angle," the cameraman grunted, slithering beneath me on his back, his camera pointing up towards my crotch.

"Little tomcat has a nice dick. Photographs nice. Balls pulled up tight enough so they don't interfere with the penetration shots. Change partners, guys. Punch him hard."

Red popped his dick out of my ass, and I saw the muscular blond step into the breach. He spit in his palm and lubed his dick, then plopped a condom on his knob and rolled it down to his bush. He plowed in deep and I would have fallen flat if the Black man hadn't propped me up by shoving his hard-on down my throat.

The four of them fucked me all over that plastic-draped stage. I mean they turned me every which way but loose. At one point they were passing me back and forth, each one spearing me deep, then making way for the next guy. I tell you, I was within a heartbeat of shooting my wad all over that camera guy. I was drooling lube like a broken pipe, my nipples were swollen up in thick points and my hole was grabbing frantically at whatever prick was poked up inside of me at any given moment.

"Final scene, men. Go for it!"

"Cum shot!" the director yelled. All of a sudden I was flat on my back, asshole snapping at the air, staring up at the camera and four bulging stiffers. The redhead erupted first, his load splashing down on my chest and neck like molten lava. He was still spitting when the Black man blasted off, creaming all over my face. The blond got my left leg and my arm, shooting hot ribbons of jism with the force of a garden hose. Finally, Harry got off, aiming his load at my cock and balls. One touch of that hot, manly load of his and I blew my own cork, laying a line from my belly button right up to my chin.

"Cut!" The guys surrounding me all stopped flogging their hogs and walked away, leaving me laying in the middle of a lake of jizz, totally dazed. I looked up and saw the camera man counting money into Lyle's hand. Lyle stuffed the wad of cash into his pocket. While I was wandering around looking for my shoes and my baseball cap all the guys who'd been fucking me up and left without saying goodbye, kiss-my-foot, or anything.

"Hey, you!"

"If you're talking to me, Lyle, you might recall that my name's Jimmy Jack." I knew he was talking to me because by now there was nobody else in the warehouse. I'm not stupid. "How'd the audition go?"

"Huh?"

"Did they like me? Am I gonna get a part in a movie?"

"Oh. Oh, yeah. You were terrific. They want you to co-star in this big war picture with a whole bunch of guys."

"Oh. What's it called."

"I don't know. *The Proud, The Hung, The Horny*—or something."

"You know how to drive?" Lyle was standing right in front of me, hands on his hips. I nodded. "Then get a move on, Timmy. We've got things to do."

"It's Jimmy. Jimmy Jack," I pointed out, wondering why he was having so much trouble with my name.

"Whatever. Get your pants on and meet me at the car." I found my shorts, ripped at the waist, with a big, dirty footprint on the backside. I put them on anyway. I never did find my hat.

When I got out to the parking lot, Lyle was in the back seat of the car, making out with this guy he called Bobby. I thought he'd been the one working the lights but I wasn't sure. He had lots of blond hair and sort of a dumb expression on his face. I didn't think he was handsome at all. I hopped in front and Lyle directed me to the "Big Pit" and told me to wait. If he'd told me what he was planning to do, I could've warned him that Deputy Billy Stallings came in for coffee and donuts every night at midnight, regular as clockwork. That was strictly his fault.

The rest is all there in the court documents. I don't know how Lyle's lawyer talked that jury into believing I was the brains behind the whole thing, but he did. And to think I went to high school with those people. They should've known better.

"Hey, Vergil!"

That was Pete, the dude in the cell to my right. He and Vergil—the guy to my left—talk across me all the time. I might just as well have been a big old hole in the atmosphere for all the attention they paid me.

"My pals Lyle and Bobbie sneaked me in a new video this afternoon. You gotta see it."

"What's it called, Pete?"

"Hell, I don't know. Wait." There were some rustling sounds in Pete's cell. "Get this, Vergil—*Jimmy Jack Hutter Takes it All*."

"That's a dumb title."

"Wait'll you see it. I'll stick it in the machine in the lounge tomorrow night. That'll get the guys stirred up—you know how they like to see some hot little sleaze get his butthole poked. Shit, they'll all be trying to screw the sofa cushions. Take my advice and don't bend over in the showers for a week or two after I show it."

Vergil laughed and said something back, but I didn't pay any attention. All of a sudden, I was starting to feel a little dizzy.

on the set

Boy Pussy

Alan W. Mills

So I wake up around eleven cuz it's bright, and my boyfriend, the one I had then, kinda envelops me like he's liquid or something, and he's warm and a little sticky, and I kiss him, his breath a bit sour from the alcohol. I'm totally hard, and his cock is fat and heavy. "Suck me off," he says, and I get in position, competing to get his sweaty sheets the fuck out of our way.

I hold his monster at the base and swallow it quick, going down, hunched over, and up again fast with no concern for romance cuz, after all, fuck it, it's a morning kinda thing. His cock still tastes like lube, you know, sweet and sour penis, with lots of MSG. His hairy nuts smell slightly rank, and I get an even better whiff of his pubes every time I sink to the base.

I breathe it in, getting a deep sample of the good stuff. I think of The Learning Channel where I learned that the sweat in the crotch and underarms and crack contains more fatty oils than in the other more open places, and it has hormones, too, and it's great food for bacteria, explaining why the smell gets so intense. Last night he reeked of pheromones. Now he reeks of creatures eating pheromones.

I suck him almost too well, and he pulls me up to kiss the creatures from my lips. I know it sounds like a gross thing, but it's really hot. If you'd ever been there, I know you'd understand. My boyfriend-at-the-time, Steve, his fat cock crushed beneath my nuts, opens his lying blue eyes and says: "Oh Davy, you're so fuckin' good!" And then he touches my a-hole with his middle finger, and it's like he's pulled my trigger. I go bang. My boy-pussy ignites and gets hot, and gets itchy, like an emotional kind of itchy, and I cover Steve's megacock with one of the condoms on the nightstand and soak it with lube and squat down, shutting my hole up with his meaty ass-plug.

His cock hurts at first cuz we've been asleep for at least five hours, so it has to be that long since he's fucked me. I adjust and open and relax, lifting my ass almost to the distant crest and wiggling my way down 'til I feel his nuts on my soft o-ring, my perfect, high-priced fuck crack that Steve helped shave only just last night.

Steve cums fast, but I don't mind. I actually have to work today. He's still panting as I climb off him and pull the sloppy condom from his cock. "Aren't you gonna—?"

"No," I say, "sorry, I don't think I can. You know how I am in the morning."

I'm down in the laundry room, pulling my unmentionables from the dryer when one of my neighbors walks in and catches me bent over. "Fuck!" he says, "I've never seen a dude look so hot in just a pair of sweats."

I look back at him with my baby-boy blues and pull the gray cotton down in the back. "How do I look out of them?"

He gets on his knees behind me and stares, cupping my firm, flawless globes in his rough, Latino hands. "Oh man!" he says, "I want to fuck you so bad it hurts."

I bend over a bit and reach back to spread my cheeks. "Why don't you give it a lick first?" And he does, sticking his tongue up inside my warm, anxious hole like he's aiming for my heart. His tongue feels good and it makes me want to get fucked, and when he pulls back to gaze at my sphincter, his eyes widen and he says, "Oh fuck, your hole is winking at me."

"I think it likes you," I say. "Lick it again and rub your cock on it to make it purr."

He does. He licks me and stands, whips his pecker out, and rubs it up and down my milky crack. It feels all warm and oily, and I back into him like a pussy in heat.

His skin is dark and soiled, and I can smell his foreskin rubbing over his swollen cock. He rubs it over my a-hole faster, and it makes me wet and horny, and then he shoots his load over my ass and onto my back, and I think: Motherfucker! Now I have to shower again!

I step out of the shower when I hear the doorbell, and I leave wet footprints across the hardwood floor as I trek across the living room.

Pulling a towel around my waist, I open the front door and it's the manager. He's kind of old but in good shape, and I say: "Don't tell me it's rent time again."

"Yeah," he says, lifting the lube. "Assume the position."

I go to the center of the living room and toss my towel to the couch. "Oh, come on, Mr. Mazer," I plead, bending over, "I got to go work soon."

"You gotta work right now for your rent, Davy." He opens his fly, letting his huge cock fall out. It already has a condom on it, and it's totally solid as he drips lube down the shaft. "I already took my pill, and there's no backing out now."

I grip my ankles and feel water drip down my back and legs and chin. I'm already starting a giant puddle, like I'm some naughty little puppy, and my building manager doesn't even care. He just gets behind me and slowly starts to push his prick inside my ass.

Now, I don't know what it is about old guys, but they always have big pricks. Yeah, big, fleshy pricks with the skin hanging off 'em. It's like they just keep growing, year after year, and never stop. Just the thought of it freaks me out, but sometimes I get so hungry for big cock, I hunt down a daddy with gray hair and a horse-cock hanging between his legs, and just say: "Please, Daddy, fuck me with your big old cock."

Mr. Mazer, he takes forever, fucking me with his huge, hard-as-a-grindstone boy-basher, and I'm begging: "Please Mr. Mazer, I gotta go to work soon!" But when my rent is fully paid, my o-ring knows it's been plowed, even if poor Mr. Mazer doesn't splooge a lot.

So, I'm freshly showered, again, and dressed and on the bus headed down Fountain. The driver scoped me out when I got on, but I didn't like something about his eyes, so I sat in the back. Some guy gets on and sees me, and he sits next to me even though plenty of other seats aren't taken.

I understand him, though. He's a young guy, like me, and he has dark hair, and he's tall and thin. "Hey," he says, and I totally know what he means, so I scoot forward and push my ass back. He touches the small of my back, and his fingers are coarse but his touch is delicate. The sensation slides down my smooth crack and I raise myself a bit to give the guy access.

I look into the rearview mirror and see the bus driver's eyes on me. Some old tranny is watching me, too, and I give both of them a really hot facial expression when my guy spits on his finger and probes it into me. My a-hole gets all happy, and the son-of-a-bitch finds my g-spot real fast and just up and tickles it like he's got talent.

I wiggle around on his finger and then we suddenly hit a pothole, and I'm all, Oh God, Thank You Cal Trans!

I get off a block from my friend's apartment and the dark-haired guy gets off with me. The first thing I notice is the bus driver's scorn. The bastard probably has a chubby that won't quit, and I bet his wife can't even deal. Oh well, I think, not my problem, but the other guy follows me, like not even discreetly, and once the bus pulls away, he says: "Is there some place we could go?"

I stop and look at him. "No. I'm late for work already."

"Oh, please," he says, grabbing the impression of his fat cock in his khakis. "You got me so hot. Your ass is like silk: warm, wet silk."

"So! That isn't my fault. I didn't ask you to play with my a-hole."

"Oh, come on, just let me fuck you long enough to get off."

When he says that, my o-ring twitches like it can hear what he's saying, but I'm not just some easy slut who does whatever his ass begs him to, so I hold my ground and say: "No, I don't want you to fuck me. Okay? You can't fuck me! Understand?"

Then I grab him by the hand and lead him behind a dumpster. I open his pants in a big hurry. His cock is hard and dripping, and he moans when I pull it out into the somewhat-fresh L.A. air. I squat down and stuff his cock in my mouth, sucking it and stroking it fast but soft, giving it lots of spit to slide along. He tries to keep quiet, but he can't—I'm bringing him to orgasm too fast. His moaning increases in pitch with the rhythm of a stopwatch, and it sounds kind of panicked, as if he's about to get hit by a car. And it isn't thirty seconds before that car hits him and he screams out, and I pull off real fast and jack the chowder right out of him and watch it go flying. Boy, is he grateful, but you know me—I just stand, kiss him on the cheek and go on with my day.

When I reach Joseph's place, he opens the door all sexy-like, with his big black chest trapped inside a tank top. You see, Joseph is famous—well kinda famous, maybe only famous in some fetish circles. You may have seen him; he goes by J.K. Junior. Personally, I think he's a stud, and when I first met him, he gave me a rich black fucking that I'll never forget. Cuz, so you can picture it, he looks like some college athlete, a football hero.

He's not super tall, more normal, and he's built, but not overly so. Just enough. And fuck, is he cute. Neatly trimmed hair, cocoa skin, excellent features. He's the reason that I'm here. "Okay," he says, "are you all ready?"

"Yeah, sure," I say. "What happens next?"

"Well, Dada's sending Bobby over to pick us up, and then we're going to North Hollywood to shoot the scene. Dada says it should take about five hours, but it'll probably go longer." Joseph smiles. "Did you shave your stuff all right?"

I pull down my shorts and bend over the sofa. Joseph spreads my ass-cheeks with his stern but sweet-smelling fingers and inspects my a-hole. "Yeah, you did a good job." I know his fingers are sweet smelling because I smelled them before, several times, each time he raised me up and put his fingers on my tongue, stretching my mouth to make room for his cock. Now his fingers rake over my crotch, his palm cupping my 'nads, my cock between the ring and the middle— you know, the fuck-you one. My shaft feels swollen next to his warm skin, and I breathe heavily as he scratches my neatly trimmed bush. "Yeah," he says again, "you did a really good job."

So, I'm bent over, wishing Joseph would shove something inside me, when the door opens without warning. Bobby Godrod steps in, stands at the threshold, and stares like he's entered the wrong apartment. "Oh," he says. "Davy Bottoms?"

"That's me," I say, aiming my a-hole right at him. "We were just checking how I did at shaving. Wanna see?"

"Actually," he says, walking in and shutting the door, "we have to be heading out. Dada's waiting."

I open and close my sphincter at him, and he notices, I know it. "Are you gonna be in the movie today? Cuz, if you're not, you can fuck me right now."

"Excuse me?"

"You heard me," I say, pushing my cock back and rubbing a drop of fluid over the head. "I've been itching to get fucked by you since I first saw you in *Rough Wranglers*."

"Sorry," he says, practically stepping up to the plate, "but you're gonna get fucked plenty once we get to the set."

We're in Bobby's SUV, heading to the Valley, and I'm checking Bobby's jock, almost sure I saw something stirring in his shorts. "What's that?" I say, and Bobby looks at what I'm drooling over.

I undo his fly, faster than he expects, and reach in for his cock. Out in the open, it looks bigger than on TV, and I say: "Dude, I knew it. Your cock is totally hard, and you wouldn't even give me a taste." I squeeze a drop from the slit and bend to lick it up.

And then I gobble his cock like a total gluttonous pig, you know, and he swerves a little, trying to stay inside the lines. Filling my mouth with spit, I rub my tongue up and down the cock in between my lips. I lift off it, the spit dripping off my chin. "Oh man," I say, my voice deep and slobbery, "I fuckin' love suckin' cock." And then I go back down, kissing his lap, and come back up to vacuum out the juice from his tip.

This is an amazing experience for me. I own the rubber version of him, but it isn't the same. When I bought it, the box said it felt real, but this is different—not better, just different. Thinking of the Bobby Godrod I keep under my bed, I reach back and rub my ass through my shorts. The unexpected pleasure makes me go wild, and as I suck Bobby Godrod's famous cock, I consider pulling my shorts down and raising my ass to the open window so I can feel the passing city blow against my o-ring. But I don't do it. Even here, on Laurel Canyon, it just might get us busted, and then I'd never get to do the movie.

Bobby has the hardest time making soup, mostly because he fears an accident, but he manages it at a signal, squinting, moaning, bucking, fighting. Shooting right into my mouth. I let him go and go, and I take it, and, as we start to move again and his cock's eruption reduces to a flow, I sit up and spit his boy-seed out the window.

Joseph's head spins to follow the flying jism. "Oh, man," he says, "Davy! You got that on some guy's hood!"

The hunk driving the Jeep behind us is mega-hot, and I wish he noticed what just happened, but he doesn't. Bobby's spunk clings to the Jeep's hood and splatters onto its window as traffic flows faster, but the stud behind the wheel doesn't let on that anything unseemly might be taking place. I make prayers about him catching on and imagine him pursuing us down into the Valley. Maybe, on a side street, he could pull us over and fuck me as a punishment. He could bend me over the spare tire of his red Jeep and ram his big, fat, could-make-him-a-pornstar dick into my a-hole and say something sweet and loving, like: "You fuckin' faggot! Take that cock, motherfucker! That'll teach you to get spunk all over my Jeep, you little shit!" Oh man, that would be so hot. So intense. But, well, of course it doesn't go down. Why is it that things like that never happen in real life?

Bobby parks in front of a grungy studio on Varna, a small, industrial looking street off Sherman Way. Inside, there's a whole crew of porn makers. I step into the front office, and Dada Cherille meets me there. "Oh Davy," she says, "I'm so happy that you made it. J.K. has told me so much about you. I can't wait to get started."

I take a moment to respond. At this point, I really need a moment. You see, when Dada takes my hand and leads me onto the set, it's a major turning point in my life. Dada Cherille, the greatest porn director of all time, my idol, my goddess, this larger-than-life persona is leading me toward my dreams. "Dada—" I say, but she cuts me off.

"Oh, please, darling, call me Charlie."

"Charlie. I almost don't know what to say. I've wanted to be in one of your pornos since I stole *Randy Raiders* from Video Carnival." Dada turns to look me in the eye and takes both of my hands in hers, in his. "Oh God," I say, "I think I'm gonna cry."

Dada grins, her full cheeks rising to greet her twinkling eyes. Suddenly she hugs me, her spiky, bleached hair touching my cheek, her warm, pillowy stomach pressed against my own flat abs. "Davy Bottoms, you are so precious. Let's you and I make magic today."

Touching my dick lackadaisically, I sit on a cold metal desk and listen to Dada describe the scene. "This movie," she says, "is called *Black Student Gang Bang*. Davy's gonna come walking into a Black Students United meeting by accident and see all thirteen of you in a circle jerk. He's gonna say, 'Oh, I thought this was the computer club,' and you guys are gonna grab him and say things like, 'This ain't no computer club, but you're in the right place, white boy," and stuff like that. And then all of you are gonna fuck the hell out of Davy is several positions until you all cum all over him. Okay, Davy, get into wardrobe while we shoot the opening circle jerk, then we're giving these guys a break and shooting you in the hallway looking for the computer club."

"Dada, I have a question," I say politely. "Why do black gang, bang videos always involve a white kid turning around the wrong corner and getting more than he bargains for?" Dada looks like she's thinking for a moment. "Why can't I just walk in and tell these guys that I want to get fucked by all of them at once? Why must it be like rape? Why can't I show the audience how much I really want it?"

"Oh, but sweety," she says, "it's not rape. You do want it. You just don't know it yet. Your idea's good, but we're gonna go with things as they are. Maybe we'll do your idea in a different video, okay?"

I smile like a five-year-old at Christmas. "That would be so cool."

Dada chuckles, then turns away from me and continues. "Okay, guys, lets get into positions, in a kind of relaxed circle. Sit on desks, or whatever, and Beau—" Dada turns to the biggest, darkest skinned stud in the room. "you and J.K. do the dialogue we talked about, and the rest of you nod or agree with what they're saying. Questions?" The thirteen black guys look at each other and shake their heads no. Dada starts again while I get up and head to wardrobe: "Alright, places everyone. Bobby, are you ready with the camera?"

I stop at the end of the set and watch Bobby handle the camera while Dada sits in a chair and stares at a small video screen that displays what's being filmed. Dada's assistant, I think his name is

Gary, yells, "Quiet on the set," and some banging on the other side of the studio suddenly stops.

"Action," shouts Dada, and Beau Cox scoots around on the top of his desk like he has an itch on his ass. I scope his giant package as he opens and closes his legs nervously, and I get an itch, too, but, like I said before, it's that abstract, emotional kind of itch that lets me know that my o-ring is ready to be fed.

"Everything's set for our party this weekend," Beau says in a deep monotone. "All we gotta, um, um, do, is—"

Dada yells: "Stop! Let's see some more excitement over this party, okay? Action!" And I turn the corner, heading down to where the wardrobe is kept, and all I can think as I hear Dada yelling again is, 'Dammit, can't we just cut to the fucking?'

I'm on my knees, sucking off the make-up guy, my finger between my thighs, playing with my pulsing a-hole, when Dada walks in, shouting, "What the hell is going on here?"

I pull off the make-up guy's cock. "I was just trying to keep myself excited while we waited for my scene."

"Goddammit, Davy! Save it for the black boys! Now, get off the floor, you dirty little slut, and get on the set. We're ready for your entrance."

"Okay." I pull up my slacks and straighten the collar of my beige polo shirt.

"Andy," Dada yells at the make-up guy, "for Christsakes, get all that spit off his chin!"

After wandering down the hallway facade, looking from one room number to another, I enter the classroom set and see the thirteen black dudes jacking off in front of each other. I looked shocked, like I'm supposed to, but it isn't acting, cuz all I can see are the thirteen huge cocks that I'm gonna get to have all to myself.

"I'm sorry, I was looking for the computer club," I say meekly.

"This ain't no 'puter club," says Beau, pulling me into the circle, his massive, shiny black cock swinging wildly and dripping lube all over the floor. "But you in the right place, white boy. Now, we gonna have some fun wit you."

I drop to my knees in front of him and start licking the bitter, warm lube from his cock. Joseph, or J.K. in this setting, grabs my blond hair and shoves his cock in my mouth, and there's a sudden blur of activity as the other black studs pull off my clothes and touch and prod me from every direction.

Sax Daily is the first man to get a condom on and shove his cock up my ass. As Sax fucks me doggy style, I joyously gag on the oversized cock of Darryl Brickhouse. And then there's somebody else's cock in my mouth—I think it's Johnny Love. He's mulatto, and I've always liked him—and he has more than enough cock for me. Then I'm sucking two cocks at once. One is smaller, Gary Bowles, I believe, and my a-hole gets a change of cock. This one's familiar. It has to be J.K. The thought makes my cock slap up against my belly.

Just so you know, it's hard to describe sex with thirteen really hung black guys. I get moved around into all sorts of positions, and I love it. I feel like a rag doll, and my guys just fuck the hell out of me for hours. For hours, while Dada yells things like: "Yeah, fuck his ass. Okay, Davy, suck his cock. Yeah, now suck his cock. Okay, Darryl, now you fuck his ass. Slow. Now hard! Fuck him hard!"

Every now and then, somebody asks me if I need a break, and I just shake the sweat from my hair like a soaking wet dog and tell them: "No, keep going, keep going," until, finally, my guys are worn-out and Dada yells at them to start shooting their thick white loads all over my sweaty, golden skin.

When they're all done, they lift me, and Joseph strokes my cock while Beau fingers my ass. Then I cum like you wouldn't believe. All day, I've been holding back, so when it explodes from my tip, my cock looks like a spitting viper, and I almost tag each black guy in the eye. I hit Dada, too. I can tell she wants to scream like she's cumming with me, but she doesn't, cuz she wants to capture live sound.

Bobby Godrod takes me and Joseph home. Before we leave, Dada hands me a check and tells me that she's never seen anything like me, and when she says this, I picture her lying back, naked, on a red velvet settee, while I suck her cock and chew on her tits. I maintain this image in my mind on the way home; it makes my dick hard again.

Back at Joseph's I say: "I think I'll walk back to my place."

"How you doin'?" Joseph asks.

"Fine. Just a bit tired."

"Hope I didn't fuck you too hard." Joseph puts his arms around me, holds me, cups my lower lip just inside his mouth. "You know," he says, "if you ever leave Steve, I'd love to be your boyfriend." He then gets on his knees and lowers my shorts. He kisses the head of my cock, and says: "This is for you."

I feel strange as my cock solidifies in his mouth, but he's really good, stroking my shaft and twisting his mouth in the same butterfly pattern I learned as a kid. And I hump forward a bit and picture a cock thrusting up into my ass, and then I squeal and pull away from his lips. He squeezes my shaft, pulling up toward the rim, then jacks it quickly, and I shoot, my creamy load striking his cheek before dripping down his cafe-mocha skin.

I stop into Stalkers for a cocktail. I lean against a wall by the pool table, and watch two trashy hustlers pass the time. I'm really zoned, as one ball hits another ball, sending that ball into a pocket. Suddenly, some would-be john says: "Hi. You're really cute." This startles me, and I spill some Cosmopolitan on my hand. "I'd pay you a hundred dollars to suck your cock."

Setting my drink down, I look at the guy and say: "I just got paid five thousand dollars to get plowed by thirteen black guys."

And I don't know why—well, yes I do—but he stares for a moment and then walks away.

Just when I'm about to give up, I stop by the men's room to take a piss. The two trashy hustlers walk in behind me and go into the stall to snort some crystal. So, I wash my hands and wait and, when they step out, I turn and say: "I'll pay you guys a hundred dollars if you let me suck your cocks right now."

"No way," says the blond one, "you gotta be fuckin' with us."

I pull out five crisp twenties and hand them to him. He just grins and opens his fly, and his buddy, his dark, ratty hair falling in his eyes, stands just to my left and whips himself out like he's needing to piss.

On my knees, I stare up at their flat stomachs and small waists. Their cocks are soft from the drugs, but I hold one of them in my mouth and smell the stinging odor of an unpampered body. As I suck each of them to erection and coax their spooge out, I decide that I should go shopping more often.

When they orgasm, their sauce spits out all watery and thin, and I let it hit me in the face, and stick to my eyelids, and get in my hair. When I walk out of Stalkers, with my hair soaked with water, I feel the cool Hollywood air on my wet face and decide to call it a day.

I'm in the tub when Steve comes in from work. He finds me in the bathroom and loosens his tie. Smiling, I say: "So, honey, how was your day?"

"Great," he says, "but I couldn't stop thinking about you."

I rise out of the sudsy water and get on my hands and knees, my hard cock just dangling above the surface. "So, sweety, do I need a fresh shaving? It's hard for me to tell."

Steve rolls up his sleeves and bends to see my a-hole. His fingers touch me, and he grabs a washcloth to rinse the suds away. "No," he says, "you look great," and his fingers keep stroking the sensitive, pink flesh, pulling the ring open and slipping inside.

In bed, Steve fucks me, slow-like. He has me on my back, my feet in his hands. He puts his weight on my legs until my feet are near my lips, and he kisses me and sucks my toes, and I suck my own toes while his big, fat cock pumps all the way into me just before humping one inch deeper, staking a claim on my prostate. And as he bears down from exhaustion, he holds his cock inside me and whispers: "Oh, Davy, I am so fuckin' lucky."

"So am I," I say, kissing his wet ear and losing myself in the way my o-ring feels all stretched out, my stomach full of cock. His body is warm and solid and large. My a-hole is so happy. So, it doesn't even matter that Steve's cock isn't the biggest I've had all day. It really doesn't. Cuz Steve's is plenty big, bigger than most guys get, and it's familiar, or was familiar, and I liked it.

the honest agent

No Small Parts

George Dibbs

"WHY DO YOU WANT TO BE THE INDIAN?" EXASPERATION MUST HAVE shown in my tone, because he winced. At twenty, Zack under pressure could look like an uncomfortable, zit-faced twinkie being scolded. "Hell, Zack," I continued, "you don't even look like an Indian."

He was tall and lanky, with long arms and a well-developed chest. An Indian costume would only make him look that much more slender. Studios these days looked for beefcake, and anyone slender was silently accused of having the "cocaine look." His red hair didn't help any.

"Chuck, I can do it. I'd be a great Indian. I made the costume, and you'd know I could play the part if you'd see me in it."

"Zack," I groaned, "the Indian is one of the smallest parts in this film." In the five years I'd been repping porn-star wannabes, the thing I knew best was that if a guy switches to a smaller part than his last one, pretty soon they decide he's going nowhere, and they don't even consider him for parts.

"Come on, Chuck—at least let me show you my costume." He reached down for his gym bag which lay at his feet. I marveled again at how his red hair always seemed tousled and yet never really looked out of place. There was a rugged, raw-boned quality about him. And, of course, he was so eager to please.

I couldn't resist. It was his natural charm as much as his dick that had gotten him parts in his two previous films, and that charm came through on the screen. "OK, Zack. Put it on and let's see what it looks like."

He shot me a look of real appreciation, and went in to the small bathroom beside my office to change.

They all had that enthusiasm when they arrived here. I had seen plenty of that since I started. But so many of them drifted away—some faster than others. Some found jobs in adult straight films, some found they could make a real living as paid escorts, some found sugar daddies, and some became street hustlers. The smartest of them got their degrees and went on with their lives. But none of them ever seemed to go back home.

Zack came back in, standing tall, grinning impishly and waiting for my approval. He was wearing the shortest, skimpiest breech-cloth I had ever seen. Tanned leather in appearance, it was really a length of thin, leather-like rope about his waist, with a flap of cloth in the front and a flap in the back. The sides of his legs showed all the way up, and the dimpled and muscled cheeks of his butt could be seen as he moved. In front, the flap of cloth ended in tasseled strips where he had slit it to give a ripple effect as he walked.

"What do you think of it?" Zack was so proud. As he walked, he moved his body so that he seemed to swing from side to side, and the breach-cloth kept rhythm to it with its rippling strips. With nothing but that on, his sinuousness was not as noticeable as I had thought. I sighed. I was more attracted to Zack Rodgers than I had been to anyone I had repped, in fact more attracted than to anyone since college. I felt a pang in my stomach. It always hurt to look back.

I grinned. "You're something, Zack. You truly are."

His eyes lit up. "Does that mean I get the part?"

"It means I'll talk to the producer and see. And with Trey Winters as the star, that means he'll have to approve you, too."

"Can I go? If they see me in this, they'll know how good I am for the part."

I've always been a sucker for puppy dogs and good-hearted souls, and Zack was a little of both. I picked up the phone. "I'll call and see if we can go over now."

With that, Zack leaped forward, came around the desk, and hugged me. He started thanking me, saying what a great guy I was, and kissing me. I realized his dick had started up. Zack was sexy as hell. His dickhead peeped out from the flap of cloth and then bobbed back inside as he continued moving against me.

I forced myself to remember what I was supposed to be doing. I reached for the phone and dialed Jerry. Zack left his arm across my shoulder and his hip rubbed against my arm.

Jerry, the producer with an Indian part in his next film, had been in school with me—so we went back a ways. Fortunately, I never had any trouble reaching him when I needed to. He had shown me the working script of this new film, and I had wanted Zack for the part of the boy doing room service. Now, I was asking if Jerry would test Zack for the Indian part.

Without thinking about it, I reached up and put my arm around Zack's waist as he stood there as I talked to Jerry. He leaned closer and I could feel the warmth of his skin. I was making my pitch to Jerry when I saw that Zack's dick was now erect, lifting the flap of his cloth.

I had seen it before, when I first asked him to show me what he had, before we signed a contract. I made them all do that. I learned my lesson early, when I signed a guy on his good looks and classy portfolio alone, never checking out the goods for myself. I discovered too late that his dick was so small it was almost microscopic. But this was different. I was not simply checking something out from a distance. I was mesmerized, because I had never been that close to Zack's before. I lost my train of thought as I looked at that magnificent thing Zack had between his legs.

Zack noticed my attention, and using only his muscles, he made his dick bob up and down, lifting and dropping the flap. I glanced up at his face and found he was grinning. I knew better but, for the first time in my professional career, I reached over and touched a client's meat.

"Are you still there?" Jerry demanded at the other end of the line.

"What?" I was holding Zack's dick by the head, feeling the shape, touching the piss slit, gently massaging under the head with my thumb.

"I've been trying to tell you to come on over now and we can decide what to do. And all I'm getting is silence at your end." Jerry sounded a little ticked.

The blood vessels and muscles in Zack's rocket throbbed under the pressure of my fingers, and he was beginning to drip pre-cum. With a real effort I restrained myself, and told Jerry: "We're on our way."

"What did he say?" Zack asked, his dick still jutting out. I had moved my hand, and now slid it around in back and moved it along the smooth and strong surface of his butt.

"He said we could come over now."

Zack's eyes lit up. "Let's go then." He paused with a grin. "Or did you want to mess around here a little while?"

That's why an agent shouldn't get sexually involved with clients. It's too hard to draw the line between business and pleasure.

"Let's go," I said, and rose from my desk heading for the door.

Zack ambled happily along beside me, his dick bobbing and the flap of cloth rising and closing. I thought to ask him to change clothes. But we were in California; I doubted anyone would notice.

On the ride over, Zack sat beside me, occasionally lifting his loincloth as if to see whether his dick was still there. Whatever it was he was checking on, it seemed to please him.

"Yep, it's still up. I've always been lucky that way. Or maybe unlucky. Back in school in Iowa, sometimes it was embarrassing to stand up and change classes because I was so hard down there. I would use my books to cover it, but guys would laugh about it and they would tell girls who would giggle and point."

"How did you happen to come west, Zack?"

He idly used the flap of cloth to fan his crotch, still happily content to examine himself.

"Oh, I don't know." He paused a moment. "There was some trouble. Nothing really bad, just some stuff. Anyhow, people said I ought to be in movies, so I came here. I didn't know anybody, and then one day I saw your ad. That's about all." His voice had an oddly unreal quality to it, like a child who isn't telling a lie but isn't exactly telling the truth either. I reminded myself that all of us have secrets. I wasn't sure whether to pursue the topic.

A car pulled out in front of us, and I swerved, almost going up on the sidewalk. The other car went on, and I stopped at the curb for a moment before going back into traffic. Someone called out: "Zack? Zack Rodgers? How you doing, man?"

Zack looked up in surprise. "Eddie? Hey, what's up, dude?" He hurriedly adjusted his cloth before Eddie got close enough to look in and see.

I was uneasy. I noted to myself that another one of the troubles with getting personal with clients is that you start to worry about them, and begin to wonder what they're up to when they're not with you.

"We're late," I told Zack quietly.

Eddie poked his face in the open window and grabbed Zack's hand and arm, hugging and shaking hands at the same time. "Wow, Zack, you ain't got much on there, my man."

Zack seemed embarrassed suddenly. "We got to go, Eddie. I'll catch you another time." His voice was friendly, but he also seemed urgent.

Eddie's eyes lit up in recognition. "Oh, didn't know this was—business."

I knew from the tone what that implied, and I wondered if Zack had been on the streets for very long before he came to me.

"You're looking good, Zack. No more problems?"

"Doing good, Eddie. See ya."

"See ya." The other boy turned and wandered down the street. We took off as soon as I saw an opening in the traffic.

Zack offered no explanation, and I didn't ask. But when we were nearly there, I asked, "Had you been sick when you knew Eddie?"

"No, why?"

"He asked how you were, and if there were any more problems."

Zack was silent for a moment. I glanced over, and then returned to watching the road. I decided that if he told me, that would be good but, if he didn't, then it wouldn't matter. Most people in gay adult films have unhappy events in their past, many of which are better left unspoken.

"Chuck," Zack began slowly, "I'd better tell you some things. And for someone as normally uncommunicative as Zack, he suddenly was a torrent of information. He told about the trouble back home—he and some boys were accused of theft of school property. Zack said he was innocent. Then there had been a fight with another boy over a girl. She had gotten pregnant, and claimed she didn't know who the father was. Zack told me that he knew it couldn't have been him because not only had he not had sex with her, he was gay and wasn't interested in her. But he had had sex with her boyfriend, in fact had been doing so for several months. Anyway, he was blamed for her pregnancy and, in light of the town's feelings that he was a troublemaker, he decided to come west.

We had reached Jerry's studio. I pulled up and parked, and we sat in the car a little longer while Zack continued his story. When he arrived in town, he knew nobody. What little money he had ran out shortly, and he hit the streets. That's where he met Eddie. Through Eddie, he met someone who took him in to live with him. Zack didn't name the guy, but it was through him that he learned about the porn industry. That's how he came looking for me. That and the fact that the guy threw him out.

"He said I knew too much about him."

I was puzzled, but waited for Zack to go on.

"He said in his job, he had to have what he called 'sex on demand.' Well, he said he had started to get anxiety or stage fright or something—anyway, he said he couldn't get it up if he thought people watching him knew he had this problem."

"I don't understand."

"Well, he never had trouble getting it up around me, and—hell, man—I can shoot four or five times a day, easy. But he told me about this problem and then he was sorry he had told me, and then after that our sex just wasn't the same. It was like he was under pressure to perform or something. So he finally told me to get out. He gave me some money and sent me to you, and that was the end of it."

I didn't question the truth of what he was telling me, but the guy didn't sound like anyone I knew. Clients usually told me who they were sending. But in Hollywood that's not unusual. Nobody ever really knows anybody, people just throw names around and claim acquaintances they never had. They throw in someone's name and say: go see him.

We got out of the car and walked into Jerry's studio. It wasn't much, but anyone wanting to make a good start in the adult gay film industry did well to start here. Jerry wasn't high pressure, he did a good job, and his films were sure to be seen by the people who count.

Inside, the secretary hardly batted an eye when Zack rippled by, his cloth apron not hiding much of what he had.

"He's expecting you," Jerry's man said, "just go on back. You know the way."

I nodded. We stepped into Jerry's office. "The film's still on, but Trey Winters is out," he said from the window, his back to us. "The bastard said he had too many other commitments, so I told him to go to hell. He may bring in big bucks, Chuck, but I'm not going to work with somebody we can't depend on."

"Who've you got in his place?" I asked.

Before answering me, Jerry turned and looked at Zack. He stared and I could hear the cash register my old school buddy had for a brain. Zack grinned back appreciatively and, with that muscle twitch, made his apron flap up and down.

Jerry burst out laughing. "Hey, fella, that's some thing you've got there." He lifted the flap and looked at Zack's dick. "I've seen a lot in my time, and I can tell you that you stack up with the best of them."

Zack practically did a war dance. I could tell this was going well. "So who did you get for the lead?"

"Dick Wagger."

Zack's face fell. "I don't think he'll want me in it." I sensed something was wrong, but Jerry didn't.

"Nonsense. He's here in another room going over the script. Let's go meet him."

As we followed Jerry, Zack whispered: "He's the guy I used to live with."

We walked into a lounge area where Dick sat alone, the script in his lap. He looked up, his eyes lit on Zack, and his face fell. But I had to give Zack a lot of credit. He went over to Dick, shook his hand, and gave him a real greeting, as if the two were best friends.

"You two know each other?" Jerry asked, obviously surprised.

"Me and Dick go back a way, and he's taught me anything I know about acting." Zack was all charm and appreciativeness. "I just didn't expect to bump into him over here."

I felt some sympathy for Dick; anyone with a fear to overcome must have a bad time in the porn industry where the camera recorded everything. I thought momentarily of Zack's last film, a bit part, but one where the director decided to do a close-up of Zack's dick—of the head of it. As the dialogue continued, the camera moved in close, until just the head filled the whole screen. Then, magically, a single drop of pre-cum appeared there, moist and glimmering. It was one of the best camera shots I had ever seen.

Zack and Dick continued talking. Zack seemed almost to be coming on to him, leaning closer and talking quietly but earnestly. He moved his right hand to Dick's shoulder, and then rested his left on Dick's knee. For a moment I felt a twinge of resentment, then realized jealousy had no place in business dealings.

"They seem to be getting along well," Jerry said. I nodded. And then a remarkable thing happened. Zack began massaging Dick's crotch area, his long fingers moving expertly as Dick gave a twitch and began to bulge under the touch.

"What are they up to?" Jerry asked. I thought I knew, but I just shook my head and shrugged.

Expertly, Zack began unfastening Dick's belt, unzipping his trousers, and the designer briefs with the large bulge were revealed. I could feel my own dick swelling, and I knew before long a damp spot would be visible. I shifted to give my pole more room. Glancing at Jerry, I saw he was watching as well. Even when you work around sex all the time, a scene like this was spellbinding.

Zack was talking quietly, his voice seeming to caress Dick as much as his hands were. It suddenly occurred to me that Zack was one of the sexiest, as well as most personable, people I had come across in a long time.

When Zack removed the briefs, Dick's cock stood up like a rocket waiting for a launch. I realized Zack was about to go down on it, and I turned to Jerry. "Do you want to waste a good shot like this?"

Jerry responded immediately. "OK you guys, let's don't waste a good thing. Come on back into the studio and let the cameramen there at least get some still shots of this. And I'll see what cameras are available." I had to smile at that. The word on the street was that Jerry only had two cameras, and one was always being repaired.

Watching the two of them get up off the couch was something to see. Zack was so hard his apron just stood out in front of him like an awning for his balls. Dick started to pull his clothes back up, then must have decided what the hell, and came half-hobbling along with Zack, grabbing his pants each time they tried to slip down. I walked behind them, wishing that somehow I could get my hands on Zack's beautiful butt.

It only took a little while for the technicians to get the lights set up. Jerry's idea of film making was to use several standard shots, so the lights generally stayed positioned for that. But it gave Zack time enough to come over to talk with me.

"I think I convinced him I wouldn't be a threat to him. His dick didn't have any problem getting up." Zack seemed pleased that he had done a good deed.

"That was good of you. Let's hope it works. But Jerry seems to like you well enough all ready, so that, if Dick should have anxiety problems, Jerry might let you take over as the star."

"Really?" he asked in disbelief.

"Sure. This is your chance to be a professional in your work. Your time to be a pro. Just do what Jerry says, and it'll all work out."

"Will you stay until I finish?"

"Yeah." I felt good that he seemed eager for me to be here. This could be the start of something good.

When they called him in for the shot a few minutes later, I decided to wait where I was. There were so many different feelings running through me, I thought I would keep a better perspective if I stayed out of the way of the main action. That way, if I was called on in a professional capacity to make some decision as his agent, my hormones wouldn't affect my decision.

When the session ended, Jerry came out first. "That's some kid you've got there. He's going to go far in this business. Got off two shots in a row. Not many can do that well, especially these days when everybody's taking something for anxiety and can't get their gun when they need to."

A moment later, Zack came out grinning. His apron hung down as it should. I figured the fun was over.

"Ready to go?" I asked.

He grinned. "I wish you could have seen it. Things went great. I was great. Hell, man, everybody was great!"

We went out to the car with Zack still bubbling over about the shoot. When we got inside, he asked, "Can I go home with you?"

"Sure," I said. I would worry about all the ramifications of involvement and professionalism and detachment later. For now, I wanted to enjoy the sheer warmth of him. I pulled away from the curb, suddenly anxious to get home.

We stopped on the way at a place I was familiar with, and I went in to get some takeout. Zack stayed in the car in that Indian outfit of his, and seemed perfectly content to do so.

At my condo, watching the sun dip down and disappear in the west, we feasted on steak fillets, baked potatoes with sour cream and butter, and a tossed green salad.

Zack sighed contentedly, finished the last of the wine in his glass, and settled down next to me on the sofa.

"I'm glad you came here," I said, putting my arm around him. He snuggled closer, loosened the thong that held his apron, and tossed it aside. He turned towards me and kissed me, his tongue finding its way into my mouth, which was as eager as his. He tasted of wine and of a sweetness I had never known before.

I reached down for his dick and found it moist. It trembled to my touch, and I moved down on it with my mouth. He sighed huskily. "God, but that's great."

I moved my hands along his body as I continued to manipulate his cockhead with my tongue. His skin had a smoothness that was irresistible. I could feel him tensing.

"I'm going to shoot," he gasped, and then cum thundered into my mouth in spurt after spurt, almost choking me. As I swallowed for all I was worth, I marveled that he was able to produce so much of the fluid, considering that this was at least his third time today.

His body lay relaxed, and his erection began subsiding. I looked into his eyes and smiled. "May I enter you?" I asked.

Zack chuckled. "Thought you'd never ask."

I began to grease myself up, both prior to the condom and afterward. Zack stayed on the sofa with his legs spread out.

"Let me face you while we do it," he said. "I want to see the look on your face when you shoot off, and I want you to see me."

I lifted his legs, putting his ankles on my shoulders with his legs spread wide, and began to lubricate him as well. I inserted first one finger and then two into him, making sure he was slick and open. Slowly, I began to insert my throbbing prong into him.

He kept watching me, but, as I reached his prostate, his eyes glazed. I picked up the rhythm and saw it was getting to him. His dick was erect again, and I wondered if it ever really went down. I began to massage it and he began to moan with pleasure. I was happier than I had been in years, and I sensed this would be a moment I would always remember. We came together in a spasm of ecstasy and collapsed into each other's arms.

I found myself hoping this was the beginning of something special.

rehearsals

Boys And Their Toys

Jay Starre

I WAS AT THE NEW BATHHOUSE ON TRENT STREET, IN CHICAGO. THE darkened hallways and strange men of the baths were a turn-on, if I was in the mood. That night I didn't think I was—until I met Donovan. Yeah. I mean *that* Donovan. Donovan Lucky.

Lounging on a marble bench in the dimly lit steam room, I was observing the parade of naked flesh with a rather jaded eye, when I first laid eyes on him.

He strutted through the steam, his tall body glowing with a deep tan. He had a dark appearance—his short hair, thick and raven black, a pair of heavy eyebrows over lidded eyes, a sharp nose and full red lips. He was a satyr in search of play. His lean body was packed with ropy muscle, and graced with a lustrous sheen of silken hair, which covered his pecs then trailed down to his flat stomach, around a long, flopping dick and down to his thighs.

I recognized him right away. I knew he lived in Chicago and had seen him once in a nightclub. But seeing him in the flesh, instead of in one of his films, was a real surprise. He wandered by the pool, towel in hand, his gaze searching the crowd.

He came toward me. I was sprawled out on my back, one leg thrown over the edge of the marble bench, idly playing with my dick and watching him. He was beautiful, but I was strangely unintimidated. I had no thought that he would be interested in me; although I am a fairly good-looking blond with a hard body, he seemed entirely out of my league. I lstared at him boldly, completely at ease.

I was surprised when he kept coming, eventually hovering right over me. My hand at my cock continued its slow massage, and my limp member suddenly began to stiffen, responding to the proximity of the nude porn star.

He leaned down and whispered in my ear. "Follow me."

I was intrigued. He turned and I got a good look at his high, white ass, the pale flesh contrasting with the deep tan on the rest of his body. It looked very fuckable. He was a top in his movies, but I had always fantasized about seeing him getting it as hard as he dished it out with that long, spear-like prick of his.

I followed that pale ass through the steam until we reached an alcove that was currently deserted. He turned to me and grinned, the satyr-like arch of his brows exciting, his teeth glowing in the semi-darkness. He sat down on the wet tile bench and beckoned for me to come closer. I did, my heart suddenly pounding as I looked down at his crotch and saw that sabre-cock rising up stiff and dripping.

His dick was big, but not grossly so. It was slim and long, and I had watched it going in and out of numerous mouths and asses in his films, always bone-stiff and throbbing. In the flesh, it was suddenly so very real. I could hardly believe it.

As I was thinking this, he reached out and slid his hand over the bobbing head of my own raging bone-on. I uttered a small cry, which sounded strange in the quiet of the steam room.

"How about if you fuck me with this hot sausage, Blondie?"

His hand caressed me softly, sliding over the sensitive head of my cock, then down the shaft and around my swollen balls. I stared down at him sitting there.

"Yeah. I mean—of course! I wanna fuck you," I blurted out.

He chuckled, deep and throaty, his hand continuing to slide over my balls, my dick and my cockhead. I was shoving my hips forward and groaning, the extent of my conversational ability at that point.

He lifted one hairy thigh and leaned back against the slippery wall, then let go of my dick and used his hands to pull apart his exposed butt-crack. Barely discernable in the near darkness was his pale ass and wrinkled, pulsing asshole.

He leaned farther back and produced a wrapped condom, his satyr-grin intense. "Come on, Blondie, I want your dick up me."

I eagerly reached out to take the proffered rubber, grazing his butt-cheek with my fingertips. With trembling hands I rolled down the condom, my legs shaking, my heart pounding.

I sat on the wet tile bench, between his legs, and smiled at him. His hand snaked around his thigh as he raised his butt and grabbed my cock.

"Come on," he growled low. With him still holding me, I leaned over him. Donovan folded his legs over my back and placed my dick at his hole. He grabbed my ass with both hands and pulled me into him. He grunted as I slipped into him.

"Yeah, I need a good fuck! I need a dick up my hole, especially a fat one like yours, Blondie. Feed it to me!" He stared up at me, his eyes wide open, the dark orbs commanding me. His tight hole alternately expanded and contracted as my cock went deeper and deeper.

I fell on top of him, his hard body wet and slippery. He laughed in my ear as our heads came together, then his tongue snaked out and licked at my neck. I held on to him as I drove my dick up his hole.

"Oh, God, yeah!" I groaned. "Your ass is so hot!"

"I need it, big boy, I need my butthole filled. Fuck me good." he said, his vocabulary about as varied as mine.

We grunted together, he licked my neck and cheek, his breath hot on my face. I plowed in and out of his slick asshole, my dick burning and throbbing, my balls churning. One of his hands began stroking his own cock between our mashed bellies. That long, hard shaft banged into my navel as he stroked it. His body lay under mine passively as I drilled him with my dick, but his hand on his cock was a rapid piston, his tongue on my face a slobbering appendage of lust.

"I'm cumming!" he growled. I felt his body stiffen, his asshole clamped around my digging dick like a vice, and his cock exploded all over my stomach and his.

I plowed on, my balls churning. Fast, hard strokes. Until I couldn't hold back any more. I pushed into him and shot my own load as deep into his guts as I could. I shook like a leaf against him as rope after rope of ball-juice erupted into the rubber. He pulled me against him and held me. We lay on the tiled bench in a pool of our fuck-sweat.

"My name's Donovan, how about you?" he whispered to me, his

hands sliding over my back and ass slowly and sensually. I was getting hard again.

"I'm Sean. You're the porn star: I recognized you," I blurted out. "But I never saw you getting fucked before, not in your films."

He only laughed and continued to caress me, his hands playing with my ass-cheeks. He gave each mound a good squeeze.

"I like butt, and yours is certainly nice. But once in a while I need to get fucked, too. Tonight I had a real craving." He kissed my cheek. "Thanks."

"My pleasure. Any time, actually," I stuttered back. His hands had slid into my butt-crack and were teasing me there. My dick was rock-hard.

"Would you like to work on my asshole some more? I've got some toys in my room." His tongue tickled my earlobe.

Toys? This was a side of the Donovan Lucky that didn't show up in his flicks! He felt my stiff prick jabbing against his gut-wall and took that as a yes. He rose up, lifting me with his strong arms, my hard dick pulling out of him.

"Come on. Let's go, Sean."

In his room, he turned to me and grinned again. His lips were soft when he leaned over and kissed me. We stood like that for a while, just kissing and caressing each other. His dick was up and hard again, sliding over my belly, duelling mine.

"Okay, Sean, now the fun begins." He chuckled, releasing me. He lay on the narrow bed in the small, private room. He grinned as he pulled out a bag from under his pillow and dumped the contents on the clean sheets. My eyes nearly popped out of my head at the display of dildos that spilled out and lay there in the garish light.

Donovan turned up the light even more, then rolled over on his belly, showing me his hot butt in the bright light. He didn't mind the light, of course, he had nothing to hide—his body was absolutely beautiful. I stared down at that fantastic ass, which swelled up from his narrow waist in two round, basketball mounds that stood out from the rest of his body in their paleness. Each cheek was creamy white, except for a barely-discernable down of dark hair that swirled across it and disappeared into the tight crack. His back was hairless and wide, packed with muscle.

"Getting an eyeful?" Donovan chuckled, his voice dispelling my awe-struck fascination. He rolled his hips and spread his legs apart, exposing his crack and that pulsing butthole I had just fucked.

"You've got the nicest ass I have ever seen," I breathed, reaching out and stroking the enticing mounds. The warm meat was both hard and soft at the same time. He raised his hips and pressed his butt into my eager palms.

"If you think my ass is so nice, use a dildo on it." He spread his legs even more and wiggled his butt.

"Which one?" I asked. My hands were so happy just touching his perfect ass, I couldn't think beyond the moment. But he had other ideas.

"Choose one, I don't care." He urged, his voice changing, the amusement becoming excited lust as I massaged his cheeks.

I grabbed the closest dildo, a long, black thing with a bulbous head that gleamed raven-dark in the bright light at one end and had a pair of simulated round balls at the other end. I slapped his cheeks with it. He rolled his butt as he gazed back at me and grinned.

"Put some grease on my hole and slide that fucker in," Donovan ordered.

I grabbed the bottle of lube on the bedstand, squirting a generous dollop of the clear fluid over his crack and butt-cheeks and watching it run down the parted flesh and pool on his big balls resting on the sheet between his spread thighs.

"Go ahead, put it in me!" he groaned, his hips writhing up and down, his lust building. I studied his body, the dildo in my hand rubbing across his flesh.

I shoved the floppy fake cock into his parted crack, rubbing the head up and down the greased skin, watching as it slid back and forth over his anal ring. The greased and crinkled rim pulsed and twitched, begging to be violated. I pointed the head at the pale flesh and began to press it between his ass-lips.

"Oh yeah, my asshole is ready for it, Sean." He was watching me over his shoulder. His face was flushed, his lips gaping, his eyes half-closed. He grinned at me through his desire.

I turned back to his ass and his greased butthole. With slippery fingers, I pressed the dildo into the center of his hole, mesmerized as the ass-lips parted and the head began to disappear. His hole swallowed the entire head in no time, just like it had swallowed my dick earlier.

"Oh god, it feels good! Take it slow at first, though," he begged. His butt had risen up to accept the thing being shoved inside it, but the rim of his hole was clamped tight behind the head of the dildo. I went slow, feeding it to him in small strokes, in and out, each time deeper and deeper. He was breathing heavily, his body tense. He relaxed as I began to stroke his back with my free hand.

The image of his ass rising in the air and taking that very black dildo practically to the hilt was so exciting I damn near came.

"You like reaming my butthole with that dildo?" Donovan crooned, his voice husky and his eyes on mine.

His dark orbs were glittering beneath those heavy brows. He was completely at ease with the dirty scene.

"You want this thing rammed up your tight hole? You want to feel it? I'll make you feel it!" I growled, shoving the dildo right to the fake balls with a sudden thrust. Lube splattered and dripped from his stretched asshole.

"Go ahead! Fuck me with it, Sean," he growled. "Do me with that dildo. I want it hard!" He shoved his ass back to meet the thing in my hand. I rammed it in and out. He groaned and yelped and wiggled his ass while I fed him the dildo in rapid thrusts. Lube glistened on the dildo, on his pale ass and swollen nut-sack, and on my hands.

I fucked him with it, while he lifted his hips and took it, all of it. I got up on the bed behind him and rammed it home, using both hands. His asshole opened up and accepted the entire dildo with slippery ease. We were both yelling and swearing and going nuts. His body was beneath me, my knees crammed between his thighs, my dick straight up in the air, drooling in time to the heavy action of my thrusting hands. I shot without warning. My balls contracted, my reddened cock filled with sperm and cum flew through the air to splatter his back and ass.

"Oh, God, oh, God," I moaned, collapsing on top of him. He wiggled out from beneath me and sat up, the dildo still planted firmly up his greased anus.

"You are one hot stud!" Donovan mumbled.

I was a hot stud? What about him?

He pulled the dildo out of his ass, his legs spread, his knees up and facing me. I watched it come out of his formerly-tight asshole, the large head finally popping out and a trail of lube drooling down from his contracting anal lips. Even though I had just cum, that sight had me horny all over again.

He reached out and massaged my shoulders, which was cool, and which was strange at the same time. He was absolutely depraved, but tender and gentle. I had never experienced such a contradiction in a guy.

"All right, I see you've cum for the second time. You can take a breather while I continue," he chuckled.

What continue? Was the guy never satisfied? His cock was stiff, flat up against his firm abs. He was already reaching for another toy, discarding the greasy black dildo.

"I'm going to plug my butt while you watch," Donovan told me. His grin was infectious, and I found myself laughing after finally catching my breath.

He spread his legs, leaned back, and began to stuff a huge butt-plug up his greased asshole. The tapered end went in easily but, as it grew larger, he grunted, gritted his teeth, and really had to push to fit the huge thing inside him. His ass-lips gaped open, stretching impossibly wide before the buttplug abruptly tapered smaller and it was inside him. The square flange was all that remained visible; his audible sigh of relief was loud in the room's silence.

"Okay, now it's your turn. I gotta have your hot body, stud." He grinned at me and moved forward, that butt-plug still firmly planted up his rear end. It was a turn-on to think of it deep inside him while he leaned over me and played with my hair and face and shoulders. He was a big guy, and even seated on the bed, towered over me.

I was still spent and thought I might not be able to give much in the way of reciprocation anyway. But when he turned around, lay back with his head in my lap and reached over to slide the head of my dick into his wet mouth, I realized otherwise. He lay there, his head in my lap, his red lips wrapped around my fat cock, and his body sprawled out in front of me. His thighs were wide apart, one of his hands down between them pressing at the butt-plug inside him, his hard dick stiff and dripping against his tanned stomach. And he was looking up at me as he slowly massaged my cockhead with his lips.

Donovan stuck out his tongue and licked at my semi-hard cock. My dick grew at once. He grinned at that and grasped my nuts with one hand while shoving my knob inside his mouth. I stared down at him while he looked up at me. He opened wide with his head in my lap and sprawled out on his back, suckling on my cock as if it were a tit or something. My cock grew hard as stone.

I blew like a volcano.

We spewed our spunk and he collapsed on top of me. He caressed my face and smiled at me.

"I think I should be able to perform up to snuff now, with that hot rehearsal behind me," he said finally.

My confusion must have been evident. He laughed.

"This was a rehearsal for a new movie I'm supposed to be starting next week."

I had to laugh too. When I had stopped I asked him what the movie was.

"It's called *Guys And Dildos*—so far, anyway. They'll probably change the name." We both laughed.

I didn't know if he was joking or not. But we spent the remainder of that night together experimenting with a few more of his toys, using them on him or me—it didn't really matter. I ended up with a new friend.

So when I was invited to the filming of his new porn movie, I wasn't surprised when I saw topman Donovan Lucky with his butt spread wide open and a foot-long greasy dildo being shoved up his ass.

I think the movie should be a success.

tops & bottoms

Tricks & Treats

Bryan Nakai

MY FIRST PORN VIDEO! OK, SO IT WAS JUST A JACK-OFF SCENE—AT least I was on film. I was sure I'd make it big next time. I hung around the set, watching the real stars do their thing. Man, did it make me hot!

The star of the film—the studio's prize stallion, so to speak— was Steve Mills. I'd have paid big money to sit on the sidelines watching Steve fuck somebody. The man was the hottest top going. Six-foot-four-inches tall, built like Apollo—I knew leather-daddies who wanted to bottom for that man. I might even consider it myself, if he ever asked me.

His cock was truly remarkable, matching the body behind it— ten inches, cut. I loved the little kink to the left when he was erect. His balls were large and heavy. He kept his pubes clipped into a neat triangle, and I suspected he shaved his chest and back. Then again, he was one of those Aryan-type blonds—maybe he just didn't have a lot of body hair.

From my lowly vantage point at the back of the crew, I mostly saw Steve's back, but that was fine with me. I couldn't believe I was sitting here watching Steve Mills in person. I could see his profile sometimes; he had that distracted "I'm fucking" expression on his chiseled face. I loved that expression on him. Hell, I loved every-thing about him. I watched him pound away on the guy who'd gotten to bottom for him today, wondering if one day it'd be me instead. I don't bottom ordinarily, but for Steve—

I memorized every inch of his lean, pale body—from the yellow fuzz on his thighs and calves to the small brown birthmark on the back of his right shoulder. It reminded me of the state of New

Mexico—kind of squarish, but with a little tail in the bottom left corner. I wondered how often he worked out to get his shoulders in such good condition. His muscles rippled every time he shoved forward. If I hadn't just jacked off, I'd have my cock in my fist watching him.

When the scene was finally completed—I was surprised at the number of takes they needed—Steve headed for the showers without speaking. The bottom went to his dressing room, walking bowlegged.

It was Halloween and I didn't have any plans or a costume. I decided to try the local bar scene and go as myself—a Native American. All I needed was a loincloth. After an hour or so of driving around, I ended up all the way across town, in one of those places I'd thought only existed in Hollywood movies.

The sign outside said "Masquerade." I balked at the cover charge, but the doorman explained it mostly went to buy cloth masks like the one he handed me. I finally shrugged, tied the Zorro mask over my face, and went inside. I stared in shock at the room before me. So help me, it looked like Rodgers and Hammerstein meets the *Rocky Horror Picture Show*!

Moving dazedly to the bar, I sidestepped a 6-foot Marilyn Monroe, a 300-pound Robin, and a Superman who looked like he'd blow away in a strong breeze. I ordered a coke with a lime twist from either Conan or Kull (I can never keep them straight), and decided to lurk until my brain grew accustomed to the mad tea party. After five or ten minutes of intense scrutiny, I came up with an objective theory: the vast majority of men did not need to run about in odd costumes!

"Nice mask, Tonto," a lean Popeye muttered, his hand on my ass. Like I said—

I took my drink and drifted towards a more interesting group clustered in one corner. These men had none of the cliched party costumes that were predominant among the rest of the crowd. No superheroes in tights, no imitation Marilyns or Madonnas. One man seemed to be wearing only body paint, but in an Escher-esque tiger stripe that made your head swim if you tried to look too closely. The man beside him was dressed as a mouse—I thought.

He wore the most ragged gray tights I'd ever seen: baggy, ripped, and stained. One of his ears stuck straight up, and the other drooped over his blond bangs. The mouse had painted his bare upper torso with gray body paint, and fastened a pointed nose with whiskers over his face. He noticed my gaze, and preened for a moment or so. As he hoisted a mug in my direction, I thought he'd already had one or two more than he should have. White men are supposed to be able to handle liquor better than we Native Americans, but I've noticed that most of them can't.

"Look what the cat dragged in," he said as I approached. I started to frown, then realized he was explaining his costume. I smiled tightly, wondering if I could slip past to hide in the corner for a few more minutes.

His companion slunk over, moving so lithely that I was certain he must be a dancer. "I'm a curious cat," he murmured in a deep voice, sliding close enough for me to put a tentative hand on his costume. It felt like paint, but I didn't have the nerve to grope him for a jock strap. The mouse sniggered into his beer.

"Rum Bum Tugger," he giggled. "Get it?"

I nodded, clutching my coke. I backed away from the cat-and-mouse game, only to collide with a young man wearing nothing but a barrel and a facemask. He smiled at my apology, straightening the wooden contraption slung onto his shoulders with a pair of suspenders.

"I'm the bottom of the barrel," he explained. "You're a top, I'll bet." He moved closer.

Whoa. "I'm—er—involved," I stammered, fighting the urge to leap for the door.

I managed to sidle away politely from the pushy bottom by pretending to study the costume of the most distant member of the little group. Man, he was big! He wore only a pair of baggy white silk trousers, a bright red sash, and those weird "Arabian Nights" shoes with the curled-up toes. He was darker than I was, but that could have been body paint. A huge white turban covered his head.

"That's Punjab," the drunken mouse stage-whispered in my ear, spraying me with beer foam. "He's hoping Daddy Warbucks will show up and sweep him off his feet."

I shot mouse a disgusted look and deliberately walked away, eyeing the brown giant speculatively. He leaned against the wall, very imposing with his brawny arms crossed over his broad chest and rippled abdomen. I thought I saw a hint of dejection lurking in his blue eyes, though. I thought about stereotypes as I made my way between the tables to his side. If there's one thing a Native American understands, it's being labeled. And in the gay world, a man that big and brawny is most likely to end up branded a top, whether he really wants to be or not.

Or, I thought, watching his eyes scan the crowd, he could just get tired of looking—just be what everyone else wants him to be. It's easier sometimes to hide behind the mask, especially if nobody seems to care what's really underneath. I know all about masks, too.

As my destination became obvious, his eyes turned my way— bright blue eyes in the dark face paint. I thought I saw a flicker of interest. Suddenly, I wanted this giant—wanted him so badly that I felt a stab of pain from my tightly wrapped balls. I moved to his side, letting my gaze wander from the broad planes of his chest to the bulk of his thighs. He would be an awful lot of man to handle, but I wanted to try.

"Are you waiting for anybody in particular?" I asked. His gaze followed the flared line of my fingers, and I saw his pupils widen as he caught sight of the thickening rod snaking its way down my left leg.

One of his eyebrows lifted. No other part of him moved.

"Other than Mr. Right, you mean?" he asked.

I shrugged, grinning. "But what if I AM Mr. Right?" I shot back. I slid my thumb underneath my mask. "Who can tell behind these things?"

He straightened, shoving away from the wall. I stared up at his impassive face.

"Listen," he began, shaking his head. "I like to get things out in the open."

The bottom of the barrel gave a sudden shriek from beside the bar. "You bitch! I saw him first!" Punjab and I glanced in that direction—the mouse and bottom were nose to nose in front of a Steve Mills poster, snarling. Punjab shrugged and opened his mouth.

I cut him off, moving in close. "Let me guess! You're gay. What a coincidence—so am I." My hand slid down the silk of his trousers, along one massive thigh. I felt his round ass tighten beneath my fingers.

"Mmm—I hope this is as tight as it feels," I murmured, giving him a squeeze. His entire body—all six foot whatever!—stiffened to attention. I didn't want to give him time to think of an excuse to back out. "Is there somewhere we can be alone for a while?"

"I—you—they've got private rooms for rent—upstairs."

I leaned closer, slid both my arms around his hips, trying to keep from rubbing body paint all over myself. My hands cupped a pair of very firm, very heavy balls. I could feel the base of an enormous shaft just above them. He was already hard.

"Lead the way, then, Punjab," I commanded with a gentle squeeze of my fist.

As we passed, the mouse suddenly leaped at the bottom, shoving him away from the bar. With a wild scream, the barrel-clad blond thudded into us. Punjab let out an "oof" as the barrel landed on his broad back. I got a foot in the stomach, and was busy gasping for air. The bottom's flailing hands jerked my mask up, covering my eyes. By the time I'd gotten myself together, Punjab had the bottom in one huge hand and the mouse in the other. Hauling them out by the scruffs of their necks, he slammed the club door behind them. Rum Bum Tugger dejectedly slunk after his mouse, presumably to take him home and sober him up.

I straightened my costume and pulled my mask back into place. After we reassured the manager that neither of us was injured, we were offered a private room gratis, as compensation. Fate does act in mysterious ways. I closed the door and examined my prize more closely.

Punjab's brawny body now glistened with sweat from his

exertion. I watched a glistening drop slip into the hollow of his navel, and wanted to lick it back out. I think that was the point when I realized I wanted a next time, without the body paint and masks. I wanted to see this man's true body, to touch him without a costume. I wanted to see if I could fill the void inside him. I wanted to make the dejection in his eyes change to anticipation.

I could tell he'd dyed his hair—it was too black for the pale skin revealed in a stripe across his neck, where the bottom had rubbed away the brown paint. Plus, there were those blue eyes. Fucking a blue-eyed blond was a major fantasy of mine—I hoped his natural hair was blond.

He studied me just as intently. I hoped getting fucked by a Navajo was one of his fantasies, too. I started to take off my mask, but he shook his head.

"Let's go by the rules tonight," he murmured, his voice thick with desire.

I shrugged. "OK, but next time I want to see who I'm fucking."

He moaned at that, but moved to the bed. I glanced at the room then—my gaze had been on Punjab's tight ass moving beneath white silk trousers as we'd come in. The manager had evidently decided on the "Little Mermaid" room. The wallpaper looked like a giant aquarium. The light fixtures were bronze lanterns. The bedspread and sheets were teal, with a seashell motif.

I stared at a huge orange clown-fish. I wasn't sure I could perform beneath all those oggling eyes. Punjab slid out of his trousers about that time, though; and I forgot the fish. He hadn't painted his legs, which were nearly as white as the trousers. Startling beneath that brown paint. Enticing pale legs under a brawny brown torso. I dove for the seafloor.

I happen to be an ass man, and Punjab had an excellent one. I lifted his smooth, muscular thighs and sighed with delight. Firm, rounded globes with a dark pucker between. Heavy balls dangling in front. I wanted to worship that ass, then and there—to cover the pale skin with kisses, to run my tongue along the cleft between those solid cheeks.

Unfortunately, my cock was threatening to rip a new fly in my loin cloth. The pain of my trapped balls distracted me until I unfastened my costume and managed to wriggle out of it. It was a tight squeeze, I can tell you. My eight inches were rock hard by then, and my balls felt like they'd swollen to twice their normal size. Punjab stared appreciatively as I maneuvered my way out of the cloth. He rolled over and put out a large hand to assist after I started cursing in Navajo. Once we'd gotten the damn things off, I tossed them onto the bed and took up where I'd left off.

Punjab moaned softly as my hands slid beneath his ass. He'd rolled onto his back, and I tugged his legs apart for another nice look at his ass. I dipped my head and inhaled the musky odor of the man—sweat, sex, and that cock-stiffening scent my biology book said was pheromones from the anal glands. I only knew I would happily become a dog if I could sniff men's asses all day without attracting attention.

I wanted to spend hours with that ass, but my balls kept interrupting and I knew I'd have to do something about them fairly quickly. I also wanted my lovely giant to have me cum inside him. So I contented myself with a few minutes, licking the skin between his balls and the tight pucker of his asshole. My fingers kneaded the muscles of his ass, wringing groans from his lips.

Then, I fished a condom from my discarded costume, and rolled it over my throbbing cock. Hoisting his legs over my shoulders, I positioned myself at his door. He really was tight.

"It's been—a long time," he gasped. I pressed firmly against his hole, taking all the time he needed but still moving forward. I felt him slowly open before me. He sighed as I entered him.

I spread his legs wider, leaning into my job. Punjab whimpered. His hips rose to meet me. I felt one big hand on my chest. All my attention was on that tight hole, though. All I really noticed was the way his hips writhed as my eight inches slowly penetrated his ass. Then I was inside.

I let him get used to the sensation for a minute, running my hands over his huge cock. It was proportional, which meant the thing had to be more than nine inches. Cut, of course—most white men are. When he sighed deeply, and his ass opened fully around my shaft, I started my rhythm.

Keeping one fist around the thick pole of his cock, I slid my other hand around to support his ass. I always felt spiritual when I fucked. My hips moved to a rhythm older than any tribal dance. My body sweated, my muscles tingled, and my mind focused to a single, clear point. I shoved forward, pulled back. My cock slid on a film of lubricant and sweat. My hands were strong and firm on the body of the man beneath me. I felt our beauty as we made love.

Punjab groaned as I increased my rhythm. My balls slapped his ass, a drum accompaniment to my dance. His cock leaked pre-cum over my fist. His hands were clenched tightly—one on my arm, the other around one corner of the pillow. His head was thrown back as he strained upwards to meet my thrusts. I watched his face for a few moments. He sucked in deep breaths, his mouth slack and vulnerable. His eyes were shut tightly, his brow furrowed as he concentrated.

I wanted him to cum first. I wanted him thinking only of me as I came inside his tight ass. My fist slid easily over his shaft, stroking a deeper groan from his open mouth. I matched the rhythm within him, pumping hard. His body stiffened, shoving forward. I felt his balls jerk beneath my belly.

Thick, hot man-juice erupted over my fist, coating his shaft with cream. I slowed my movements, milking his cock. He quivered, whimpering, as I took him to the edge of discomfort, pulling every ounce of cum from his balls. When I was certain he was dry, when the purple head of his cock was too sensitive for me to touch—only then did I gently slide my hand back to the base of his shaft, holding him in a firm-but-gentle grasp. I bent over his quivering belly.

"Now make me cum," I ordered. My hand moved beneath his ass, pulling him upward, opening him completely to me.

He moaned, and I felt his hole spasm around my cock. I pounded his ass, slamming against him hard enough to make him grab the edge of the bed to keep from sliding off. He was gasping for air by the time my balls spewed their load into the waiting condom, deep within his ass. As he felt the hot cream spurting out, he cried out, arching his body towards me.

I stayed within his ass for as long as I could. Then, I slid my wilted cock gently from his hole, lowering his legs to the floor. I leaned over him, my lips finding his. The body paint began to smear from his sweat. He met me hungrily, his mouth open. Our tongues wrestled together now that our bodies were too tired. At last, I had to come up for air.

"That was fantastic," Punjab murmured, rolling to his feet. A huge, pale swath striped his back where the bottom's landing had rubbed away the paint. I ran an appreciative finger up the white skin, from his lean waist—to the New Mexico-shaped birthmark on his right shoulder blade.

Steve Mills! Steve the Super Top! I was glad I was still sitting on the edge of the bed.

When I didn't respond, Steve shot me a quizzical look. I swallowed hard, trying to get control of myself again. This man needed a top more than ever, now.

"Yeah," I managed to rasp, "yeah, it was really something."

I leaned close, looking into the blue eyes. "How about a re-match without the disguises?"

His face fell. "I really don't—"

I stripped the black cloth from my face. "I don't know if you noticed me this afternoon, but I would really enjoy showing you why the studio hired me."

Steve stared at me without speaking. I saw hope blossoming deep in his blue eyes.

"Actually I watched your scene," he said, his eyes never leaving mine. I felt a dopey grin stretch across my face. "You don't mind that I—"

"Like to catch instead of pitch?" I closed the distance between us. "Did I act like I minded? I love fucking big men, especially when they've got asses as nice as yours."

Steve lowered his six-foot-four-inches back to the bed as I pressed hard against his chest. "Now get ready for that rematch, Punjab," I muttered. "Daddy Warbucks is home."

director's assistant

Grunt Work

Derek Adams

"HEY, MARK."

I looked up from a dog-eared sheaf of director's notes that I'd been struggling to decipher. "Morning." I waved at Bill, one of our camera men.

"Who's the blond Adonis?" He looked over his shoulder at the dazzling young man who was hanging out down at the far end of the studio. "That is one fine arrangement of chromosomes. Is he for real, or did he just shed his wings and drop down out of the clouds?"

"I seriously doubt he's heaven-sent—unless he got delivered to the wrong address," I retorted cynically. "I literally found him when I got here this morning. He was asleep in the doorway."

"I'd like to wake up some morning and find that sleeping in my doorway," Bill chuckled, grabbing his crotch and giving it a squeeze. "So, what catastrophe caused him to be sleeping in front of this dive? Or does he just like the great outdoors?"

"Oh, he gave me the typical sob-story. He grew up in a small town, knew he was queer from an early age, so he came to the big city hoping to become an actor. I suspect he thought he'd walk down Hollywood Boulevard and get whisked away to a major studio by some producer who'd sign him up to be the next Keanu Reeves. I admit he's got the face and the body, but so do thousands of others just like him. Some of 'em even have talent. Of course, this poor bastard didn't even get a job waiting tables at a greasy spoon. He told me he ran into a guy who suggested that he definitely had what it took to star in one of our little epics, so here he is. I suspect he's never even seen an X-rated video."

"So why didn't you just growl at him and scare him off like you do everybody else?" Bill teased.

"He told me he hadn't eaten in two days."

"So you took him out and bought him breakfast, right?" I nodded. "I always suspected that under that crusty surface there lurked a sentimental slob who was just waiting for an opportunity to bust out into the open."

"Screw you, buddy." I gave him the finger. "If Jason decides to let him do a scene, I hit him up for the five bucks I blew."

"And if he doesn't do a scene?"

"Then, I guess I'm out five bucks. I don't really care. I just had the distinct pleasure of sitting across the table from him this morning, watching him shovel two complete bacon-and-egg breakfasts into that perfect body." It was true, the guy—Chris, I think he said his name was—was stunningly handsome. His hair was the color of corn silk, his thick-lashed eyes were as blue as a summer sky, and his cheeks were flushed with pink. His boyish aspect was offset by a prominent, chiseled jaw and a long, slightly aquiline nose.

He hadn't been in the city long enough to lose any of his farm-boy vigor. His tanned arms were thick with muscle. Prominent veins networked his forearms and snaked across the full curve of his biceps. His chest and shoulders were putting a serious strain on his old T-shirt. His lower body was doing things to a faded pair of jeans that should have been against the law, and the bulge in his crotch promised to be very photogenic. All in all, if I could have afforded to feed him, I would have kept him for myself.

Unfortunately, I could barely afford to feed myself and my cat. I'd been laid off from my job at a mainstream studio about six months ago and this stint with Jason Carr was all that was keeping me going.

Bill, my cameraman buddy, had told me that the director was looking for an assistant. I didn't know exactly what a porn director's assistant did, but for six hundred a week, under the table in cash, I was willing to find out. Most of my duties turned out to be chasing after props and trying to keep track of Jason's hieroglyphic notes regarding aspects of production. I also got to spray the boys with mineral oil and water during the shoots, so the job wasn't a total loss.

"Good morning, gents. Are we ready to go?" Jason Carr strode in, his high-heeled boots and teased-up hair completely failing to make him look like the tall man he aspired to be.

"Morning Jason," I said, following him. "I got a new guy here looking for a job."

"Everybody's looking for a job," he retorted. "Tell him to fill out a form and we'll call him."

"Thanks for nothing," I muttered. The door swung open again and I groaned audibly when I saw who stalked in. Ken Hughes was a notoriously difficult person to work with—always snarling at the production crew and harassing the hell out of his co-stars on the set. He was tall, dark, hairy—built like a Greek god and as handsome as the devil but easy to hate. He always seemed to have a chip on his shoulder that was damn near as big as his legendary cock.

At thirteen and a half inches—I once saw him measure it on the set to prove the point—he had the biggest damned dick I'd ever laid eyes on. It was a mean-looking piece of meat—gnarled with thick veins, heavily hooded and bigger around than my wrist. To give him his due, the man was a sexual titan—he could get it hard and keep it hard for as long as it took to shoot a scene. On the down side, he used the damned thing like a weapon, treating his sex partners like assault victims. More than one unlucky bottom had ended his movie career after a session in the sack with Ken Hughes.

"I see we're privileged to work with the Prince of the Pricks today," Bill whispered, sidling over next to me and giving me one of his 'why me' looks. "Wonder who his lucky co-star's going to be today."

"Rick Winters, at least according to the cast list."

"Well, I hope he gets here sober and able to function. Of course, given his usual level of performance, it's pretty hard to tell if he's awake, or even alive on camera. I've got a feeling it's going to be a long day."

We got the lights cued and the set arranged, but there was no sign of Rick Winters. When I called his apartment, his roommate told me that Rick hadn't returned from a party he'd gone to the night before. I relayed the information to Jason and he sent me scurrying for a replacement. I canvassed another guy we'd hired for the film, but he'd heard rumors about Ken's technique in the sack and refused to have anything to do with him. I went back to Jason and filed a report.

"Is that number you found out on the doorstep this morning still here?" Jason asked hopefully.

"He's in the office," I admitted.

"He doesn't know our leading man, does he?" I shook my head. "Good. Go get him."

"Jason, he's a nice kid," I protested. "I don't think its right to throw him to the wolves like that. I was thinking we could pair him up with a nice guy like Pete or Lance—break him in easy."

"What are you, his mother? I've got a film to make, and I've got to pay for that human tripod over there whether he screws or not. I can't afford any delays." Jason obviously wasn't in the mood to listen to the voice of reason. "What's his name, Mark?"

"Chris," I muttered, wishing now that I'd chased the poor bastard away this morning.

"Chris!" Jason barked. "Get over here." Chris came bounding out of the office, smiling eagerly. "Still want to be in pictures?" Chris nodded and his hair cascaded down over his eyes like a golden veil. "I want you to meet your partner in a very important scene. Get over here, my friend."

"You won't be sorry you gave me a chance, sir," Chris burbled, his voice brimming with enthusiasm.

"Jason might not be sorry, but I've got a twenty that says the kid will be," Bill hissed into my ear.

"Ken, could you come over here for a minute please?" Jason's tone had shifted from 'famous director in charge of all he surveyed' to that of "man begging favors from the gods.' Ken strolled over sullenly, his hands jammed into his back pockets, stretching the fabric taut across his monumental member. "Ken, this is Chris."

"Presentation of the sacrificial victim," Bill whispered. I nudged him in the ribs with my elbow.

"Oh, wow," Chris gushed. "I know you. I saw your picture in a magazine once."

"Yeah, right," Ken snarled, his lips curling back from his perfect teeth.

"I did, really," Chris chattered on, unaware of Ken's notoriously bad temper. I had no doubt that if the poor fool didn't shut up, Ken would lash out at him and end his career before it even got started. "You've got the—"

"—biggest dick I ever saw," Bill winced under his breath. That was the worst thing you could say to Ken Hughes. His entire career was based on the size of his prick and what he could do with it, but he would fly into a rage if people talked about it when the cameras weren't rolling. Maybe he secretly thought it made him some kind of a freak. The dude was weird.

"—saddest, gentlest eyes I've ever seen. I've still got the picture," Chris concluded, reaching out to shake Ken's hand. Bill and I exchanged a look, then Bill went back to his video camera. I hung around, waiting for Ken's response. He didn't say a word. He even shook Chris's hand, which surprised me. Usually, he touched fellow performers with his dick and that was about it.

Jason gave them the set-up and called for quiet on the set. The concept was simple enough—they walked into the room with the big bed and took off their clothes. Chris was enthusiastic, stripping to the buff in about fifteen seconds flat. The boy was amazing, every muscle straining against his golden skin. He had gorgeous arms, a nicely developed chest with big pinky-brown nipples, and a concave belly with a perfect six-pack of abs. His legs were long and sinewy, swollen with muscle at thigh and calf. The entire, delectable package was rounded out with an ass like two ripe, sun-kissed melons. All in all, Chris was my recipe for a wet dream.

By the time he was out of his shorts, his fat prick was already reaching for the sky, the mushroom head puffed out full and tight. Downy golden fuzz clustered around the base of his hard-on, but other than that he was as hairless as a newborn baby. I had the distinct suspicion that if you bit him, he'd bleed vanilla cream.

Ken looked like he always did—hot, manly, studly, dangerous, whatever. All you had to do was pick one of the words used to describe him in the magazine layouts and he definitively embodied it. He was such a stunning specimen of manhood, it was a pity he was such a shit. His body was beautifully proportioned, muscular but not overly bulked up. He was hairy in all the right places—silky chestnut hairs curled across the expanse of his sculpted pecs and trickled down his washboard belly in a fine line, ending in a profusion of dense curls at the base of his huge prick. His arms, legs and bubble butt were also liberally feathered with more of the same dense growth, making him heaven for anyone who liked hairy men. No razor had ever touched him below the neck, that much was quite clear.

"Ready, Bill?" Bill gave Jason a thumbs-up gesture. "Okay, fellas, go for it." Ken just stood there, muscles tensed, waiting for Chris to come to him. He didn't have to wait long. The blond was so eager to please he was practically wagging his tail. He bounded across the room and stood in front of Ken, looking at him, his innocent blue eyes open wide. I was standing just out of camera range, watching everything that went on.

I guess I expected Chris to grab Ken's cock, drop to his knees and start sucking. He didn't. Instead, he reached out and put his hand tentatively on Ken's chest, his fingers tangling in the hairs that curled between Ken's pecs. Then Chris traced a line up along Ken's throat to his chin, followed the line of his jaw back to his ear, stroked the thick column of his neck and rested his hand on his shoulder. Never once did he take his adoring eyes off of Ken's face. Finally, he leaned forward and kissed Ken chastely on the lips. Ken's fingers slowly squeezed into a fist.

I flinched, waiting for the fist to connect. Instead, the fingers relaxed and curled around the blond's neck, slowly pulling Chris's face down to the swollen nipple crowning Ken's left pec. "Suck my tit," our star growled, tightening his grip on Chris's neck.

Bill was hovering above the spot where I was crouched, filming all the action. When I saw those succulent red lips brushing against that rubbery bud of flesh, I felt a tingle in my groin. This was no passing tit-nibble—Chris was focusing all of his concentration on making love to it. One of his hands was pressed against the small of Ken's back, the other rested on the swell of the big man's biceps. From where I stood, I could see his fingers trembling. Now that I noticed it, Chris's whole body was vibrating.

Ken's body language surprised me too. Usually at this point in the action, he was flogging his pecker, working to get it hard so he could move in for the kill. This time, however, his hands were otherwise engaged, one still against Chris's neck, the other exploring the lush curves of his hairless ass. A quick glance at his crotch showed that his cock wouldn't need any fluffing today—he was already obviously aroused, his monster meat slowly rising up between his tautly muscled thighs.

Finally, Ken pulled the blond's head back from his swollen tit. "You know the drill, kid," he growled huskily. Chris looked up at him, bewilderment clear in his sky-blue eyes.

"I've—I've never—uh—" He blushed, his cheeks flushing scarlet. "But I want to," he blurted. "Really, I do. Just tell me what to do." His smile made even my stony heart palpitate. Ken must have been caught up in his spell as well, because his massive prick started pointing at the ceiling.

"Suck my cock," Ken rumbled, his voice coming from deep in his chest. Chris got down on his knees and got his first good look at Ken's dick. His expression was priceless—he looked like he'd never sucked cock before in his life. He kept looking up at Ken like he expected him to give instructions. To my surprise, that's exactly what he did. Ken wasn't a talker, but he started giving out orders in a deep, sex-heavy voice.

"Start with my balls, man. That's it, lick 'em, get 'em all nice and wet. Oh, yeah, that's good. Now open wide and swallow those big fucking balls. Yeah, you can do it. Pull on 'em. Drag 'em down nice and tight. Stretch those cords to the limit, man. That's real good."

Chris was gripping Ken's thighs, kneading the straining muscles while he sucked the man's big nuts, following Ken's directions to the letter. Ken's cock angled higher and higher, the bloated head touching a point about two inches above his navel. A big drop of honey oozed out of the piss-hole and slowly drooled down, splashing on Chris's forehead. It was a nice touch.

"Now my cock. Suck my cock," Ken said hoarsely. Chris released the man's big balls with a wet smacking sound and watched the cum-bloated orbs rise to hug the shaft of his big cock. Then he began licking along the swollen shaft. His pink tongue darted like a lizard's as he worked his way from the hairy base out to the hooded knob.

"Chew that cock-skin," Ken commanded. "Catch it between your teeth and pull on it. Oh, yeah, that's it. Stretch it out. Now, stick your tongue in there. Push it up against my knob. Do it!" Chris wrapped both hands around the pulsing shaft and started working the spongy mass of tissue looming in front of him. His pink tongue wedged under the fleshy overhang and traced the rim of the crown. Ken actually had a smile on his face at that point, which had to be a silver-screen first. I hoped Bill had captured it on tape for posterity.

Chris swallowed almost half of Ken's huge organ before he backed off and went back to polishing the knob. His lips were stretched tight as he started bobbing back and forth, working the top three or four inches of Ken's butt-buster till the man's eyes were rolling back in his head.

"Let's have some fucking, guys," Jason called out from his perch on a ladder off to one side. "Ken, pick him up and throw him on the bed. Mount him and do your stuff."

Ken reached down and pulled Chris back to his feet, but he didn't just throw him on the bed and fuck him. He turned him around and pushed him gently onto his hands and knees. Then, he knelt down and started rooting around in his crack. I'd made several films with the man and he sure as hell had never done that before. Seeing is believing however, and I was definitely seeing.

Chris was crouched down on all fours, whimpering softly every time Ken touched him. When Ken finally got his tongue wedged inside the tight channel, Chris's whole body began trembling. After a few minutes of tongue work, Ken switched to a finger, which he was barely able to push through the tightly clenched ring of Chris's ass muscle. Chris moaned and looked back over his shoulder at Ken, his eyes brimming with tears. Jesus, if the dude couldn't manage a finger, Ken could never hope to fuck him. I began to think the whole shoot was going to end up being a bust.

Ken displayed remarkable patience, rubbing Chris's belly and nibbling the nape of his neck as he kept on fingering his ass. He pushed in slow and easy, finally breaching the guy's sphincter and sliding a finger into him up to the webbing. Ken's huge stiffer was angled high, and the head had worked its way out of the hood, glowing crimson in contrast to the pale ivory shaft. Something was definitely up with him. He was treating the young blond like a real person, not like an adversary to be fucked into total submission. I began to think I might have to revise my opinion of the bastard.

"You gonna let me fuck you?" Ken growled. Chris looked over his shoulder at the man who was fingering his tender ass. His expression was perfect—a mixture of apprehension when he glanced at Ken's huge prick, and pure unadulterated passion when he locked eyes with him. The kid was mesmerized. Hell, so was I. Even Bill was starting to breathe heavily behind the camera.

"Uh huh," Chris said breathlessly, his rosy cheeks flushing scarlet.

"Are you getting all this?" I hissed at Bill, reaching down to adjust my burgeoning hard-on.

"I'm getting it," he snapped back, elbowing me aside. "Damn, those two are hot enough to melt paint."

"You ready?" Ken asked. Chris nodded and crouched back down on the bed. He stretched his hand back to Ken. Their fingers slowly intertwined and Ken rubbed his cockhead along the blond's spit-slicked crack. When he was lined up with the target, his hips thrust forward slow and easy, relentlessly stretching Chris's asshole open.

Chris gasped when the head popped inside of him, but he voiced no other protest as inch after inch of Ken's thick, veiny prick disappeared up his backside. Ken used his free hand to stroke Chris's sweat-streaked back and ass, showing a concern I didn't think he was capable of.

After Ken had him loosened up a bit, he crawled onto the bed with him, pushing him down onto the mattress. "You doing okay, buddy?" Ken whispered in his ear. Chris nodded and Ken picked up the pace. His hairy ass was poetry in motion, the knotted muscles shifting and flexing as he humped, plunging his cock in and out of Chris's hot ass.

"Roll over on your side," Jason ordered. "I wanna see some cock pumping here." Ken wrapped his arms around Chris's chest and rolled both of them onto their sides. He hooked a hand behind Chris's knee and scissored his legs wide apart, giving the camera a great view of his fat prick pistoning in and out of Chris's hole. Every time he drove it deep, Chris would squirt clear, viscous juice onto his washboard belly. His mouth was open, his soft grunts and groans making it clear to the whole crew just exactly how he felt about getting his ass reamed.

The bed frame was starting to creak and I could tell that the end was near. I put away my spray bottle—they didn't need any artificial sweat to make their bodies glisten at this point—and watched them as they got ready to blow. Chris's swollen hard-on was twitching and flexing, his balls drawn up so tight they weren't even budging when Ken's nuts butted against them. His eyes were closed and his lower lip was drawn up over his teeth as Ken laid in to him, finally bringing his signature battering-ram technique into play.

I'd never seen Ken looking so good. The hairs on his body stood on end, his muscles were pumped, and the veins in his arms and neck stood out like cables. Ken's face was buried against Chris's neck and it was clear that he was kissing him—another first. They were both snorting and bucking and gasping for air, making all sorts of wonderful animal noises that would play very well on the final cut of the film. There would be no need for dubbing or extraneous music on this tape.

When Ken wrapped his fingers around Chris's dick, that was it for the dazzling blond. Chris shrieked his pleasure as he blew cum in a high arc that cleared his head and splashed onto the headboard of the bed. Ken kept on humping, jacking Chris till he was drained dry and his smooth torso was criss-crossed with thick white strands of jizz. Then Ken pulled his cock out of Chris's butt and pushed the young blond's hand down onto his dick. Chris peeled off the rubber and pumped the pillar of flesh until Ken started pumping out one of his trademark wet-shots.

The first blast shot out the end of his dick like a high pressure hose, splattering the wall above the bed. Chris's eyes got wide and he pointed Ken's cock straight up in the air for the second shot. It was equally impressive, arcing high in the air and splattering down on Chris's already sticky chest.

"Man, that's hot," he sighed, pumping the man's enormous stiffer harder and faster. Ken didn't disappoint—after a couple of minor shots, he erupted with another gush of scum that had Bill tilting his camera high in the air to catch the full arc of it. Chris flogged Ken's cock till it went soft, then scooted around and curled up against him, burying his face against Ken's hairy chest.

"Cut and print," Jason crowed triumphantly. "Thank you gentlemen. We'll break for lunch now." Well, if those two heard him, they didn't pay any attention. They were starting in with deep, tongue-twisting kisses, the kind of kisses that usually only lead to one thing. "You ain't getting paid for this, you know," Jason razzed. Ken flipped him off without even coming up for air, and we all went out to lunch and left them on their own.

It had been a hell of a morning. I won a twenty-dollar bet and I'd actually seen Ken Hughes really getting it on instead of punishing some poor guy with his prick. I didn't know whether to think of myself as a talent scout or a matchmaker, but then Jason sent me out for half-a-dozen pastrami sandwiches and I was reminded that I was just the grunt. Still, I did feel pretty good about having brought fresh meat onto the set, not to mention the fact that the meat had managed to tame the savage beast it had been tossed to.

About the Authors

DEREK ADAMS (Grunt Work)—The author of the popular Miles Diamond erotic detective novels, and over a hundred erotic stories, Derick lives near Seattle.

BARRY ALEXANDER (Dream Date)—Barry is the author of *All The Right Places* (Badboy Press, 1998). He has also been published in *Skinflicks* (Companion), *Casting Couch Confessions* (Companion), and *Friction* (Alyson). Barry lives in Iowa.

SAM ARCHER ("You've Got Fan Male")—Sam's work has appeared in *In Touch* and *Freshmen* magazines. A Louisiana native who now lives in Arkansas, Sam has spent most of his 35 years as a writer, hitchhiker, and house guest.

JORDAN BAKER (That's Why They Call It Acting)—Jordan has had stories published in *Indulge, In Touch,* and *Hustler*, as well as in numerous literary magazines. He lives in Arkansas.

MICHAEL CAVANAUGH (My Brilliant Career)—This is Michael's first published story. He has been a waiter, doorman, model, and writer. He lives in Seattle, Washington.

BILL CRIMMIN (The Big Tip)—Bill was first published in *Casting Couch Confessions* (Companion). His stories have also appeared in *Loveseats* (Nocturnis), *Sons Of The Moon* (Nocturnis) and *Altar of Eros* (Idol Books). He is a Londoner.

IAN DESHILS (A Bare Market)—Ian lives in Michigan with his life companion. This is his first published work. Ian served in the U.S. Army, worked as a sheriff's deputy, and spent time as a draftsman with Douglas Aircraft Company.

GEORGE DIBBS (No Small Parts)—George was first published in *Casting Couch Confessions* (Companion). A self-described beach-bum, George loves surf, sun, sand, and skin. Southern Alabama's golden beaches and the Gulf of Mexico are his home.

VIC HOWELL (Body Worship)—Vic's work has appeared in *In Touch, Mandate,* and *First Hand* magazines. His stories of Southern boys have appeared in *Skinflicks* (Companion) and *Casting Couch*

Confessions (Companion). He's a Georgia native.

DAVE MACMILLAN (Big Brother)—Dave edited *Casting Couch Confessions* (Companion), and the forthcoming anthologies *The Altar Of Eros* (Idol Books), *Loveseats* (Nocturnis) and *Sons Of The Moon* (Nocturnis). He lives in Atlanta ,Georgia.

ALAN W. MILLS (Boy Pussy)—Alan is a California-born writer and poet living in West Hollywood. He's also the editor of *In Touch, Indulge,* and *Blackmale* magazines. His stories have appeared in *Friction 2* (Alyson) and *Skinflicks* (Companion).

BRYAN NAKAI (Tricks & Treats)—Bryan was first published in *Casting Couch Confessions* (Companion). He is a Native American living in Albuquerque with an Anglo physicist.

LANCE RUSH (The Next Big Thing)—Lance's work has appeared in *Blackmale, Cruisin,' Daddy, First Hand, Guys, Hombres, Latinos, Options,* and *Torso* magazines. In addition, his stories have appeared in *Friction 2* (Alyson) and *Skinflicks* (Companion). He is a New York writer, poet and playwright.

JD RYAN (A Tiger By The Tail)—J.D.'s work has appeared in *Casting Couch Confessions* (Companion) and in *In Touch, Bunkhouse,* and *Honcho* magazines. He lives in South Carolina .

SIMON SHEPPARD (At The Adonis)—Simon is the co-editor, with M. Christian, of the anthology *Rough Stuff: Tales of Gay Men, Sex and Power.* His work has appeared in *Skinflicks* (Companion), *Casting Couch Confessions* (Companion), and many other anthologies. He lives in San Francisco.

JAY STARRE (Boys And Their Toys)—Jay's work has appeared in *In Touch, Mandate,* and *Bunkhouse* magazines. Born in Los Angeles, Jay emigrated to Canada at nineteen. He presently lives in Vancouver. He is now a personal trainer and full-time writer.

CHAD STEPHENS (Fund "Raising")—Chad's work has appeared in *In Touch* and *Hot/Shots!* under the name Charlie Stevens. He has also sold a video script. He resides in Redondo Beach, California.

MICHAEL WILLIAMS (Star Power)—Michael's work has appeared in *American Bear, American Grizzly, Indulge* and *Men* magazines. A former New Yorker, Michael now lives in San Francisco with his lover.

companion press sex book catalog

BAD BOYS Of Video #1
Porn Star Interviews
By Mickey Skee
224 pages, 5-1/2 x 8-1/2
ISBN# 1-889138-12-6
$12.95 Softcover (Photos)

BAD BOYS Of Video #2
Porn Star Interviews
By Mickey Skee
224 pages, 5-1/2 x 8-1/2
ISBN# 1-889138-19-3
$14.95 Softcover (Photos)

**The "BEST OF"
Gay Adult Video 1998**
By Mickey Skee
208 pages, 5-1/2 x 8-1/2
ISBN# 1-889138-10-X
$12.95 Softcover (Photos)

**The "BEST OF"
Gay Adult Video 1999**
By Mickey Skee
208 pages, 5-1/2 x 8-1/2
ISBN# 1-889138-14-2
$12.95 Softcover (Photos)

**The "BEST OF"
Gay Adult Video 2000**
By Mickey Skee
224 pages, 5-1/2 x 8-1/2
ISBN# 1-889138-21-5
$14.95 Softcover (Photos)

CAMPY, VAMPY, TRAMPY
Movie Quotes
By Steve Stewart
212 pages, 4-1/4 x 6-3/4
ISBN# 0-9625277-6-9
$9.95 Softcover

CASTING COUCH CONFESSIONS
17 Gay Erotic Tales (fiction)
Edited by David MacMillan
192 pages, 5-1/2 x 8-1/2
ISBN# 1-889138-17-7
$14.95 Softcover

COMING OF AGE Movie & Video
Guide, By Don Lort
216 pages, 8-1/2 x 11
ISBN# 1-889138-02-9
$18.95 Softcover

The Films of KEN RYKER
By Mickey Skee
152 pages, 8-1/2 x 11
ISBN# 1-889138-08-8
$18.95 Softcover (Photos)

The Films of KRISTEN BJORN
By Jamoo
152 pages, 8-1/2 x 11
ISBN# 1-889138-00-2
$18.95 Softcover (Photos)

THE FRESHMAN CLUB
18 Erotic Virgin Tales
Edited by David MacMillan
192 pages, 5-1/2 x 8-1/2
ISBN# 1-889138-27-4
$14.95 Softcover (fiction)

FULL FRONTAL, 2nd Edition
Male Nudity Video Guide
Edited by Steve Stewart
144 pages, 5-1/2 x 8-1/2
ISBN# 1-889138-11-8
$12.95 Softcover

GAY HOLLYWOOD, 2nd Edition
Film & Video Guide (non-hardcore)
Edited by Steve Stewart
352 pages, 7 x 8-1/2
ISBN# 0-9625277-5-0
$15.95 Softcover (Photos)

**HOLLYWOOD HARDCORE
DIARIES**
14 Erotic Tales (fiction)
By Mickey Skee
192 pages, 5-1/2 x 8-1/2
ISBN# 1-889138-15-0
$12.95 Softcover

LITTLE JOE SUPERSTAR
The Films of Joe Dallesandro
By Michael Ferguson
216 pages, 8-1/2 x 11
ISBN# 1-889138-09-6
$18.95 Softcover (Photos)

PENIS PUNS
Movie Quotes
By Steve Stewart
118 pages, 6 x 4-1/4
ISBN# 1-889138-07-X
$5.95 Softcover

RENT BOYS
18 Erotic Hustler & Escort Tales
Edited by David MacMillan
192 pages, 5-1/2 x 8-1/2
ISBN# 1-889138-25-8
$14.95 Softcover (fiction)

SKIN FLICKS #1
15 Gay Erotic Tales (fiction)
Edited by Bruce Wayne
192 pages, 5-1/2 x 8-1/2
ISBN# 1-889138-16-9
$12.95 Softcover

SKIN FLICKS #2
18 Gay Erotic Tales (fiction)
Edited by David MacMillan
192 pages, 5-1/2 x 8-1/2
ISBN# 1-889138-26-6
$14.95 Softcover

STAR DIRECTORY
Over 2,000 Porn Star Videographies
Edited by Bruce Wayne
384 pages, 5-1/2 x 8-1/2
ISBN# 0-9625277-22-3
$18.95 Softcover

SUPERSTARS #1
Porn Star Profiles
By Jamoo
204 pages, 5-1/2 x 8-1/8
ISBN# 0-9625277-9-3
$12.95 Softcover (Photos)

SUPERSTARS #2
Porn Star Profiles
By Jamoo
224 pages, 5-1/2 x 8-1/2
ISBN# 1-889138-20-7
$14.95 Softcover (Photos)

THE VOYEUR VIDEO GUIDE
To Gay Softcore Videos
Edited by Steve Stewart
144 pages, 5-1/2 x 8-1/8
ISBN# 1-889138-05-3
$12.95 Softcover (Photos)

X-RATED Gay Video Guide
Edited by Sabin
448 pages, 5-1/2 x 8-1/8
ISBN# 1-889138-03-7
$12.95 Softcover

companion press order form

PO Box 2575, Laguna Hills, CA 92654 USA

Phone: (949) 362-9726 Fax: (949) 362-4489

Please include your phone number or <u>E-MAIL ADDRESS</u> (for questions about your order):

PRINT Name

Address

City _____ State _____ Zip _____

PLEASE PRINT CLEARLY. USE EXTRA SHEET OF PAPER IF NECESSARY

Qty	Order or ISBN # last 3 digits only	Title	Price (each)	Price

SHIPPING & HANDLING CHARGES—BOOKS ONLY
U.S. Shipping & Handling Charges (U.S. ONLY)
First book $4.00. $1.00 for each additional book.
Canada Shipping & Handling Charges (Canada)
First book $5.00. $1.00 for each additional book.
Outside U.S. Shipping & Handling Charges (Outside U.S.)
First book $20.00. $1.00 for each additional book.
RUSH FedEx Delivery Charges (U.S. ONLY)
Check one and ADD to above charges ❏ Overnight, **Add** $35.00
❏ 2nd Day, **Add** $25.00 ❏ Saturday Delivery, **Add** $45.00.
CREDIT CARD or MONEY ORDERS ONLY for rush delivery.

Subtotal	$
Discount or Credit (if any)	-
California Residents add 7.75% Sales Tax	$
Shipping & Handling See left for rates	$
ADD RUSH FedEx Delivery Charge	$
TOTAL	$

Check Payment Method
❏ Visa ❏ MasterCard ❏ American Express ❏ Money Order
❏ Check (U.S. only) **(Allow 6-8 weeks.)** Make check payable to COMPANION PRESS.

VISA   MasterCard   AMERICAN EXPRESS

Credit card # _____

Exp. date _____

X Signature required for all orders

I certify by my signature that I am over 21 years old and desire to receive sexually-oriented material. My signature here also authorizes my credit card charge if I am paying for my order by Visa, MasterCard or American Express. We cannot ship your order without your signature.

❏ **Here is my $5. Please send me your complete book flyers. I do not wish to order at this time. (I understand that my $5 will be refunded with my first purchase).**